CITY OF SHARKS

CITY OF SHARKS

'There's a crack in everything, that's how the
light gets in.'
— Leonard Cohen, 'Anthem'

IAN ALEXANDER

Library of Congress Control Number:		2017907994
ISBN:	Hardcover	978-1-5434-0084-7
	Softcover	978-1-5434-0083-0
	eBook	978-1-5434-0082-3

Print information available on the last page.

Rev. date: 05/11/2018

To order additional copies of this book, contact:
Xlibris
1-800-455-039
www.Xlibris.com.au
Orders@Xlibris.com.au
745557

CONTENTS

CHAPTER 1

CONFESSIONS

Perth, Summer 2030

Diana is ushered to a corner table at an out-of-the-way, dimly lit eating place, Santorini, discretion guaranteed. No telescreens here: the Orwellian devices that watch, listen, and report back to HQ. They've recently been installed under the auspices of the President – the Australian Parliament couldn't resolve the issue – in every house and commercial premise. In the name of national security and moral standards.

Santorini is only open to 'approved' clientele and is under police protection. The only other places that are exempt from telescreens belong to the politicians, who've become even better at placing themselves above the laws they make.

Diana surveys the wine list and orders an expensive red, one which her lover will appreciate too. He pays the bills. With taxpayer's money. She waits, sampling the full-bodied Shiraz, grateful for time to wind down from a hectic week.

She checks her watch for messages and hooks into the backlog. She ignores those to do with work and replies to a couple from friends, ruefully thinking that she's in danger of losing contact due to the pressures of work and now *this*, the affair, but rather than talk about

1

her personal life, she instead posts news of the political highlights of the past few days onto her Facebook page.

And after all, personal observations on Facebook are almost a thing of the past in the new surveillance environment. In any case, Diana has plenty to draw on: she works as an adviser to State Premier, Wayne Cloke.

Diana never intended the affair; it's not part of her *modus operandi*, but once they were working together, desire got the upper hand. Desire for a man she found personable, funny, and apparently genuine in his appreciative comments.

He approaches Diana at the restaurant table. 'You get better looking every day, darling, what's your secret?'

Diana smiles and kisses him lightly on the cheek, noticing his eyes look a little glazed. His hand brushes, almost strokes, her body and maintains contact in a manner he would normally reserve for their private moments. She would love to respond in kind, but her instinct tells her otherwise; he's behaving very differently from when she saw him this morning.

'Steady on man, that's for later . . . are you OK?'

'Sure Diana, I'm on top of the world!' Wayne returns, 'I feel fantastic, best I have in weeks!' he says in a mildly hysterical manner while smiling broadly, pouring himself a glass of red and downing it in one gulp. Refilling the glass and taking another heavy swig, he turns his attention to the menu.

After the meal, they take a cab to Wayne's parliamentary flat. Diana feels pleasantly mellow but is puzzled at Cloke's otherness. Did he get stuck into the booze at an earlier function? She knows what he's like after too many drinks, but this is quite different. *What is he into?* she wonders.

As if to answer her question, as they sit on the couch, Cloke reaches into his jacket pocket and produces tablets, telling her he had one earlier and suggesting they both take some now.

Diana is flabbergasted. She knows that Perth – a city servicing a vast hinterland that includes a mining frontier – is full of users, but at thirty-two, she's wary. She's enjoyed a few binges in the past, still has the odd joint when off-duty, but knows that drugs aren't good for her health, and in any case aren't 'form for either a State Premier or his adviser.

'Wayne, that's crazy, and why have you already had one? What's going on here? Are you turning into an addict?' she asks in a tone conveying concern for her boss.

Oblivious of this, Wayne shrugs and takes one of the tablets anyway, heightening his already off-beat mood. He becomes amorous; Diana abandons her solicitous concern and responds with a kiss. They head for the bedroom, and it's not long before they're making love. But Diana is not sure that's what it is: the encounter misses their usual close connection, it's not satisfying, and Cloke seems to be getting his pleasure from an imagined experience.

Afterwards, Cloke doesn't dwell on the sex but instead looks at Diana with a slightly crazed expression and says, 'I want to tell you about the deal I've done with JD on the casino.'

He's referring to John Dick, boss of ABC Constructions, one of the State's biggest builders; the casino is the city's second.

'What are you on about, Wayne? A deal with a Labor Party mate, one of our biggest donors, to build the casino? God, talk about shades of the past!'

As a political aficionado, Diana is well aware of the WA Inc cronyism of the 1980s. A scandal that ended up costing Labor its ten-year hold on the State government, it started with the award of contracts for the State's first casino to big Party donors.

'Yeah its all right, the contract's not in his name. Any rate, this deal goes one better. You'll love it!' he predicts, now semi-delirious and wildly off-target. He forges on. 'Get this, Dick's set up a personal fund for me. Millions of retirement dollars, and like the contract, all totally undetectable.'

Diana feels a sense of unbelief. She knows the Premier often sails close to the political wind; she's heard rumours about deals, but whenever she's raised questions, he always produced plausible answers, and up till now, she's taken him at his word. Up till now, she thought, well hoped, he wasn't into anything dodgy. She wrestles with this revelation.

'God, Wayne, if that's true, it's not just corrupt, it's criminal!' she screams at him. Then, seeing his wry smile, she figures he might be pulling her leg. 'You bastard, are you bullshitting me again, or have the drugs fired your imagination?'

'This is not imagination, Diana. I'm telling you God's truth.'

Cloke's completely serious, even putting his hand on his heart. He reaches into his work files and extracts a document. 'Have a look at this!'

His eyes are wild and excited as he hands over an email to his private address containing details of a decoy building company and a bank account number.

Diana is shocked, thinking of stories she's heard about ecstasy as the truth drug. She responds vehemently, 'Christ, Wayne, that's disgusting, you must be mad. You've got to give up this crazy scheme.'

But Cloke's energy has drained, and he's asleep with the discussion unfinished. Diana's worried and unable to sleep. A few hours later, she looks at the solid form next to her with increasing anxiety and disgust. But she reminds herself she does work for him and automatically reverts to her role.

Should he still be here? she thinks cloudily, reaching for her watch and turning on the bedside lamp.

'God, it's 3:30 a.m.!' she shouts involuntarily. She prods him. 'Wayne, wake up, you were due home hours ago!'

'What the hell?' is all he can manage, and then, 'shit, yes! I'd better get in touch.'

Diana hears the panic in his voice as he reaches for his watch and switches it on. Or tries to, then remembers it's not working. He turns to the old-fashioned phone, not many of these left now, on the bedside. He puts his finger to his lips as Diana looks on with a mixture of anxiety and anger.

'Hello, darling, sorry to break your sleep. Yeah, I'm still at Parliament, the meeting'll be over soon,' he says, winking at Diana. He pauses to listen to a reply, and while Diana can hear the high-pitched tones on the other end, she can't make out the words.

Wayne responds with an apparently effortless continuation, 'well, my watch is dead. See you within the hour, darling!'

With that, he puts the phone down and disappears for a shower while Diana calls for a government car.

She's increasingly perturbed. Her feelings have been further rankled by the apparently effortless way Cloke lied to his wife. Maybe she'd be better off out of this dangerous liaison.

Where had it all gone wrong? she wonders. Had she made a mistake in moving from her previous work as a journalist with the city's, in fact now the country's, only daily news-sheet, the *Worst Australian?* If she hadn't done that, she would never have been asked to contribute to his policy review and attend *that* briefing. His eyes had been very much on her during her spiel; she could feel his scrutiny, even when he was out of her sight-line.

Afterwards, Cloke had made a beeline for her and told her he was very much taken by her policy ideas. He also made it clear that he appreciated her engaging looks and charm. Only days later, he offered her a job as journalist and policy advisor in his office. Diana accepted eagerly, seeing it as a golden chance to get closer to Cloke and to the centre of political action.

Now, she asks herself, *at what cost?*

As Cloke emerges from the bathroom, dressed and towelling his hair, she offers, 'Wayne, your car'll be here soon, but look, surely Yvette will be even more on her guard after that call?'

'No worries, Diana.' Wayne shrugs off her concern.

'Wayne, for God's sake! Not only are you drug-fucked, you're in danger of being sprung by your wife, *and* you've broken all the corruption rules you claimed your government would obey!'

'Diana, don't be like that.'

'Wayne, I've had enough. I'm shattered. You're no better than the politicians you dragged before those inquiries. In fact, you're worse. I want to end this relationship . . .' Diana trails off, almost in tears.

'Diana, come on!' Cloke pleads. 'Don't say . . . you can't believe that. Look, there's a place for you in all of this . . . come on, darling!'

'As if I want to be your partner in crime. Get lost, you prick!'

Diana feels her anger rise, adding to her emotional stress. She gets her belongings together and leaves the flat pronto. Her driverless car – all politicians and their staff are issued with them – is parked nearby and she asks it to head for home, fast. The vehicle races down the city's near-empty pre-dawn roads for a few short kilometres and drops her at the door of her flat before parking itself.

Diana's dramatic departure leaves Cloke bereft, with dents not just on his drug high but his ego as well. Worse is awaiting him when he reaches home.

His long-suffering wife greets him, 'and just who were you meeting at the flat at midnight? Diana, I wonder?'

Her assertion startles him, as in his drug-fuddled state, he hadn't realised the number of the flat's phone had earlier shown up on his wife's phone.

'How did you know about Diana? God, she *told* you, didn't she?' Cloke demands.

'That's for me to know and you to find out,' she informs him coolly, 'but if you don't end the affair today, we're history, Wayne!'

Thinking mainly of the political embarrassment a divorce in these circumstances could cause, the threat is enough to prompt Cloke into a confession and a promise to end the affair.

CHAPTER 2

THE WASH-UP

A few hours later, with no more sleep under his belt and coming down from his drug trip, Cloke is desperate to speak to Diana. He communicates just as the day is beginning at 6, the time she usually gets out of bed. Not this morning, however; she only fell into a fitful sleep at half-past four.

She eventually hears her watch beep while still half asleep, but is brought to full alert by Wayne's spiel about being sprung and his promise to end the affair. He tells her he doesn't intend to keep this promise.

Diana has trouble keeping her emotions in check; while she is glad to be out of the increasingly dangerous liaison, she is also devastated by the realisation that the man she thought she loved has turned out to be a real operator, on several levels. Holding back tears, she manages 'Wayne, you're only thinking of yourself here, you callous bastard. As I told you last night, our relationship is over!'

'You what?' he asks, failing to recall their conversation. 'Look . . . I'll give up the drugs, I'll talk to JD . . .'

'Why should I believe that? In any case, you won't go back on your deal, or so you said last night.'

'Did I? Well, some things are harder to get out of than others, but why desert me in my time of need?'

'Wayne, I had no idea you're into drugs, and I can't believe you've done such a self-serving deal with JD. And you're treating your wife worse than me by the sounds of it!'

'So it was you who told my wife about us?'

'Why the hell would I do that? You're talking rubbish, Wayne, and you know it. And by the way, sex with you last night was meaningless for me, there was no connection. Now I can see why, you're just out to use me,' Diana tells him evenly.

Cloke's anger gets the better of him, and he ends the conversation abruptly after telling Diana she's no longer welcome in either his bed or his office.

'Talk about a politician ducking for cover!' she splutters.

Losing her relationship is bad enough, but she hadn't counted on also losing her job.

Distraught, Diana gets in touch with Chris Burnside, an old friend.

'Diana, it's not even six thirty yet, what's up?'

Diana tearfully tells him of the wash-up. Chris knows about the relationship, had warned against it, but his advice fell on deaf ears.

'God what a story, Diana, can I help?'

'It'd be great to see you, Chris, to talk this through.'

'Well, I need to be at work by 10 at the latest, but how about I meet you for breakfast in an hour or so?'

'OK, see you at my favourite café sometime after eight.'

While showering and dressing, Diana reflects how she and Chris first met as students a decade or so back, through the campus branch of the Labor Party. Chris is ten years older than her – he'd gone travelling and pursued other interests before enrolling. They immediately hit it off and discovered they had similar interests and outlooks: Diana was studying journalism, Chris, politics and law. Their friendship developed quickly as they swapped notes on politics and events.

They started going to parliamentary debates, and while Diana enjoyed the verbal exchanges, she was bemused at the name-calling and schoolyard behaviour. Chris was more receptive to the shenanigans: the experience spiked his interest in politics.

During their student years, Diana had resisted the occasional push from Chris to take their friendship from platonic to intimate; she had love interests elsewhere. She did believe in love, then at least. She observed Chris – a restless ladies' man if ever there was one – go through a series of short-term lust-driven relationships, a habit he had pretty much adhered to since, barring a few unplanned complications along the way. Diana pushed away the thought that she might now be cast in the same mould.

The café isn't far from Diana's apartment in Highgate, a trendy residential enclave just north of the city. One that has spawned many a local and state politician over the years. Diana enjoys her part in local Labor Party branch proceedings but regrets Chris's recent decision to resign from the Party as it means she can't share as much gossip with him.

It's a short walk from her pad, but a longer journey for Chris, who commutes from Fremantle, some way west. Diana waits anxiously at a small table near the café's bar to shelter from the summer morning heat, fanned by a searing easterly. Climate change on steroids, forecast maximum today 47 degrees, continuing another blistering early summer heat wave.

When Chris arrives, Diana jumps up eagerly and hugs him, barely holding back tears. They move to an outside table in a sheltered nook. Through now streaming eyes, Diana tells of the affair's denouement. She's glad of a sympathetic ear from Chris, but the effect is spoilt for her when he chips in, 'well, I did try and warn you off Cloke . . .' His voice trails off as Diana gives him a hurt look.

'Jesus, Chris, there's no need to rub salt into the wounds!'

'I'm sorry, do tell me more.'

Diana is pensive for a moment, then tries ruefully to explain the relationship and what sucked her in.

'Well, everyone says Cloke is charismatic,' Chris offers.

'Yes, but what a con man he turns out to be.'

Diana is distraught again on the verge of tears. Chris says jokingly, 'Maybe it goes with the territory?'

'Certainly seems that way!'

Over coffee, Diana shows Chris the document Cloke had brandished so proudly the previous night. Chris is fascinated, telling her it relates to information he already has through his work. As state officer in charge of casino licencing, he vets applications and makes recommendations to government.

He reveals that he recommended the licence go to Kerry Cinnamon, a powerful Sydney-based property developer.

'What about Cinnamon's international criminal connections?' Diana objects.

'Sure, but our departmental guidelines insist that licence assessments be based on financial strength alone. In this area, Cinnamon is well qualified, and the rest, well, the police look at criminal records and the like, but they gave him a clean bill of health too. They say the rumours of criminal links are just that, *rumours.* Mind you,' Chris adds, 'the investigating police are part of the purple circle that intertwines police and criminal activity.'

'Hmmm,' muses Diana. 'What a web! But hang on, why don't you and I use the info from Cloke to expose *his* corruption?'

'Steady, girl, it might be OK for you now, but I still have work responsibilities. Shit, I could be linked to any leak on the casino!' he adds nervously.

'Well, OK, but we have to do something!'

'I agree, but give me time to think about it. I've got to get to work now anyhow.'

He gets up to leave, extracting an e-cigarette from his bag.

'Still on the old nicotine, I see,' teases Diana.

'Once an addict, well, at least I'm trying to give up tobacco!' He shrugs and blows her a kiss on the way out.

Diana watches him affectionately and notes he lights up as soon as he's in the street. She stays to finish a much-needed second pot of tea. Half an hour later, she leaves reluctantly. She walks via Hyde Park, the plain trees in full leaf, casting welcome shade on the paths that wind around the lakes. She stops momentarily to watch a clutch of ducks with their ducklings enjoying the morning sun on the sparkling water. Shards of light bounce in her direction. At moments like these, Diana feels it's good to be alive, but the feeling fades as she recalls the unexpected losses of the past twenty-four hours.

Once home, she tidies up records and retrieves information from her computer while she still has access to the office system. She's grateful that Cloke has so far failed to notify his office of her sacking.

Around midday, however, the party is over when she receives official notification of termination. But she's happy with what she has retrieved and puts the results on an external disk drive, with a copy on a thumb drive. She then deletes it from her computer.

When she leaves her flat, the mercury is already topping 40 degrees, summer weather par excellence. She's preoccupied and only vaguely notices the shimmering heat haze around the approaching light rail vehicle on nearby Beaufort Street. She catches the new tram – one of Cloke's more popular initiatives – to the terminus and walks through the city to her parliamentary office.

She ponders how much the CBD has changed in the fifteen years since she got her first job at the Sunday press. She takes in buildings that are ever taller, construction of which has left few reminders of the past. King Street, a heritage area that has kept most of its original buildings, is now all but swamped by high-rise offices, apartments, and hotels in the vicinity.

C'est la vie, at least in Perth, she reflects. Chris will tell you a different story about the community's resistance to high-rise in Fremantle if you give him half a chance. But she knows that despite this, even Freo is starting to look a bit like central Perth, a characterless and bleak copy of a midwest US city.

At the office to collect her belongings, Diana finds most of her fellow staff – now former colleagues she realises with a shock – sympathetic. Those closest to her are outraged. Some joke about resigning in solidarity, but word of her affair seems to have spread like wildfire, and that means there's little love lost among other jealous souls.

Over a cuppa, there's speculation about who Cloke will recruit to replace Diana and how they will deal with the increasing flak the government is facing. Diana knows they will face a whole lot more when news of the casino deal comes out, but she keeps mum on this.

She leaves feeling flat, but knowing it's a good time to end her first foray into the murky world that is politics. Well, end her formal involvement, that is.

Later that day after leaving his office, Chris decides to add to the dossier of politically explosive material Diana has on Cloke and his cronies. Having thought the matter through during the day, and realising he can't resist this opportunity, he feels the tension in his stomach as he puts the information together. He takes several breaks to indulge his smoking habit and goes well over his daily quota of five. It's doing his health no good; his doctor has been urging him to give up for years. He's cut back and tries the e-cigarette when he can bear it. But he's addicted to the nicotine, and besides, it eases his tension.

After several hours of assiduous work, he phones Diana, and they go over the details via a computer connection. Next morning, Chris meets his press contact; the journalist is impressed, but says he'll need corroborating evidence to make the story stick. Chris stresses that he must have a guarantee of anonymity for the sources before he can provide any more.

He knows that his job will evaporate, and Diana will find it extremely difficult to stay in the public sector if they are identified with the leak. After some discussion and a call to the paper's editor, the journalist agrees to the condition, Chris hands over the incriminating documents and unsourced departmental material. They sign an agreement, and the journo is on his way to what he hopes will be the scoop of the year.

CHAPTER 3

CLOKE AND DAGGERS

West Perth, Saturday evening a week later

Cloke downs his double scotch in one draught. It soothes him temporarily, but as he sees JD approaching, he orders another two from the hovering club waiter. JD had made it clear that this meeting was a must, and Cloke wasn't in the habit of going against his wishes. As State Premier, he couldn't afford to.

Cloke has had one hell of a week, trying to keep the lid on the increasing rumours circulating about the casino deal and having to answer hostile questions not just from the opposition, but also from increasingly sceptical colleagues in his own Party as swell as fending off the press. So far, the journalists had held off publishing anything, but Cloke suspected it was only a matter of time. Cloke was usually good at handling a hostile press, but this week, he seemed to have lost control of his usually smooth persona. Not to mention his personal life and the dust-up with his wife following his mea culpa over Diana.

The drugs didn't help, and even though he hadn't been caught out, colleagues close to him noticed his behaviour was unusually erratic and were questioning why. Not only had his habit ruined his love life, it was now threatening to destroy his political career. He had been under the influence when he drew up the casino deal with JD.

Enemies and factional heavies in the Cabinet had demanded details of the deal. Cloke had been evasive in his answers. His denials were only believed up to a point, and he had been forced to promise a full report.

And in his office, he had to justify Diana's sacking to his restless staff without spilling any political beans; that made life that much more difficult again.

Now JD approaches, a weary look on his rotund face.

'G'day, Wayne. You're right into it, then?'

'True, JD, but you'll be pleased to hear I've ordered one for you too.'

'Good man, Wayne, I think I need it as much as you.'

JD slides into his seat, barely capacious enough to hold his huge form. He leans back, cracks the fingers in his hands, and is able to raise a smile for the occasion. They exchange civilities until the waiter delivers the drinks. Wayne makes it clear they want to be left alone in their small booth at the far end of the members' private room. Far from prying eyes and the omnipresent telescreens.

'JD, what d'you mean summoning me here?' Wayne now asks in an affronted tone.

Leaning forward and speaking in a low but authoritative tone, JD tells him, 'listen Wayne, the bloody cat's out of the bag. I've had the press onto me all afternoon, asking about the bloody casino contract. They know something about our deal, they said enough for me to know this is not just rumour-mongering. They may not know it all, but they seem to know enough to sink us both. What the fuck's going on? Remember, none of this was going to be traceable?'

JD's already ruddy complexion goes redder; the veins in his neck bulge as he struggles to contain his anger. Cloke goes pale. The same press inquiries are reaching his office.

'That's impossible, JD,' he blusters.

'Well, the impossible often seems to happen in your political domain!' JD counters. 'Either way, you're going to have to take the heat on this.'

'Shit, JD, where can I go with this? If I admit it, I'm stuffed. If I deny it, they'll roast me when it all comes out!'

Cloke slumps in his chair, polishes off the whisky, and looks pleadingly at JD. JD is not moved but smiles benevolently at the man under pressure.

'Look, mate, *you've* got to sort this. I suggest you think about resigning.'

'You what? No way, I think our deal should be cancelled. It's the only way to keep my fractious Cabinet happy!' Cloke returns in a desperate but louder voice, attracting the attention of a group a few booths away. Heads turn in their direction.

'Hang on mate, keep it quiet.' JD motions with his hand, and the group returns to their drinks. 'Look, the deal is going to stay in place, otherwise I'll have to give the press *my* version of events, and I can tell you, if you think they've got you now, my contribution will put you in a much worse light!'

Cloke goes paler; he's in too deep and is in danger of drowning in the whirlpool of political scandal that has taken down so many of his colleagues.

JD presses on, 'look Wayne, there can be life for you after politics if you just do the right thing. The cash will still go into your account. No one needs to know. Five million is a pretty generous retirement fund on top of your bloody parliamentary perks!'

Cloke slumps back again, apparently regretting having ever accepted JD's offer to be his principal backer. The run had been great while it lasted, but now? Flexible Constructions calls the tune.

CHAPTER 4

CHANGE IS IN THE AIR

Sunday morning, a week later

'Blue sky. Hot sun. Forecast, 45 degrees and fine,' the telescreen in Chris's flat announces. No rain for months in a metropolis thirsting for water in the ongoing throws of an apparently endless summer.

'Bloody climate change,' mumbles Chris as he tries to pry his eyes open, only alerted by the incessant intonation of "it's 8:00 a.m., get up now" from the telescreen announcer, whose glib enthusiasm for the continuing hot weather he finds little short of nauseating. He'd love to turn it off, but that can't be done. Chris is reminded of the slogan under which the telescreens were installed:

Be Ever Vigilant

Chris sweats under the flimsy doona, the sun blinding him as it shafts roughly through the slats of the broken venetians on the poky bedroom window. Paint flakes from the wall under the intense heat. The Fremantle heritage apartment was acquired twelve months ago after the complicated separation from his wife. The two-bedroom place is as badly maintained as any in the sleazy high-rise ex-state housing block, chosen by Chris for anonymity and price, certainly not amenity.

Chris notes its already 40 degrees as he struggles to clear his head, the aftermath of a boozy session at one of the city's trendy e-bars. Chris, seasoned public servant, community activist, and underground corruption-fighter, knows that Perth is about Blue Sky in more ways than one: his mind picking over the many dramas that are being played out under the blue sky of Perth

Perth, a city where dodgy land deals have become a way of life. Right from 1829, when Captain Stirling and his band from England arrived in search of a fortune from the infant Swan River Colony, the place has been a land scam. Selling limitless prospects to flocks of unsuspecting buyers but delivering limited results for most.

Chris is in danger of being depressed by this chain of thought.

'Ah, the hell with it,' he says, climbing out of bed. 'I'll fight the land sharks another day.'

Chris pads around the unkempt flat, a space he is just beginning to enjoy. He's been a Fremantle resident for fifteen years, but has only just acquired the flat in the centre of his favourite city. Until then, the prospect of being tied to a mortgage had not appealed to him, but with a recent promotion to a highly paid public service job, he had been convinced to take the plunge.

Emerging from the shower, Chris ignores the signs of a beer pot as he glances at his otherwise lithe and lanky reflection in the mirror while throwing on shorts and the obligatory Freo weekend summer gear – shorts, protest T-shirt – state-approved only allowed. This one bears the slogan:

THINK BEFORE YOU ACT

Ironically, this is something Chris is not good at, especially during or after one of his increasingly frequent binges. But it's something he aspires to. To complete his outfit, there's sandals and socks, a habit ingrained by the English parents.

He heads out jauntily for a morning coffee on the cappuccino strip. He recalls how Fremantle used to have a laid-back, almost hippy vibe, but has gone progressively up-market. Its status as a heritage city has almost gone as high-rise buildings take over the city.

As he takes in his surroundings, his mood is broken as he sees the multi-storey building opposite, one that many in the community opposed, as it dwarfs the surrounding historic buildings. This is an issue that Chris's beloved Fremantle First has in the past engaged. But the organisation was outsmarted by a coalition of interests, including the City Council, that promoted high-rise as the way of the future.

Vast tracts of city land were set aside, but this attracted only a few developments. So the development industry pushed for even taller buildings, and recently, a State government redevelopment authority (the FRA) moved in to accelerate the city's makeover, starting with a thirty-storey tower. This was bitterly opposed by Fremantle residents and even some in council, but government went ahead regardless.

Chris is glad that he is no longer a Councillor, a post he held for a few years in the time before high-rise projects got the nod. This was too much for Chris, who figured the odds were stacked against him and the city's heritage. Little did he know the horrors in store, like the office tower that blocked the view of the harbour from the café.

Still, the cafes survive and are a godsend, Chris reflects as he takes over a table in the sun. He dumps the espresso and takes a long drag on his first e-cigarette of the day. The heat of the sun courses through his long, languid body, making him feel almost healthy. But then he coughs, laughs, and coughs some more, swearing that he'll soon give up. But nicotine and its greener alternative help him relax, escape reality.

CASINO FRAUD: PREMIER RESIGNS.
Early election set

But even as he takes in the news posted on the telescreen, he knows there's no lasting escape. He grimaces at the screen. Remembering he's being watched, he soon turns his grimace into a lopsided smile

The screen asks:

What caused the government's downfall?
Arrogance and corruption!
The Premier was paid off –

'Jesus, God, what the hell?' he exclaims, draining the rest of his coffee and listening intently.

He knows the information he and Diana supplied to the press two weeks back would make an impact, but this?

The telescreen outlines how, after Cloke's resignation, Elaine Hipper has been given the dubious mantle of acting Premier. A social worker by background, Hipper was recruited following her term as Mayor of Subiaco, where she was popular and built up an enviable reputation for integrity.

She was inducted into Cabinet soon after her election and quickly showed leadership potential. Bravely wielding a new broom, she is now attempting to sell a government supposedly free of corruption, with an election due in three months' time.

'Some hope,' snorts Chris. 'Even this electorate is not that gullible.'

Still reeling from the news, he looks around at others buried in the news or lighter pursuits and thinks, *You don't know how much I had to do with all this!*

He also recognises the corpulent figure of Doug Dodge shuffling into Joe's coffee shop across the road.

Dodge is accompanied by several others, one of whom is a burly figure Chris has seen before but can't quite identify. Could it be Jack Sizall, shady developer with links to the underworld, one that Chris has recently heard Dodge is taking money from to help shepherd one of his projects through the approval process?

Dodge is a notoriously incompetent businessman and frequently into corrupt deals. He and Chris were on the council at the same time, Dodge is still there. He's a familiar figure in Joe's, where drug dealers, here-today, gone-tomorrow entrepreneurs, nightclub owners, corrupt cops, and officials gather. They're guaranteed safety from prying ears as the broken telescreen somehow never gets repaired.

Dodge has done many a deal in Joe's, enough to keep the money rolling in at a rate sufficient to compensate for the losses his other business interests accumulate.

Chris muses on the murky world of politics. Would Cloke manage to avoid criminal charges? The matter would go to the Corruption Commission but this so-called independent watchdog is still under the thumb of the police.

The cops are the key to this, they must be, he muses.

They've got privileged information, just like the politicians. The police rackets in drugs and prostitution protection are small beer compared to corrupt pollies and business types, and Chris wonders which way the wind will blow.

The sudden ringing of his watch cuts into his reverie. Diana's face comes up on the screen.

'Well, that's Cloke gone, now who's next?' she says in a breathless tone. 'It's time we got together for a celebration, don't you think, darling?'

'Diana just be careful what you say, you never know who might be listening in.' Chris is thinking of several incidents of politicians and public servants being brought to grief by authorised call monitoring by the corrupt authorities.

'OK, OK, Chris, but what about tonight? You owe us that,' returns Diana impatiently.

'Really . . . I mean, see you there,' struggles Chris, and he ends the conversation. Then he wonders how he can change his evening appointment: a phone hook-up with his estranged wife to talk about the son.

His relationship with Diana is fluid enough for him to occasionally put her off. But he realises that won't work tonight; he needs to find a diplomatic way to put his ex off.

As he ponders this and prepares to leave, he sees Dodge emerging from Joe's opposite, and as their eyes meet, Dodge gives Chris the fingers-up sign.

Typical, Chris thinks, refusing to get riled. He is able to smile at Dodge in return.

Dodge has the capacity to get under Chris's skin: from his time on council, Chris knows that Dodge is one of the most corrupt Councillors around. Not only that, but Dodge is an arrogant and objectionable character. He's always hostile to Chris, the more so after Chris exposed a scam Dodge was running. But these days, Dodge's influence in Fremantle is on the wane.

'Well, every cloud has a silver lining. At least Dodge is now on the sidelines,' reflects Chris as he wends his way home after a visit to the markets for his weekly fruit and vege supply.

Later in the day as Chris takes an evening stroll once the intense heat of the sun has gone, an idea crosses his mind.

Christ, I could stand for Fremantle as an independent. I'll get on to the Community Coalition.

The coalition is a group of Freo locals promoting community-based people for political office. They've had a modicum of success in the latest council elections, but not enough to get a majority of seats. And they haven't yet found anyone prepared to run on their ticket for Parliament.

Chris has been a key part of the coalition during his many years as a local resident. He's developed a good profile, something vital for an independent seeking to break into politics. This contrasts with the discreet way he works for the Department of Casino Control. But in both his work and his community activity, he's driven by a strong sense of social justice.

As part of the coalition's leadership team, Chris's most famous hour came when he exposed a planning approval scam where Dodge accepted from the developer an extensive trip in the name of electoral research. This in the lead-up to the vote on the approval of a controversial multi-storey car park. The relevant state authority somehow held this was not a conflict of interest. Hence no action against Dodge. The car park was approved by council later in the year. Chris' group staged a week's sit-in of the Mayor's office. Newly elected Mayor Paula Muscatelli had not supported the car park, although she left the door open for a scaled-down version.

She figured those in opposition to the car park had considerable voting power. She was reluctant to call the cops in to break up the sit-in, bad for PR. She negotiated with Chris. Some said afterwards that Chris had given in to the Mayor's considerable charm. Certainly Chris seemed smitten by Paula. Especially when she set up a meeting to discuss the council decision.

Despite the cynics, a scaling down of the size of the car park resulted. Paula even campaigned for a temporary moratorium on future parking structures. But that was too much for the new conservatives elected at the same time.

Chris's enthusiasm for a parliamentary seat diminishes a tad as he reminds himself Fremantle has been Labor for decades. But then, they are on the nose after the casino scandal. So this could be the time for Chris to dust off those still-present, but submerged state political ambitions.

I'll tell the coalition and the press about how I helped break the scandal, he thought. *That should help convince them a campaign is at least worth a go.*

He's now eager to tell Diana about the idea, but resists. He knows she needs space. But then he weakens and transmits a cheeky message about wanting to discuss some new career ideas. He's later delighted when she responds that she has plenty of ideas that will advance his career as vice-buster.

CHAPTER 5

CELEBRATIONS

Diana is in fine fettle that evening and wears a glamorous, revealing dress, one of her favourites. It emphasises her hourglass figure and shows off her smooth back to perfection. She gives Chris a warm and intimate smile as they meet outside Rory's restaurant.

Apparently in another world, Chris gives her a tentative hug, failing to comment on her appearance. Diana regards him with disappointment when all he offers is to order a drink.

'No, Chris, I'm paying tonight and I'll order the best champagne to start with.'

Chris is unmoved. A deferential waiter approaches their table, deliberately booked by Diana to be as far as possible from the telescreen. The waiter bustles off to get the drinks.

'What's eating you, mate?' Diana probes as Chris almost slumps in his seat.

'Oh, Christ, I'm sorry, Diana. Just that my ex went a bit crazy when I finally got hold of her. I'd been trying to get in touch to cancel the phone hook-up we'd scheduled for tonight to discuss family issues. Brought back all the crap we went through and why we're not together any longer.'

'Sorry to hear that, my sweet,' Diana responds, then reprimands him, 'but come on Chris, get into the moment! Here we are celebrating our great political –'

She trails off as the waiter approaches triumphantly, bearing two glasses of the best champagne the place has on offer, Gaston Chiquet 1989. Diana takes an appreciative sip and nods enthusiastically when the waiter asks if they would like the rest of the bottle.

'Anyway, here's to us!'

Diana raises her glass, and in a last ditch attempt to get Chris into the right zone, rubs her leg against his. She knows his predilections. This succeeds only too well in chiding Chris out of his gloom. He relaxes and smiles sheepishly. They clink glasses and enjoy the golden bubbly liquid.

Diana resumes, 'I was joking about Cloke, of course. But it's reminded me of the treacherous path we're on, exposing this corruption business.'

'*Don't* remind me,' Chris intimates by his grimace.

'Thing is though,' Diana ploughs on, 'I've just cracked a job with Richard Right, Leader of the Opposition and Premier in waiting.'

She smiles, knowing Chris will likely be uneasy about her working for the conservatives. But she sees it as an ideal opportunity to get a close look at the opposition's *modus operandi*.

Making the offer, Right was aware of her Labor sympathies, but advisers can be viewed separately from their political masters. In Diana's case, her good looks and even her efficiency had swayed him. In the hope that he could trust her, possibly befriend and bed her, Right also thought she would prove a handy weapon in the upcoming campaign.

'Fuck! Why?' Chris responds.

'Talk about fraternising with the enemy'. Diana's smile evaporates.

Chris tries to retrieve the situation, 'even though that's the pits, it'll give you a very big window on the Right government, assuming they win the election.' He looks serious for a moment before a wry smile lights up his rather sombre features. 'But we'll have to be bloody careful how we use the information you get,' he concludes.

'And just who said *you're* going to get any information, young man?' Diana teases.

Later, over coffee, following a sensual shared plate of oysters and a brilliant fish dinner, Chris looks out contentedly from their table on Rory's Terrace high above the city. His eye is drawn to the mouth of Fremantle harbour where the sun's last rays bounce spectacularly off the maritime museum, still failing to improve its stolid appearance.

Closer to them the river gleams, the sky's few clouds clinging to the horizon, vivid with red and indigo reflections. Over the past half-century, the Swan has become putrid under the influence of nutrients flushed in from upriver industries, farms, and septic tanks. But tonight, you could ignore that and just admire its tranquil beauty.

And the same's true at five the next morning as Chris wends his way home along the river from Mosman Park, whistling lightly in the aftermath of a memorable night between Diana's sheets. The sex was wild and raunchy, and they experimented with many new positions. They playfully agreed over a shared after-cigarette that should they fail in their political mission, they could make a fortune updating the Kama Sutra.

Chris pulls his battered red petrol-driven Nissan – a vehicle he plans to trade eventually on an electric one, as petrol vehicles are on the way out – into a parking bay and embarks on a walk. It takes him past last night's rendezvous and then along the riverbank. His only company a few early joggers and the odd lazy pelican, that look at him askance from atop jetty posts.

How does that Ogden Nash ditty go? he wonders. Is it:

Ah what a wonderful bird is the Pelican,
His beak can hold more than his belly can . . .

And then? I must look it up . . .

Walking back to his car some thirty minutes later, puffing from the pace he thought he should keep, Chris is surprised to find a note under his windscreen wiper, flapping in the morning easterly.

'*Many a whistle-blower meets a sad end,*' it informs him in an unusual classical script.

'Christ, they're on to me already,' he exclaims

As he travels slowly down to the strip for coffee, he glances about nervously. while keeping a watchful eye on his rear vision mirror. It's only as he calls Diana that he remembers the script on the note matches that which she sometimes uses.

'Got you, lover boy?' laughs Diana as she answers. 'Couldn't resist when I saw your car there. I was on my way to see my son, Peter.'

'OK, you'll get yours.'

'Looking forward to it! See you next weekend, sexy.'

A reminder of their planned trip south.

CHAPTER 6

POLITICAL CAPERS

As she approaches Parliament House, Diana's stomach churns as memories of the days after Cloke sacked her flood back. She's here for her new job with the man who stood most to gain from Cloke's departure, Opposition leader Richard Right. Her mood lightens as she envisages the new political adventures that await in the world of conservative politics.

Right swans out of his den as she comes into his dreary office suite, and he almost falls over in his enthusiasm to greet her.

'Diana, welcome, now you finally *are* in the right place' he jokes weakly, extending a flaccid hand in her direction.

'Thanks Richard'. She smiles, not impressed with his egotistical sense of humour or his limp handshake.

But she is soon into the job: there is an election strategy meeting today, with Diana expected to contribute some 'left of field' ideas. She barely has time to find her desk before being shepherded in to nearby Party HQ to meet the brains-trust of the Liberal Party. Some cynic observed "trust me, the Liberals have no brains at all!"

But this is the group that will, now with Diana's seasoned advice, steer the Party in the upcoming election, based on the slogans which emerge from that meeting:

DO THE RIGHT THING – VOTE FOR
RICHARD'S LIBERALS

one which came from Right who could think of little outside himself.

LIBERAL: THE PARTY FREE OF VESTED INTERESTS

from Diana, she thought tongue-in-cheek, but taken seriously by the brains-trust.

Diana soon immerses herself in the different ways of the Liberal Party. She finds them more assured but less professional than Labor. The reasons for this become clearer as she works with Chris towards the breaking of a new political scandal far more momentous than the one they have just busted open.

CHAPTER 7

MUSICAL CHAIRS

Diana leaps with amazement as her new boss, Richard Right, appears on the six-lane road out of the incessantly spreading fog. Is that a sword on his forehead? What's he doing here anyway?

'I know all about you,' he hisses, advancing on her beneath a blackening sky.

She shrinks back at first, but then dares him to proceed.

God, what will he do? *she thinks with panic, her emotions taking over from her instincts.*

Sweat breaks out all over her aching body. Snakes hiss beneath her feet, the night darkens further as the fog blankets everything to the horizon, now near enough to touch. And in a moment so too would be Right, who grabs the sword from his forehead and advances menacingly. She makes to get away but finds her feet unaccountably heavy, bogged down as if in mud. It's as if she has smoked one joint too many.

'Off with her head!' Right screams. Her slow get-away now becomes impeded by an impossibly steep rocky slope that looms out of nowhere as the road disappears into the fog. Music, with Wagner's stamp on it, blares and she can't get this thought out of her mind, despite the approaching spectre of Right, now wearing a helmet with horns, Brunhilde-like, as he swings his sword in a wide arc above his head.

In fact, she thinks, her musical reverie continuing as Right bears down on her, the music reminds her of the Budapest Opera where, on a recent holiday, she had sat through five long hours of Siegfried. *Her partner at the time had remarked that the canapés and passing parade in the two intervals were much more interesting than the music through which he frequently slept.*

The Wagner music comes to a crescendo just as Right is about to strike.

She's suddenly half awake, sweating, cushions lying askew across the floor. She's frightened, still not able to grasp the fact that she had been experiencing another nightmare. She hears a thumping nearby which confuses her. She half-realises the nightmare is over. Then the thumping becomes louder still and is accompanied by voices calling her name. This almost jerks her awake.

'What the heck?' But then realises the noise is outside this foggy nightmare world.

'Bloody hell! Someone's at the door.'

She trudges from the leather sofa in the TV room where she falls asleep in front of her favourite programme, *Spartacus.* It's now 9:20 p.m. Diana thought it might have been Chris. But then recalls they're off down south together tomorrow.

She's taken aback when she finds Premier Elaine Hipper at the door flanked by two MPs, Judy Doorknock and Yoni McNamara. They glance up at the departing hover helicopter provided for transport.

'Oh, hi, come in.' Diana tries but fails to sound casual and cool. She regards them warily, blearily, the nightmare still clouding her brain.

Since losing her job with Cloke, she's maintained her social link with these Labor politicians; they empathise with her rough treatment and understand that while her affair with Cloke may have been misjudged, it certainly didn't justify her sacking. And they've become friends, even given her new job with Right. Friendship in politics can cross unexpected boundaries, occasionally for genuine reasons. Other times for pragmatic purposes. If Diana had to guess, she would've said that this visit was a mixture of both.

'Are you all right?' inquires Elaine

'Yeah, just a nightmare . . .'

'Hey, we won't be here for long, just want to talk. But first we commiserate with you on your job with Right!' She smiles broadly.

Diana grimaces.

'Right was my nemesis in the nightmare! Bastard was about to behead me!'

As if to illustrate the drama, Diana strokes her neck and throws back her head, showing off her long locks to full advantage. She laughs to relieve her tension.

'Well, I never realised he treated his staff that badly!' Elaine jokes. 'Funny, but your nightmare does make our visit especially well timed.'

'How do you mean?'

'Well, we can explain, but can we sit down first?' requests Yoni, the sort of politician never short of goodwill.

Diana gestures them to the lounge. She doesn't mute the TV as it will effectively mask the telescreen's hearing range. She offers red wine, this one a pinot from her cellar. It lubricates the conversation, one which will have a big influence on the political calendar.

Diana strikes a deal with Elaine and Yoni. The terms? Feed whatever politically sensitive information she gleans concerning the coming election campaign. In return, Elaine promises her a key job. That'll be some interval after the election, on terms and timing of Diana's choosing.

Even if this might mean switching from a job in government to one in opposition, Diana is keen to return to her real political home. And becoming increasingly excited by undercover political work.

The next day, Diana and Chris cruise south on the beltway that helps propel their car, Diana's driverless Tesla, at a safe speed of 160 kph.

Diana tells Chris of the deal. He reckons she's done well, very well indeed, and can no longer contain himself. He excitedly tells Diana about his plans to stand for Parliament.

'Perfect,' she comments, 'if you're in the Parliament, the Liberals will be under even more pressure.'

'Yeah, only problem is I was hoping you would work for me, darling!'

'In your dreams, baby!' Diana shoots back.

Even if she hadn't struck a deal with Hipper, she instinctively knows that to work with Chris would destroy their blossoming relationship.

They soon clear the worst of the traffic and before long are looking down on the canals of Mandurah from the new super bridge that takes them over the Inlet.

Once a sleepy holiday village on the outskirts of Perth, Mandurah has been swamped by city-bound commuters and retirees. Many were recently attracted by the massive extensions of Florida-like canal developments. The wetlands had won international recognition because of their unique ecology, but this mattered little to developers who regarded the wetlands as little more than mosquito-filled muddy swampland.

Diana and Chris are headed beyond the mud and ooze, as far south as Nannup, a small ex-timber town with enough hippy connections to make Fremantle look passé.

Stopping at the aptly named Florida Bakehouse for a never-to-be-bettered slice and coffee, Diana's growing sense of peace is shattered by a clutch of hard-revving motorbikes rumbling in, carrying several members of the Death Cheaters bikie gang, notorious for their involvement in the State's cocaine supply. Often at war with another gang, Hell's Gift, led by Bert Lilliano.

The riders in fading leather stake their claim on the place loudly. Diana's shocked to see a person she recognises as Jack Sizall, shady businessman, car importer, and crime boss.

He's hard to identify with his face obscured by a heavy leather jacket, collar turned up despite the heat. Diana recognises him from the way he sits, slightly aloof, surveying the scene. Just as when he was in her office for a meeting with the Premier earlier in the week. He had come in to talk cars; he's the State's biggest car dealer. Despite Sizall's never-to-be-repeated offer, Right in the end went with Tesla dealer John Views. This because he wanted to distinguish his cars from Labor's and because he hoped the deal would persuade Views, regular donor to the Liberal Party, to come good again for this latest unexpected election.

A few minutes later, Diana and Chris are back on the beltway, its sixteen lanes – eight in each direction – stretching relentlessly to the horizon.

Great, less than an hour to go, used to take two, she thinks. Then her mind returns to the bikers. 'Just what was Sizall doing there?' Diana asks.

No reply from Chris. He's deep into music, seamlessly directed to his ears from the car's central console. Seeing his preoccupation, Diana waves a shapely arm in front of him. Chris reluctantly turns his attention to her as she repeats the question.

'Well, there would have to be the usual coke deals going down,' Chris replies, 'dunno, we might get a better idea tonight. The bikies have a get-together in Nannup this weekend.'

'Jesus, just let's hope the cops don't turn up.'

'They're already there I hear. See it as another opportunity for some digging,' Chris offers.

'Don't you ever get out of the investigative groove?'

'Try me later' is all Diana gets in reply before he switches back to the music.

Chris has had his music fix by the time the car reaches the Big Bong, a laid-back Nannup hotel. Sure enough, they passed a contingent of motorbike police waiting at the entrance to the town. The bikies wouldn't be far behind, especially as they'd driven down the winding Blackwood River valley from Balingup, described by the tourist blurbs as 'one of the prettiest drives in the south-west'. Apart from there being too many dark huddles of pine plantations along the way, Diana for once agrees with the PR.

After dumping their luggage, Diana takes Chris up on his offer of trying him later. Their sex continues the Kama Sutra theme, and they enjoy their bodies intertwining in new positions.

Later still, they head for the wide hotel bar, which opens on to a well-honed verandah with jarrah flooring and wire railings. Several drinkers laze around the space, and a few gather around the hotel bong, in this new era of legalised soft drugs, albeit strictly controlled by the state.

To the amazement of many, the Cloke government moved to allow licensed premises to become legal pot-smoking places similar to the well-known cafes in Amsterdam. The conservative backlash to these measures had been strong, expressing the usual moral outrage and predictions of social breakdown. That hasn't happened, but the killjoys are whipping up a fair degree of hysteria on the topic.

Diana has done her bit to steer Right away from plans to reverse the legislation, by arguing successfully that following the expected election victory, their first one hundred days should concentrate on positive not negative measures.

Meanwhile, it's business as usual at the Big Bong. And knowing the nature of this place, a police raid would only stop the more obvious manifestations of smoking in any case. Even before the reforms, guests were untroubled lighting the odd joint in this laid-back atmosphere. Which is just what Chris does as they slump into one of the comfortable lounges.

Feeling totally relaxed, they head for dinner at the local pub. They're not surprised to find the bar full of bikies, but hadn't counted on the 'raunchy ladies' show that was in its final act, accompanied by raucous encouragement, stamping and cheering from the predominantly male audience. The ladies strut their stuff provocatively and stark naked, apart from a postage stamp, just enough to cover the pubic region.

Diana is disgusted at the carry-on both on and off the stage. She's of the firm view that such entertainment is the worst form of female exploitation for the sexual gratification of men. In contrast, Chris is disappointed that they hadn't got to the pub earlier. He's aware that this won't go down well with Diana, but finds it hard to cover his excitement. His political correctness doesn't extend as far as Diana's, especially after the loosening joint.

After the show, they both note how the ladies fraternise enthusiastically with the bikies, relishing the crowd of bearded men – with a few tough-looking bikies' molls thrown in – that surrounds them like a phalanx. This behaviour indicates that they are well-known or even a part of the bikie world.

The topic of female exploitation dominates Chris and Diana's dinner conversation, with Chris admitting that raunchy ladies under the control of a bikie gang isn't necessarily the best way of progressing gender equality. That's a goal he genuinely believes in, regardless of the stirring in his loins that the well-built catwalk girls brought on.

After dinner, Chris and Diana go for a long walk by the river that winds through the edges of the town, sometimes spilling its banks in winter and flooding much of the low-lying area. Still slightly hazy from their smoke and well-plied with a Margaret River chardonnay they enjoyed with dinner, they are at first indifferent to the shouting and muffled noises in the distance as they head towards the town's camping area.

But the noise becomes impossible to ignore as they come closer to the source. Police lights are flashing on top of several vehicles, which are closing in on a group of militant bikies. From the noises and shouting, it looks like the cops are raiding the bikie enclave.

'Now fancy that,' chirps Chris, 'I wonder if they were tipped off about this one.'

It's common practice for the bent cops to warn the bikies ahead of such raids. Yet the show must go on.

Chris and Diana seek a better vantage point, breaking into a run on the narrow approach road to the camping area. Their progress is temporarily halted by the squeal of tyres and looming headlights of a battered Jeep. The vehicle appeared to have gotten out of the camping area well ahead of a line of police. It accelerates rapidly as it sweeps past Diana and Chris, but Diana spots a familiar figure in the driver's seat.

'Bloody Sizall! Well, that answers your question,' Diana asserts. Funny how the key figure is let leave so easily!

Chris and Diana note that the next day's *Worst* makes no mention of Sizall in their extensive coverage of the raid, portraying it as a 'Police Crack-Down on Bikies Drugs Bonanza'. A substantial amount of cocaine is reported as found at the bikies' camp.

'I guess that is only a tiny proportion of Sizall's stash,' Chris comments over breakfast in the sunny porch of the Big Bong. 'He would have left just enough behind at the camp to make the raid look respectable. The Jeep would've been loaded to the gunnels.'

He goes on to read to Diana an article with a comment from Hipper to the effect that this incident showed how serious her government was about outlawing the bikie drug trade.

'Yeah, sure, as if anyone will take that seriously in the wake of the scandal,' crows Diana. She's well aware that previous governments had sworn to outlaw bikie gangs such as the Death Cheaters in a typical West Australian response to lawlessness – *a ban*. But like other bans, she knows that this one has no chance, especially given the links between the police and the bikies.

'What does my new boss have to say?' asks Diana.

Chris quotes Right to the effect that if elected, his government would move quickly to widen police power ever further and hence be far more effective in 'rooting out' bikie-led crime.

'God, he's sillier than I thought.' Diana smiles reflectively. 'Maybe I can help him sound a bit more sensible next week.'

'Yeah, but just don't tell him about Sizall,' warns Chris.

'Chris, as if.' She looks reprovingly at him. Suitably chastened, he quickly changes the subject.

After breakfast, they walk into town for a lazy coffee and then to Nadine's place. She's an old acquaintance of Chris, and Diana knows her independently. Nadine escaped the city years ago and has become closely involved in the local alternative community as well as pushing environmental and other issues affecting the area. Her HQ is a charming old weatherboard and corrugated iron cottage in the centre of town. Originally belonging to a mill worker, it consists of the standard two rooms off each side of the hallway, neatly extended by some early hippy dropouts 1970s style at the back, opening out into a couple of large rooms and an earthy kitchen.

'Come on in, you old bastard,' yells Nadine, an energetic and upfront redhead in her forties. This from the back of the cottage on hearing the knock at the front door. The door's set under a bull-nosed verandah that wraps around most of the house.

'And that makes two of you, Diana, you must be a bastard to still be mixing with him!'

'Well, I reckon that makes three of us,' jokes Chris as they go for the old group hug.

Hugs follow all round as they meet or renew contact with Nadine's circle, all here for the weekend fun. Many Chris has met before at similar gatherings which Nadine calls two or three times a year. They are a mixture of locals and city professionals. All have brought food to a cook-up which had already started in the kitchen. The smell of pumpkin soup, home-baked bread, and dope soon fills the air.

The weekend meanders on, its easy-going rhythm only broken by a semi-serious political discussion in which several of the group offer to help Chris with his campaign in return for his promise to attend to a number of local issues.

The issue of top priority to Nadine and the locals at present is a proposal for a mega pulp mill. The mill looms as a further threat to the rapidly diminishing forests, although it's being promoted as the only answer to declining jobs in the timber industry. Before its closure decades ago, Nannup's mill was on the brink for years owing to automation and the lowering of the mill's previously lavish timber quotas. These quotas were the main reason that the heart had been ripped out of much of the surrounding jarrah and marri forests: jobs at a very high environmental price.

And while much of what remained of the magnificent old-growth jarrah and marri around Nannup and the karri beyond is officially protected, extensive stands of magnificent trees are still being logged.

A pulp mill would only increase that. The project has been around for a number of years. It's now being strongly promoted with government and opposition falling over each other with hollow promises to support the mill while protecting the forests. A storm of community protest is gathering, and Nannup is its epicentre.

'So, Chris, we know you'll help us on this one when you're an MP up there on the West Perth Hill,' says Nadine as she closes the discussion that gathers around the topic over lunch.

'Goes without saying,' returns Chris. 'Besides, if I refuse, that's curtains on weekends down here!'

'You got it, kid!' from Nadine as she lights one of the biggest joints Chris has seen in a while. Now there was one forest product he has no problems with!

A talking point later in the day is a fracas between some bikies and Nadine in the local pub, when for a laugh – she imagined – she asked one of the bikies for a dance. Several of the bikies' molls took her on one side and stomped on her feet with their heels to warn her off their men.

'Town's not the same since that mob increased their visits a couple of months back,' explains Nadine to the crew. 'But I'll crack a dance one of these days!'

'Well, meantime, darling, you'll just have to dance with me,' offers Chris. 'I work for the government, a far more corrupt outfit than the Death Cheaters!'

'Many a true word said in jest,' affirms Diana who has been talking with Martin, Nadine's on-again off-again lover. They all get into the dancing at that point, and the party is back on the rails.

CHAPTER 8

ELECTION GAMES

Two months later, Premier Hipper calls the election. It's a dirty campaign, more so than usual. Despite desperate advertising and promotions announcing the government's intention to become squeaky clean, the mud from Cloke's adventures sticks.

The steady stream of leaked intelligence from the Right camp – gained by Diana and passed on to Hipper as agreed – is reckoned by pundits to have limited the swing. And influenced the decision of some voters to say, 'A pox on both your houses,' and vote for a mixed bag of independents and Greens. But in the end, Right has the greater number of seats, which leads to a minority conservative government dependent upon a small clutch of sympathetic Independents – of whom Chris was definitely not one – for their survival.

Chris records a convincing win in Fremantle, and that sets the media – even the stern telescreen news – into something of a feeding frenzy: he's the new local hero. His campaign on local issues appeals. He scores a substantial share of the primary vote, mostly torn away from Elias McRafferty, the long-standing but essentially dull local member. This slashes McRafferty's usually unassailable lead, and Chris's vote builds to overtake McRafferty's with a steady stream of preferences.

Days of hard partying follow, interrupted only by contact from the major parties trying to garner Chris's formal support to shore up their embarrassingly low number of seats. He rejects the approaches, determined to stay independent, and not get drawn into deals that he could later regret.

Chris fantasises about holding the balance of power – that is, having the deciding vote in a house evenly balanced between the major power blocks. The numbers just don't stack up that way.

In the upper house, an anachronistic leftover from colonial days, the story is different. Here, independents and Greens do gain the balance of power, and that gives them an important say. But the Liberals have control of the Treasury benches and the State budget, the real key to political power.

Hipper holds on to leadership of the Labor Party, despite several challengers coming forward, including the former police Minister, part of the small Cloke stable still present in the Parliament. But the former Minister's association with Cloke counts strongly against her.

Messages of congratulations to Chris appear in Fremantle shop windows. Business owners fall over themselves to get Chris's attention, but he's aware that they have their own agendas and accepts no compromising favours.

'Hey Chris, you gonna get me that job as government caterer?' Joe, the wily proprietor of the café, asks only half-joking, when Chris drifts in a few days after the election. 'Free coffee forever if you do!' he oozes ingratiatingly.

While Dodge, sitting at his usual table just inside the entrance, adds, 'yeah, and a bloody good thing the new government will be for Fremantle. Only what a fuckin' pity we've got you as our new MP.' He obviously isn't happy this morning. 'You'll trip up soon enough,' Dodge continues, but Chris is in an ebullient mood and Dodge's barbs are not reaching him.

'Give over, Dodge,' he responds, 'you're the one headed for the fall. I hear you've been taking bribes from Jack Sizall.'

Dodge visibly pales and stammers.

'Er, no, you've got the wrong person there, boyo.'

'Oh, do you mean that it was someone else Sizall bribed or that you got the money from someone else, like Lilliano?'

Chris is delighted with Dodge's suddenly changed demeanour; he's struck a raw nerve.

'Fuck you,' fumes Dodge and goes back to his breakfast.

Nice to get the better of Dodge for once, thinks Chris with a chuckle.

CHAPTER 9

DOWN TO BUSINESS

After the election, Diana decides to stay on with Right, taking a raincheck on Hipper's offer. This is a hard decision for her, torn between her thirst for information on the operations of the new government and a new wariness of her boss.

Right drunkenly approached her on election night, inviting her to a back room at Party HQ.

Diana was cautious, asking, 'er what are we going there for?'

'Oh, don't worry, Diana, I just need to have a confidential chat about your role now that it seems certain I'll be Premier.'

'Well alright then,' she replied doubtfully.

Once they reach the room, however, Richard approaches and puts his hand on her backside, then moves closer as if to kiss her. Diana steps away, shocked.

'Excuse me, Richard, that's just not on!'

'Oh, Diana, relax, just a friendly peck.'

'I'm not up for any of that nonsense, Richard. I want our relationship to be purely professional.'

'Well, that wasn't the case with your former boss from what I hear,' he slurs.

'What I did then with Wayne and what I do now with you are totally different. I didn't sleep my way to the top, whatever you might think!'

'Well, girlie, I shee. Look I should apologishe, but you're damned attractive to me!'

'That's as may be, Richard, thanks and please don't call me girlie. So patronising!'

'You women are so demanding!'

With that, he flounces out and back to the rapidly developing party as the returns improve. Diana waits until she recovers from the emotional shock. She takes her leave early.

Not the ideal start to the new era! she thinks reflectively as she's powered home by the Tesla.

But the first post-election meeting of the brains trust gives her a taste of what's to come. At a discussion over lunch, Ken Thumper, developer and Chair of the Party's Strategy Committee, coincidentally a major financial contributor, opens to Right with 'OK, Richard, don't forget who's first in line for those road contracts, like the Rockingham-Midland Highway we're gunna build.'

'And you know who's gonna build the next stage of that bloody Hills railway, and I don't mean Flexible Constructions,' chimes in John Tough. Tough Engineering, another big donor, is a company that aims to go beyond roads into public transport.

Richard smiles obligingly, knowing the die is already cast.

Despite Perth's overwhelming addiction to cars and freeways, trains are fast becoming the new major capital works. First, there was the modest $300 million Joondalup railway in the 1980s: the first suburban rail line built in any Australian city for years. But one that proved extremely popular for the government of the day and helped them get re-elected in the 1980s by virtue of holding on to marginal seats in the vicinity.

More recently came the Mandurah line, a project completed early this century. Railways are rapidly becoming the new pork barrel in WA politics.

But in the past, the conservatives were far more interested in road-building and spent billions extending freeways and major roads across the city. The road-building extravaganza went under the unlikely title of *Transform WA*. Transform it into what? Land development heaven perhaps, since the new roads helped open up even more land.

But political gamesmanship on either side comes at a price: under Cloke, the cost of a new hills railway project had blown out to an embarrassing and budget-stretching $3 billion, a doubling of the $1.5 billion original estimate.

Right had been informed by strategists that his new government was stuck with completing the project, and in any case, abandonment at this stage would prove politically embarrassing. More importantly, if he was going to be allocating large rail contracts, then he had to ensure they went to the biggest donors – *whoops,* he thought, *correct that for public consumption to the most proficient and economical contractors.*

In the face of these possibilities, Diana's enchanted to think she has struck scandal gold again. The thought is especially delicious since the government's been elected on a platform of honesty, inspired by Diana's very own slogan. But she would be strategic with her use of the information, give them enough rope.

Besides, Diana has been given the job of drawing up Richard's personal agenda for the first hundred days of government, and for the moment, she needs to concentrate her energy on that target. That and keeping Richard's hands off her; even after she knocked him back on election night, she can sense he hasn't got the message. A hundred days, a target more difficult than she would have thought a few months ago, Right heads a minority government, and it would only take one Independent to cross the floor and the government would fall.

So a lot of Diana's time is spent with Richard and his acolytes in the parliamentary bar, a place where bored parliamentarians and their hangers-on frequently gather. Diana is careful with her consumption, conscious of her figure and the need to get home safely. Many in this crew get disgustingly drunk as the long-sitting nights accumulate. And some take the same approach to her as Richard, becoming overfamiliar on more than one occasion.

This irks Diana and frequently prompts her to take her leave and work in the office on the programme. With that and the continuing harassment from Right, Diana is not sure she'll even make it to the hundred days. It now stretches before her like a life sentence.

CHAPTER 10

SAUCY BUSINESS

Keeping an eye on government is one of Chris's preoccupations as a new MP. But he's surprised to find that there are only twenty-six parliamentary sitting weeks scheduled for the year and only three days per week. He also finds out quickly there is a lot more to being a politician than attending Parliament, and sometimes those sixty days could be twelve or fourteen hours each.

Chris finds he understands why so many members take refuge in drink during and after sitting hours. On late and often boring sitting nights, Chris discovers, to the detriment of his health, that a casual drink often leads to a serious drinking session.

It's a Wednesday and Chris has the mid-week parliamentary blues. He has no interest in the debate (on the restructuring of the Potato board) going on interminably in the chamber, so he makes his way to the bar. He looks around the room and, not seeing anyone he wants to sit with, makes his way to a corner table and catches up on the day's news.

He's not seeing much of Diana as she's nearly always busy on Right's latest agenda. And he's often busy on his own crowded programme. Their paths occasionally cross in the corridors or even in the bar, but while they nod to each other politely, they've agreed this is best for protection of Diana's reputation; in any case, their relationship is in a static stage. They only manage to catch up on the occasional weekend, and then they're too tired to continue the Kama Sutra routine. Chris is restless and prone to be thinking of moving on. Diana's too busy to think about the future.

The TV news doesn't hold Chris's interest for long, and as he looks up, the elegant Sarah Kingswood, MLA, walks into the room and makes her way to the bar to order a drink. His interest is piqued: with his roving eye, it hasn't taken long for Chris to pick out the most attractive women in the Parliament, and Sarah is definitely amongst them. Not only that, but her political star is on the rise in the government. Like Chris, she's only been in Parliament since the election and is tipped as a future Minister; at Diana's urging Richard promises a Cabinet renewal after the first hundred days in office. Women were severely underrepresented in his post-election ministry.

But Chris also recalls how Diana warned him off Sarah; she's married, attractive, and by all counts, not averse to affairs. Not only that, but as Chris well knows, she's on the conservative wing of the government. Her initial parliamentary speech damned what she described as the left's 'obsession with stopping development in this great State'. She was particularly critical of moves to stymie the pulp mill, moves which Chris is right behind.

Despite all this, Chris smiles invitingly at Sarah as she turns from the bar, drink in hand. Sarah returns his smile with insouciance, but makes her way over to his table and says,

'Ah, the member for Fremantle, Chris, how are you?'

'Bored, I'd have to say, but will you join me, Sarah?'

Sarah hesitates; they've only met in passing in the corridors.

'You're not nervous of being seen in my company, surely?' Chris goes on.

'Well, you have been giving government a hard time.' Sarah's tone is neutral.

'But I haven't said anything much about you, Sarah!' Chris tries, mockingly.

'It'll only be a matter of time I should think,' Sarah replies drily.

Chris motions to a seat opposite him, and to his surprise, Sarah takes it. As she sits down, she smooths her dress over shapely legs and looks quizzically at Chris. His pulse rate shoots up, but he tries to remain cool.

'There's plenty I could say about the government, but we could steer our conversation away from party politics tonight!'

Sarah visibly relaxes at this suggestion and asks how he is adapting to parliamentary life.

'Well, I've discovered it's not all it's cracked up to be.'

'I'll drink to that,' returns Sarah brightly.

She raises her glass, Chris does the same, and both quaff a good measure of wine. Chris is drinking red tonight, one of his favourite Frankland Shiraz varieties, the only disadvantage of which is the high sulphur content and the morning headache that often follows. He knows he should drink less and also turn to organic varieties, but old habits die hard.

Their conversation turns to wine and other topics. Chris is excited that he and Sarah seem to click; there's a spark between them despite (or because of?) their political differences, and they share the common gripes of newcomers.

As they leave the bar to return to the debate an hour later, Chris is chuffed when Sarah agrees that they should do the same again.

'Sooner rather than later, I suggest,' Sarah adds, in case Chris thought she was just being polite.

Chris stops in the corridor to chat to a female colleague and watches Sarah's sashaying movements with a keen eye as she returns to the debating chamber. The colleague raises an eyebrow at Chris and says, 'just remember the dangers of sleeping with the enemy, Chris!'

'*Alright*, I was just looking,' returns Chris, blushing.

'Well, I'm not sure if I believe you, you seemed on very friendly terms when I popped into the bar earlier.'

Chris had been oblivious to people coming and going, so engrossed was he in his conversation with Sarah, and so taken was he by her company.

'Come on, I have to do something to pass the time.'

His colleague's reply is drowned out by the ringing of bells, summoning him to return to the chamber for a vote. He puts up both hands palm upwards to indicate the end of the conversation and takes off swiftly. A lucky escape there, he thinks as he bursts through the door and tries to decide which way to vote on a clause of a bill he knows very little about.

Meanwhile, Diana also finds that, despite her best efforts to stay cosseted in here office, more than a modicum of her time is spent with Richard and his acolytes in the members bar. Richard demands her presence, telling her he needs her advice on tap.

Badly pissed and hungover MPs become such a common sight to Diana that she accepts them as a fact of parliamentary life. And there are plenty around one night early in the first week of the new sitting as the police Minister makes his way unsteadily through the crowded bar in her direction.

Diana vaguely wonders through her growing white-wine haze whether she should remind him that her speech, that is his speech, on the Prostitution Control Bill is coming up in twenty minutes. She is of the mind that the government line – more police on the ground equals less crime – should not be pushed too strongly and has constructed the Minister's speech accordingly.

The Minister, who often shows no sense of propriety, comes closer and drapes a languorous arm over the back of Diana's chair. His erratic manner indicates that the bar's supplies of his favourite single-malt whisky have taken a big dent in the last few hours.

'What about this, Diana?' he starts, then pauses as he points out a paragraph in bold on the second page of his copy of Diana's carefully prepared speech notes. He seems to forget what he was saying in mid-sentence, and Diana senses he's losing the plot.

'Are you shuggesting I shay that prostitutes will get more police time?' he slurs.

'Minister, with respect' – not that she feels any – 'that means the criminals behind prostitution, not the pros themselves,' Diana joins in the badinage.

'Well, all I can shay ish that I don't want any of *my* girls put out of business,' he says pointedly, then his already ruddy face goes a deeper shade as he realises he has said too much. He laughs nervously, trying to cover his embarrassment. 'Only joking of course!' he grins in an ungainly effort to convince Diana.

Diana has heard rumours of heavy political connections in prostitution, and she realises this is no joke. It's another priceless piece in the jigsaw to know that the ambitious Minister is directly involved. Diana judiciously plays the innocent and goes along with the joke while making another mental note for a later debriefing.

'I know that, Minister!' she manages. 'Anyway, maybe you need a strong coffee before you get on with that speech?' she goes on, seeing the opportunity to bring the conversation back to where it had started.

'Great idea!' he slurs.

The Minister slumps down in the chair opposite, next to Bridget, his press officer. Diana is becoming good mates with Bridget as they swap notes over the foibles of their bosses. Bridget hadn't heard the exchange between Diana and her boss since she was busy with another conversation at the time. She simply raises a 'watch it girl, he's usually pissed after dinner!' eyebrow in Diana's direction as the Minister leant over her.

Now, Bridget smiles and starts fussing over her boss. She gets him an extra strong coffee to help him put on a semblance of sobriety. She later tells Diana of the time when, towards the end of Cloke's premiership, the Speaker was so sozzled that he came to grief while trying to silence the all-too-common uproar in the house. An over-enthusiastic and mistimed blow from his gavel propelled him from his pulpit to land him on the clerk's desk below amid a wild scattering of papers and people.

Later that night, Chris and Diana do connect for a change. Over supper, Diana gives Chris a humorous account of the Minister's unwitting revelations. Chris is delighted to have some more potential ammunition, and he laughs along with her.

But Diana is only too well aware that there is a serious side to all of this, even though few politicians are called to task for overdoing the grog. She wonders if Chris – with his liking for alcohol – will survive this regime. Chris is oblivious to this line of thought as he downs another glass of whisky, which brings his consumption to danger level considering the red wine he consumed with Sarah earlier.

In an effort to mask his growing befuddlement, he asks Diana, 'why d'you think the press stays quiet about all this drinking?'

'Maybe because they don't like pointing the finger at something so close to home! There are heaps of heavy drinkers amongst my journalist colleagues, that's for sure. And tell you what, I can see why they get into it up here – tonight would have been a bit of a nightmare for me without it,' Diana replies.

'Hmm, I reckon the unwritten rule is that it is OK to drink as long as it's kept in the family,' reflects Chris. 'Drunken behaviour is frowned upon, but grog is an accepted part of life up here.'

'Well yes, but don't get too precious about it, mate!' Diana points to the glass of scotch Chris has just had refreshed. 'There's quite a few politicians who've retired early due to the demon drink.'

'Hmm,' says Chris, colouring slightly, 'but talking about retirement, the superannuation scheme up here is incredible. I could retire with a couple of million dollars up-front, or a yearly pension of over $100,000 after only serving eight years! Packages like that are only matched by the ridiculous bonuses paid to private sector bosses.'

He goes on to tell her that he was amazed to hear his new colleagues whining incessantly about how poorly compensated they are for all their hard work. He'd been told that this topic came under more scrutiny and led to more animated discussion in the Party rooms than did any policy matter.

'Now I know the real reason you decided to go into politics!' laughs Diana.

'Hell, no. I want to go one better and get a sinecure like head of the FRA when I retire!' Chris jokes.

He's referring to the job currently held by Fred Chewis, ex-planning Minister appointed by Cloke before his demise. Hipper had been tempted to sack him, but found it would have been incredibly expensive to terminate his very well-paid contract.

CHAPTER 11

BUSINESS AS USUAL?

Down at the FRA's Fremantle office, Chewis is coming to terms with the change of government and what it would mean – his major concern is always for himself.

When he was planning Minister, a phone conversation with the Premier had gone like this:

> *Premier: I hear you're trying to block that new city office proposal?*
> *Chewis: Well, Wayne, it's right against our policy on central city parking. We are committed to keeping the number of cars down in the city centre. This development has ten times the number of parking bays allowed for at that site.*
> *Premier: OK, but you fucking well know it's going to give that part of the city a boost and create lots of new jobs. And it is sponsored by government agencies and some big-time Party donors.*
> *Chewis: Yeah, but surely the fucking donors have had enough favours for now?*
> *Premier: Fred, do you want to keep your job as planning Minister?*
> *Chewis (faltering): I, er, sure, Wayne.*
> *Premier: Well, just approve the bloody development will you or you'll be out of the Cabinet in a flash!*

Chewis: *Er, yes, I see what you mean, Wayne [long pause] . . . hmm . . . yes, why not? A few extra cars in the city streets won't make any difference compared to the economic joy that development will generate for us in the lead up to the next election.*
Premier: *Good to see you've got the message, Fred, and in time, you'll see how your decision pays off!*

And so Chewis kept his job, and the cronies continued to make economic hay while the sun shone. Soon afterwards, the story about the doubtful car park approval came to light, but it was never verified. Chewis was persuaded to quietly step down from Parliament, comforted by his new job as head of the FRA. Cloke figured that Chewis would respond appropriately to the demands of the big boys in the property market.

Today, Chewis is faced with another important decision. The FRA is under political pressure from Dodge and his council mates to endorse a controversial application for a new brothel in the city.

For his own reasons, Chewis is keen to progress the application but not be seen to be doing so. He dictates a note to his secretary – secretaries being a luxury these days, but not yet for the big boys.

He also dictates a press release praising the government for its anti-prostitution legislation and pointing out the brothel should be outlawed for this reason alone.

Some Fremantle Councillors have previously expressed support for the brothel despite vigorous community opposition and much outcry from Chris as Fremantle MP. Mayor Paula Muscatelli, who also has a seat on the FRA board, has so far kept her options open on the issue: on the one hand, she made some critical remarks, but on the other, she let it be known that she would not be able to vote on the matter, as her family owned property nearby.

At the Fremantle FRA board meeting, Chewis opens discussion: 'board members, I think the brothel application should be refused, due to the Port's need to acquire more property.'

Chris scratches his head at this pronouncement and looks around the table, noticing some other members look equally surprised. Chewis takes this in and continues, 'members, let's face it, we do need to remove the danger and inconvenience caused by residential properties close to the working port. The houses can be converted to suitable commercial uses, and that doesn't include brothels . . .' He smiles and trails off. Lying comes easily to Chewis after many years of practice in Cabinet.

A perfunctory debate follows, with Chris bemusedly expressing support for Chewis. Sgt Bill Murkitt, the Fremantle police representative, chimes in with 'While the properties are being acquired, we should seek out these suitable uses you mention, Chairman.'

'Too right,' replies Chewis. 'We'll set up a working party to investigate that further after we've got the houses.'

What are they up to this time? Chris thinks. While he has yet to meet Murkitt, the track record of Fremantle police in this area is hardly squeaky clean. But he keeps his counsel.

Mayor Muscatelli enters the debate briefly: 'I can't vote on this because of my nearby properties, but I want it on record that I'm not at all happy with brothel proposals in Fremantle, especially this one. Despite many on my council supporting the application, I have to take wider community views into account.'

On hearing this, Murkitt audibly groans. Chris also takes note and wonders if this application is the scam Dodge was working on when he spotted him in company at Joe's café recently. Maybe Sizall's long-time rival, Bert Lilliano, is behind it? Maybe Murkitt is dealing with one, Dodge with the other?

As he listens to the Mayor's comments, Chris starts to wonder if she, whose good looks attract his eye, is changing her political spots. She was elected on a middle-of-the-road platform against a candidate he would rather have seen win. Before he finishes this line of thought, the recommendation to acquire the properties is unanimously adopted.

While approving noises come from the community and the local press at the unexpected outcome, Dodge and his supporters are positively spitting chips. The FRA has become the main obstacle in the way of their plans, but that won't stop the backers blaming him. Dodge is a bully, well-practiced at hurling random abuse at bemused constituents, but not so well equipped to deal with the mob of heavies behind the application. Their underlings double as bouncers at late-night venues in the city, using the clubs as outlets for drugs sourced through bikie gangs.

It's time for Dodge to try and put the fire out, and he starts by going to see Mayor Muscatelli, having been under the impression that she would either support the brothel scheme or keep quiet about it. Paula is agitated, making it clear that she wants the scheme scuttled. Dodge tells her she has no right to oppose the brothel considering that a majority of her Councillors support it.

'In any case,' Dodge goes on, 'you owe me a political favour. Don't forget how much help I gave to get you your bloody job.'

Paula is taken aback at his effrontery.

'You might have been on my election team, Dodge, but I don't owe you any favours. I don't do business that way. I suggest you go and talk to Bill Murkitt.'

Dodge storms out. When he makes contact with Murkitt, he is relieved to find that they talk the same language. Murkitt promises to get the ball rolling at the FRA, but in return insists that Dodge give him the lion's share of his 'commission' once the brothels are operational. Dodge reluctantly agrees. What choice does he have?

Some days later, Murkitt seeks a meeting with Chewis under the pretext of properly introducing himself as the new police rep on the board. They meet in Chewis's spacious dockside office at the top of the recently completed thirty-storey building overlooking Fremantle harbour. Like the board-room on the floor below where last week's meeting was held, it offers spectacular views of the city, the coast, and the development corridors to the north and south, the ocean westwards and the sprawling metropolis to the east.

Residents complain that the building is totally out of scale and character with the heritage structures in the city's adjacent West End. Not only that but before the offices were built, ships docking in the harbour were seen from the city towering over old colonial buildings like the railway station. Ships looked just as if they were sailing in to dock at the platforms. The development removed the magic of this unique element.

At first, Chewis is wary of Murkitt.

'Well, Bill, to what do I owe this honour?'

'Oh, I thought we should get to know each other better, Fred, so that we can build a more co-operative relationship between the FRA and the police.'

He's referring to the FRA plans that would relocate the police from their long-time site near the Fremantle markets. This to create space for expansion of the markets, restoration of the historic sloping walkway up to the old Fremantle Goal, and expansion of nearby Fremantle oval, home of many a classic Aussie Rules match.

An expanded facility would become the long-term HQ for the Freo Dockers who've been playing 'home' matches some distance away. It would be a popular move, following the Docker's finally winning their first Premiership cup in 2024.

Part of the plan is to install the police in the office complex on the harbour front. But the police are reluctant to move from what they regard as their own home ground, and so far, they've stalled by simply refusing repeated FRA requests to discuss the matter.

'Good idea, Bill, maybe we could start by opening up discussion on our redevelopment plan?'

'Sure, Fred, but you know the police hierarchy are adamantly opposed to moving?' Murkitt adjusts his fading tie, with its characteristic skull and crossbones, as if to emphasise the point.

'And what do you think could change that?'

'Well, we are off the record here?'

'Of course, these meetings will always be off the record as far as I'm concerned. I guess that suits both of us, gives us room to move if you know what I mean?' Chewis does his best to smile pleasantly.

'That suits me perfectly Fred, but you know that matter of the brothel and the compulsory acquisition that came up at the recent board meeting?'

Chewis nods.

'Well, I thought the FRA just might be able to see its way clear to installing a health centre there instead of the brothels. I mean, massage is an essential health service if you see where I'm coming from?'

'I get your drift, Bill. Hmm . . . A health centre? Now of course, the FRA would *never* agree to a brothel, but health centres are a different matter.'

Chewis winks. Murkitt winks back.

'I wonder if the public will buy it though,' Chewis muses.

'Well, they just might if we make the approval subject to the usual police checks on the centre's bona fides.'

And so the seeds of a deal are planted that allows Chewis to have 'his' brothel, in return for the police moving to the harbour front. Murkitt is happy, Chewis is happy, and soon the local police Superintendent and the developer will get their cut, and they'll be happy as well. Oh, what a wonderful world.

CHAPTER 12

TVTV

'The little shit!' shouts Gabor, the irrepressible wily chief and TV producer, as he slams the phone down after another long and difficult conversation with James Ambognas, also a producer.

A very prickly producer with a reputation not so much for creating programmes, but more for creating organizational problems. His political agenda is often confused, but he's made it clear to all and sundry that he regards the new Premier as the man of the moment. He's already made a pitch to be Right's media advisor, but so far Diana, who knows Ambognas and his reputation, has managed to block his approaches.

'I'll murder that bastard one of these days,' Gabor jokes to Greg Jones at the next desk.

'Good idea, Gabor, but TVTV won't be able to afford to defend you!' Greg responds. 'Hey, man, it's time for that interview.'

Greg is a bearded Perth identity, bon vivant, and man about town who runs the program *Planning Exposure*, a weekly round of planning issues. Because of his anarchistic approach to life, Greg is often at odds with Gabor and TVTV management. As a result, they've made periodic moves to keep his rather wacky programs off the air. But these days, if such action is threatened, rather than arguing the toss, he goes around them uploading his programs onto the Internet via U-tube.

Gabor is the mainstay of TVTV, the community-based production house and TV station that makes and broadcasts programmes on Channel 61.

The station is often preoccupied with the typical money and ego battles of a community-based organization. Apart from Gabor, TVTV is largely run by volunteers, who produce programmes that give otherwise disenfranchised communities a voice. The job is made difficult by a lack of money. There's precious little public funding, and sponsors for programmes are few and far between.

Their job is made even harder by Ambognas, miffed that Gabor has left him out of a new monthly programme on politics, dubbed *PolySpeak*. The show is hosted by Jones, who has a keen understanding of how the community is often screwed by the political system. Jones also has a reputation as a stirrer and is instantly recognisable from his funky appearance – voluminous bushy beard of which an orthodox jew would be proud, offbeat clothing, wild hair, and outlandish hats.

Ambognas is threatening dire unspecified consequences if Gabor doesn't let him in. Gabor refuses, and in any case, the first batch of programmes is about to go to air. These are to feature the clutch of new community-based MPs.

Chris is first cab off the rank and is currently in the studio. Given the momentous and unexpected nature of his election win and the subsequent high degree of public interest, the programme is going live-to-air, with Gabor directing the cameras and organising the technical side of the broadcast.

The interview goes well: Chris comes across as a man of the people. Greg has skilfully brought out his sense of humour, which oils the interview wheels beautifully. They have covered Chris's background, his history as an activist, and the story behind the revelations that brought Cloke down and propelled Chris into Parliament.

Greg: Now Chris, tell us about your programme in Parliament. How are you planning to deal with this fusty old institution?

Chris: Well, I don't intend to get bogged down, Greg, I'd like to see the procedure up there changed so that it is less formal, less adversarial, more open to genuine discussion.

Greg: Sounds good, but can you convince your fellow MPs?

Before Chris can reply, a loud voice off set is heard,

'That prick shouldn't be allowed into Parliament, let alone try to change the culture!'

Gabor turns angrily to see a coat-clad Ambognas burst into the studio, brushing aside the door attendants, and advancing rapidly shouting abuse at Chris and anyone else in his sightline.

'Fuck off, Ambognas,' Gabor yells, and then belatedly. 'Cut transmission for Christ's sake.'

The techs are already on to it, and transmission stops but not before the damage is done. The techs keep the cameras rolling, realising the drama is worth recording. 'Reality TV with a difference,' observes one of them wryly.

Chris gets to his feet, hoping to find a quick exit; he's shocked at the violence of the man's invective. He sees a man with a mission, the sort of person who'll stop at nothing to achieve his ends.

'Must be upset at the election result!' Chris quips, but he can't be heard above the increasing melee.

Several people try to stop Ambognas, but he takes a knife from his coat and makes a dash towards Gabor. As he sweeps past, Chris deftly shoots a foot out and trips Ambognas, who falls heavily onto the knife. He yells in pain and clutches his stomach as blood forms a pool on the studio floor.

All hell breaks loose as Gabor moves in and delivers a sharp kick to Ambognas's balls. He groans heavily and writhes in double agony.

Gabor reaches to retrieve the blood-covered knife, but Greg grabs him and pulls him away.

'Come on, Gabor, do you really want to carry out your murder threat?'

'No and you *can* let go of me now Greg,' Gabor assures him.

The cops have been called, and an ambulance can be heard wailing down the street. Ambognas is rushed off to emergency. For long afterwards, he nurses a sore stomach and particularly sore balls. The police waste little time and charge him with attempted assault with intent to cause bodily harm.

They take Gabor at his word when he tells them there is no footage of the event as he ordered the broadcast to stop as soon as he saw Ambognas burst in. In order to keep them schtum, Gabor winks at the cameramen as he spins this line.

But this later lands Gabor in difficulty with the long arm of the law. That night, TVTV broadcasts dramatic footage of the incident on their news segment and, after that, are able to sell the footage to other media outlets. The media are keen, especially since new star MP Chris features in the action.

Commercial TV channels, and other media come to the party and pay TVTV healthy fees for 'exclusive' coverage of the event. The upshot is that, thanks to Ambognas, TVTV experience a sudden change in their financial fortunes.

But this may not last for long. The police are testy, first because Gabor apparently lied to them about there being no footage of the event. Gabor protests innocence, saying he didn't realise until later that the cameras kept rolling after the broadcast was cut, and the cameramen say they didn't hear the police question Gabor. The police have trouble with this story and threaten to charge Gabor for withholding evidence, but they are also dark that the footage was broadcast at all, holding that it has prejudiced the trial and should have been handed to them on request.

So while the new-found wealth means TVTV can launch a whole raft of new programmes (or pay their chief more, Greg cynically suggests), they also have to hire lawyers to keep the police at bay. To help, they are flooded with a new wave of volunteers, anxious to find out whether community TV is this exciting all the time. Gabor and his team heave a big sigh of relief when Ambognas is forced to resign from the committee. He tries to convince the police to charge Gabor with assault, but they just laughed when they saw the graphic footage of Gabor's swift kick.

For Chris, it's an unexpected outcome: he loses a big slice of his airtime but emerges as a hero for his quick tripping of Ambognas. He also becomes the main eyewitness for the media and plays a big part in subsequent coverage of the event. Interstate and international interest soon turns the whole thing into a media circus and much is made of politics wild west style.

Chris escapes to Nannup for a few days to avoid further unwanted media attention. He contacts Diana to see if she can join him, but she's too busy, accompanying Right on a visit to the State's north-west, where the latest mining boom is under way. This time, it's the opening of a long-deferred iron ore mine to supply the apparently insatiable Chinese market.

After the drive down to Nannup – this time he takes the direct route, as fast as his old rattler will take him – Chris heads straight to Nadine's and finds her at home brewing a cuppa.

'G'day, you bloody media junkie!' is her greeting.

'You're in fine form, I can see, you political groupie!' he returns as they hug.

'As always, Chris. Hey, after a cuppa and the obligatory joint, how about we pursue your new agenda, helping us out down here with some local political problems?'

Chris groans inwardly as he recalls *commitments* made during his recent pre-election visit to the town. He reflects how much easier it is to make commitments before a poll than it is to follow them through later!

'Christ, Nadine, you never lose an opportunity!' he says in an aggrieved tone.

'You're the one who wants to be the pollie, Chris,' Nadine reminds him, laughing and jabbing him in the chest.

'More fool me,' says Chris ruefully, as he mock-kicks Nadine in return.

'None of your city political tactics here, ma-aa-te!' cautions Nadine in an obvious reference to his recent fracas at TVTV. Nadine has deliberately used the take-off pronunciation of the 'mate' favoured by Party heavies. This exchange and the joint that follow soon help Chris to the realisation his new 'rural' political project could be fun if he keeps his sense of humour.

Later in the day, Chris is looking forward to a well-earned quiet drink. But he soon finds that the town had been captivated by the story of his well-timed trip of Gabor's assailant, and he's recognised everywhere he goes.

A mixture of admiration and mock humour greets him at the pub:

'Geez, mate, you should be Minister for police after that!'

'Where's the TV coverage for this visit, mate?'

'That knife attack will stand you in good stead for Parliament!'

These are typical of the jests directed at him over the weekend. Once Chris realises what he has let himself in for he decides to go with it and starts to enjoy his newfound celebrity status. He even has a badge made by one of his hippy mates at the local screen printers, reading:

YES I'M THE TV TRIPPER

On Sunday, Chris wears the button with relish, and it elicits a variety of responses, with most taking it in good humour.

Back at TVTV, Gabor is working on an interview with John Chipper, the new Minister for forests. They are also planning to invite key ferals in the hope that the session might provide action to match that which Ambognas had provided in the first broadcast. This time, Gabor decides to keep the police informed of his plans. As usual he is attempting to play the system both ways. Greg suggests Gabor would make a great politician.

CHAPTER 13

PERTH – A CITY FOR CARS

As he heads down the freeway for the third time that day, off to another meeting, Chris has plenty of opportunity to reflect on the time he spends driving around the metropolis. His car sports bumper stickers galore, but his favourite says simply **Perth: A City for Cars.**

Designed by an artist friend of his in the early nineties, he has kept one on his car ever since.

These days, he's frequently chided over the sticker for apparently supporting car use in a time of global warming, rising petrol prices, and impending fuel shortages. But Chris tells anyone who expresses concern that the sticker is designed to be read ironically to remind us of what Perth has become, not what he would like it to be!

Chris swings his Nissan onto the bridge into South Perth where the freeway snakes its way along the foreshore. The river is ruffled by an early afternoon sea breeze. He guns his old faithful close to the 100 kph speed limit; anything faster and the car threatens to shudder apart.

He reflects on how the freeway has only left a sliver of foreshore in place of the wide riverside park of old. It alienates the suburb from its western river foreshore. Above the incessant roar of the traffic, he asks his passenger, 'Hey, Francine, what do you reckon South Perth was like before the freeway?'

Francine Burt, his newly appointed young research assistant on the end of the question, looks at him sceptically and comes back with 'OK, old man.'

She smiles to make it clear she has her tongue-in-cheek. 'You know I'm too young to remember, but I've studied a bit of history. Oh, and I haven't told you I've read most of Tom Hungerford's stories of old South Perth too! So when I say South Perth before the freeway would have been intimately connected to the River, quieter and maybe a bit more innocent, it's not a complete guess . . .'

'Fair enough,' Chris breaks in suitably admonished. 'Yeah, that's right, sorry, I'd forgotten that one of the chapters in your PhD deals with the impact of the freeway on South Perth. All the more reason for publishing it, I reckon!'

Francine winces; she isn't ready to re-visit it, having only completed last year after much painstaking work. She then embarked on some overseas travel, only recently returning to Perth. Her thesis is an 'alternative' critical history of the Main Roads Department. Chris was impressed when he read it, and it played a big part in her getting the job.

'You should talk to Greg Jones who was born and bred here. He calls himself a son of the South Perth soil, and in the sixties, he used to raid the nests of the red-capped dotterels on the foreshore. And even when the freeway went in, you could run across the four lanes easily if you were agile. Just try it today.'

His reverie is cut short as a Perth-bound electric train shoots past them between the concrete barriers of the median strip, almost finished in its journey from Mandurah.

'Hey, Chris, forget about roads for a minute, wouldn't it have been brilliant if we could have somehow gotten that railway to connect Mandurah to Fremantle rather than Perth?' asks Francine.

'Right on!' says Chris approvingly. 'A few of us pushed that idea for years, but no one listened. But if you think of a way we can still get Fremantle in on the rail act, let me know!'

'I'll work on it, Chris.' Francine smiles.

They're building on an earlier discussion on whether they should travel to the meeting by train or by car. Francine had questioned Chris's frequent use of the car; after all, he advocated public transport over the car. He had already caused a bit of a stir by opting to keep his battered Nissan rather than take a new electric car offered to all MPs as part of their salary package. He argued that MPs shouldn't be driving subsidised new cars and asserted that his Nissan had a few more years in it yet. Never mind the emissions the car churns into the air.

Today, his meetings are in suburbs off the railway line, so the car seemed the best option. But in later discussion over sandwiches with Francine, he decides that in future his day's travel would use bike or public transport. This would mean more travel time since bike and public transport journeys take longer, especially where destinations aren't directly served by rail. Patience would be called for, a commodity Chris is often short on, but his new modes of travel might also be good for publicity. Political opportunism? Never!

They come off the freeway on a ramp overlooking Rockingham station. Ironically, this meeting is about Perth's obsession with making things even easier to get around by car.

The proposed Rockingham-Midland Highway is routed through serene wetlands. According to the publicity, it would be fabulously engineered, with provision for public transport, but it would still hack right through valuable wetland and a well-used park.

The plan has been around for years, but the community successfully resisted attempts to build it. Yet during the election campaign, Right has stated categorically that his government would build the road.

Chris responded during his election campaign, 'this highway will be an environmental disaster: it will destroy a fantastic wetland and rip through the heart of the community. It will generate unwanted traffic in an area now relatively free of it. The road was taken off the map, but Right wants to reinstate it under pressure from noisy constituents, the car lobby, and the Mad Roads Department, er, sorry, I mean the Main

Roads Department! I will continue to fight with the community to stop this road!' (Cheers).

Today's meeting is designed to come up with means to achieve just that. This was to prove difficult, as the pro-road lobby, heartened by the government's announcement, unexpectedly turn up in force waving placards and chanting, 'What do we want?'

'Rockingham-Midland Highway!'

'When do we want it?'

'Now!'

For years, conservatives in this part of suburbia had been running a slick, well-financed campaign to convince residents that there would be chaos and mayhem on other local roads if the highway were not constructed.

Looking around the pro-road crowd, Chris is surprised to see Ambognas with a video camera crew. Ambognas had arrived at the scene early on. Out of hospital for a week or so he's yet to have his day in Court. Ambognas is filming people drifting into the meeting and interviewing figures from the contrived opposition. Chris guesses that this would be for Ambognas's proposed new TV show *Social Conflict*.

Gabor had briefed Chris after Ambognas's attack at TVTV. The concept for the show had been approved when things were running more smoothly between them, but when Ambognas resigned from the Committee, the show had been cancelled. Since then, however, Ambognas had outsmarted TVTV by convincing another channel to put on his show with MRD as sponsor.

'Hell, what's your "friend" doing here?' asks Francine as they survey the scene. She recognises Ambognas from the publicity after the attack.

'Bloody Ambognas is no friend of mine!' Chris replies edgily, failing to pick up her irony. He's anxious to avoid Ambognas and so they divert to the back of the small but increasingly restless crowd and then make their way through to the meeting organisers.

'Chill out Chris, I've heard the full story from Mike in the Fremantle office.'

Mike Dean is Chris's Electorate Officer, trouble-shooter. Like most EOs, Mike has good PR skills, the front line when constituents come looking for help with personal and financial problems. Such constituents are often desperate, having already tried all other avenues of assistance. Many believe that MPs, even backbenchers, can somehow override the bureaucracy. Or that they have the ear of government and hence are able to magically solve their problems. *If only,* Chris thought on days that he encountered them.

At the protest scene it's decided to defer the meeting to a time and place without Ambognas's company. But as the anti-road activists are about to disperse, a wall of slogan-chanting pro-roaders confront them. They are clearly being egged on by Ambognas, intent on getting as much footage of 'conflict' as he can whip up.

Ugly scenes seem sure to follow, but Chris and the anti-roaders are by now mindful of the set-up and beat a hasty exit through the nearby bush. Ambognas is left standing like a shag on a rock having already got little else but shots of 'What do we want? Rockingham Highway! When do we . . .'

Back in the Nissan, Chris and Francine exchange smiles and get into an animated conversation about the whole road protest scene. Francine recounts how back in the 1950s, when the bulldozers first started reclaiming Mounts Bay on the CBD's front doorstep for a freeway interchange, one lone person, Bessie Rischbieth, was at the scene.

She's sporting an umbrella to stave off the inclement weather and a sign of protest as the the trucks dump sand into the water. Bessie, of course, was ahead of her time in Perth, passed off as mad by many, reflecting her derisive treatment in the parochial local press.

By the seventies, anti-freeway campaigns had emerged in Perth, centred on inner-city Perth and Fremantle. These campaigns had some successes leading to cancellation or scaling down the city's ambitious road plans. But other projects had gone ahead regardless.

And 'bigger and better' roads are still in fashion. It worries anti-road activists like Chris and Francine that people are demonstrating in *favour* of road-building, just as the anti-roaders are running out of steam.

'We've got to change that culture!' said Francine, as Chris drops her on the cappuccino strip.

'Well, that's after we get your PhD published!' offers Chris.

'Huh, some people never give up!' Francine replies as she pulls the door open, smiles widely at Chris, and heads to join a group of gorgeous-looking friends at a coffee table in the fading evening winter sun. To the world-weary Chris, it looks like she's in for a night of fun. He shrugs and drives away, faintly jealous of Francine's social scene.

CHAPTER 14

MORE BUSINESS AS USUAL

In his city offices a few weeks later, Premier Right, Fred Chewis, and several other notables have a clear view of the Perth city foreshore, or at least what's left of it. That's a pool of murky green water surrounded by abandoned building sites.

This development project was all but abandoned by Cloke's government, after a previous administration carved into a heritage-listed park for an inlet to be surrounded by high rise development. 'Bringing the river to the city' was its selling point. Selling point indeed. The newly created waterfront land was sold on incredibly favourable terms to government cronies, on the promise of future building.

As the economy nosedived, the promises soon evaporated. The result was masses of vacant land with a few public facilities and walkways constructed by the FRA. With no buildings adjacent, these are windswept and uncomfortable places.

As they look out on this mess, Right observes, 'well it's time to get the ball rolling on *our* project in Fremantle,' Right says, fixing Chewis with his eye, 'but these must remain secret!'

'But of course, Premier.' Chewis replies demurely.

The plans envisage a Fremantle makeover: high-rise apartments and commercial buildings of up to one hundred levels grouped over the railway, behind the nineteenth century Fremantle Station.

In the Premier's view, this will provide the iconic statement many in Fremantle's business and development community have been waiting for – the buildings will be the tallest in Perth and really put the city on the map. Or so they think. Many in Fremantle will be aghast and will argue that the buildings will not just overshadow the historic city, but will make a mockery of it and will kill off its status as a tourist-drawcard.

The investment and publicity opportunities offered by the development are so appealing to the power-brokers that they are prepared to risk any community reaction and political flak. And politicians love to be audacious. The meeting breaks up half an hour later, with all agreed on keeping confidence until the Premier's announcement, expected in a few weeks.

But the agreement is shattered a few days later when some enterprising soul within the FRA leaks the plans to the press. Right is furious. He's on to Chewis.

'Fred, you're going to have to resign over this stuff-up or I'll be forced to sack you. And you'll get plenty of crap from me in public. I can't afford to be associated with the slip-up.'

For once in his working life, Fred has prepared the ground; his contract ensures his existing parliamentary pension will be doubled on his stepping down from the FRA job. And this he will do as soon as the plan is 'approved', that is, ratified by the FRA.

'I already have my resignation letter prepared for the board, and the arrangements are in place for the handover. Who do you fancy as my replacement?' Chewis asks confidently.

'That's for me to know and you to imagine, Fred,' comes Right's cagey Reply.

Imaginations run wild in Fremantle, too, when the leaked plans hit the press. Chris is stunned and needs little prompting to publicly condemn the idea. The local news weekly, the ***Fremantle Messenger***, interprets his opposition this way:

High-Rise 'Monsters' a Death Threat to Freo – Burnside

The *Messenger* also rails against the proposals in its editorial. But the community is not at one on the development – the Chamber of Commerce labels the proposals as 'visionary' and Councillor Dodge calls the buildings 'iconic'. Mayor Muscatelli, however, is quoted as saying she is 'shocked' at the proposed scale of the buildings and 'outraged' at the community not having been informed. But she also says the redevelopment concept should be properly evaluated.

The FRA board is due to meet again a few days later. In the lead-up to the meeting, Bill Murkitt arrives early and sits in a patch of warming winter sun streaming in through the harbour-side window. He's quietly picking his nose and pondering the future of the brothel deal as Fred Chewis walks in. Fred is armed with a stack of files.

'Now there's a nose I can't pick!' says Chewis.

'I hope not,' returns Murkitt, only mildly embarrassed.

Murkitt's thick skin is a product of the tough, corrupt police culture in which he thrives.

Murkitt turns his attention to the updated FRA Agenda that Chewis hands him.

'Fred, I need to talk to you about this sub-committee report, but I think the redevelopment plan will cause more controversy today,' Murkitt offers. 'I *was* surprised to read about it in the press.'

Chewis nods and colours slightly, mumbling something about employees you can't trust.

'But I reckon the idea of high-rise over the railway behind the station is great,' Murkitt continues, 'it'll complement the new police HQ beautifully, as well as providing some handy apartments nearby. Think of the fun we'll have there!'

It's obvious who is number one in Murkitt's world. Even though Murkitt's parents were from poor backgrounds, they escaped poverty through education and small business. Like them, Murkitt regards success in life as within reach of anyone through self-improvement. He just adds a bit of what he rationalises as 'good honest graft'. He goes on, 'of course the community reps want the whole high-rise scheme canned.'

'Yeah,' replies Chewis, 'but what are the chances of you neutralising that Chris Burnside, Bill, before he gets to be more of a bloody nuisance?'

'Fucking Burnside, he's so predictable!' protests Murkitt. 'But I know he has a few weaknesses. I'll play on those to get him out of the way,' he adds darkly.

'Steady on, Bill. Christ, we don't need that sort of talk. Not yet anyway! How about you just work on causing him and his feral friends some minor trouble? No names, no pack drill, right?'

'Right,' says Murkitt, relishing the challenge. 'Now, on another front,' he goes on, 'would you have picked the recommendation of the sub-committee report?'

'*Ne*-ver!' replies Chewis, tongue firmly in cheek.

'After all, what could be more natural,' Murkitt continues, making a quotation gesture with his chunky fingers, 'in Fremantle than another health centre?'

'Especially when a spa and massage facility is added,' Chewis laughs.

'Subject to the usual police checks of course!'

'OK, that's great: the whole package should get board approval today, don't you think?' asks Chewis, anxious to get the deal completed so the blood money will start to flow his way. He has many debts to pay, a result of his profligate Parliamentary lifestyle. The Chairman's generous stipend helps, but that's on the way out, and despite the perks he's due on stepping down, he still needs more income to cover his pied-a-terres in Nice, San Francisco, and London. Not to mention the three yachts to keep up.

'No worries,' says Murkitt.

At the board meeting, the health centre sails through with near-unanimous support.

It's a different matter when they reach the high-rise item, and Chewis nearly loses control of the meeting under sustained attack from Chris. Chris starts vociferously, but is distracted by Mayor Paula Muscatelli, sitting opposite. He loses his way slightly, the more so when she crosses and uncrosses her shapely legs.

Chris finds himself in mind of all sorts of possibilities for himself and Paula. Admittedly, he's also interested in Sarah Kingsmill, but she's going to take careful cultivation.

He recalls that Paula has a reputation as a man-eater, but this only increases his interest. He also knows that Paula is open to approaches from either gender, and he finds this intriguing. With an effort, Chris drags himself back to the business at hand.

Chewis threatens to cut Chris short as he starts to ramble, and this brings Chris back sharply to his attack. He finally gets into his stride. 'This redevelopment plan is a travesty, an architectural and economic disaster in waiting. And what about the links between board members' business activities and the current plans? I notice nobody has declared a conflict of interest, and yet I see several potential cases

Chewis cuts him short. 'Mr. Burnside, you may be an MP now, but we're not in Parliament here – I'll not allow broad unsubstantiated accusations like that – stick to the plans and stop this innuendo.'

Chris is taken aback, but he's made his point and it's struck home: fellow board member Jack Short colours visibly. He's head of the local Chamber of Commerce and a director of Flexible Constructions, possible bidders for the redevelopment project.

Chris comes back to the debate. 'Mr. Chairman, I won't say any more on that point, but I have to say that I think you deserve censure for not informing the board of this disastrous plan before it got to the press. I move that the plan be dropped altogether!'

Chewis scowls and calls him to order for 'reflecting on the Chair without due cause'. Chris demurs, but reckons he has stung Chewis where it hurts, and that he is also still smarting from Chris's win at the polls where he defeated a mate of Chewis's, the former Labor member for Fremantle. That same person was appointed to the FRA board for a special five-year term by Cloke before his demise and was now looking askance at Chris as if to say he thought his attack way over the top. But before he can get to speak, Chewis himself chips in, 'I'm warning you, Mr. Burnside, you may have already gone too far.' He seethes with barely controlled anger. 'As to your suggestions of any conflict of interest, you know that all members are required to declare any potential conflicts at the start of each meeting. No one has signed the register today, and that is where the matter rests,' he adds forcefully, cynically aware that the general nature of the discussion means no one had to declare an interest in any case. But it's a good line for the press.

'And as to the press, what they happened to get hold of was a very early draft, it wasn't even ready to be tabled here. It would have been tabled when it was ready, but as it is you and others have gone off half-cocked without bothering to check the facts or to consult me.'

A few around the table look embarrassed.

Chewis continues in an injured tone, 'I've already launched an investigation into the leak and respectfully assure you that if it turns out to be one of our employees, I will personally carpet and fire the culprit.'

'Sure, sure, Mr. Chairman,' responds Chris. 'But that still doesn't excuse the fact that we weren't informed about the study to start with. I'd be interested to know what other members think.'

'Well,' says the former MP for Fremantle, 'I must say I do agree with you, Chris, about the board not being informed at the right time. But I don't think our Chair needs to be censured as this leak was not authorised. And I don't know where your accusation of vested interest comes from. I see the board as fundamentally honest. If they are involved financially in any development, it is only because they believe in the good of the city!'

'You can't really believe that naïve crap!' Chris growls.

'Well, I happen to have more faith in human nature than my fellow community representative here!' the former MP returns, attempting to sound disingenuous. 'But regardless, I do agree that it's regrettable that this hit the press before we knew about it. I for one insist that future initiatives of this sort are brought to us at their inception, not halfway through their development. It's something that shouldn't happen again.' He pauses. 'I think the whole concept should go out for immediate, formal, public input.'

This unexpected, if lukewarm, support heartens Chris as do sympathetic noises coming from several others, particularly Mayor Muscatelli. Chris smiles encouragingly in her direction. He wonders how Chewis will handle the situation now that his potential allies seem to be turning on him.

The former MP continues as the hubbub around the table dies down

'But the way forward? Well, the current plans come as a shock, but unlike Mr. Burnside, I don't think they should be abandoned. Remember, we're sitting on a goldmine with all that railway land going begging,' he says emphatically. 'Now, while I'm a big fan of heritage, I see bold redevelopment as a key to lifting Fremantle out of the economic doldrums. I think the public will respond far more positively than the prophets of doom would have us believe. I agree with the Mayor that the merits of the idea need to be investigated further.'

The Mayor smiles warmly at Chris and takes the floor. 'Well, Mr. McRafferty, I do think the idea needs to be investigated, but I don't share your optimistic outlook on its benefits. The plan we've seen confirms my worst fears about the excessive powers of the FRA. The body is not popular with Fremantle residents.'

In her recent rise to power, Muscatelli had run a clever campaign building on this resentment. While espousing a pro-development line that suited the large contingent of voters, she carefully cultivated the anti-government feeling that the FRA's establishment had crystallised. She was a sharp operator, and one who often caught people short with her changes of direction. Her political alliances could be temporary and shifting, as she was now demonstrating.

'So I rather share Mr. Burnside's feeling about this planning exercise, and, Mr. Chewis, I think you have to take a share of the blame for the position we're in.'

Chewis grimaces at this turn of events and protests. Chris is delighted, as he'd thought Muscatelli was different; after all, she was from a Fremantle family who were long-standing conservatives. And yet he knows she is likely to take advantage of any stuff-ups Chewis makes.

'I stop short of censure, Mr. Chewis,' Muscatelli continues coolly, 'but I suggest the board express disquiet at the way in which the Chair has allowed these plans to be developed without any reference to the board. Furthermore, with the development concept itself, whatever its final scale, the planners have shown total disregard for heritage. Mr. Burnside is absolutely right to say these proposed buildings would belittle our beautiful city. In fact, the Mayor waves an arm at their surroundings, I think that *this* building is already too high for Fremantle. However,' she pauses and looks around at the expectant faces, 'I do want to see the idea of railway land redevelopment explored further. However, the community should get some social dividends from this project. I think an arts centre and some affordable housing should be included.'

This last suggestion brings gasps from around the table. Paula isn't known for her support of Burnside and seemed lukewarm on social dividends. But as the only female on the board and a powerful and attractive one at that, the other members stay unusually quiet despite any misgivings.

The mostly middle-aged male board is certainly aware that Paula is looking at her best, flaxen hair well groomed, and sporting a brief low-cut outfit that emphasises her well-rounded breasts and rides high over her shapely legs. Chris finds he is failing in his efforts to keep his roving eye off her. He brings himself back to her argument with some effort as she goes on, 'I propose that the board express deep concern over the preparation and release of these plans, demand a full public explanation from the Chair and ask the planners to prepare some more modest plans for public consultation within the next two weeks.'

She gracefully crosses and uncrosses her long legs while managing to reveal a generous glimpse. Members shuffle their feet and pretend not to look, but they take it all in eagerly. She smiles again in Chris's direction, which has the immediate effect of weakening his shaky resolve. He is now considering Paula with a mixture of admiration and disbelief. The ideas she is espousing are far more in accord with his own than he had dared to imagine.

'Mr. Chairman, I protest!' This from Ken Short. 'The Chamber of Commerce is of the view that these criticisms are an over-reaction. We welcome the economic opportunities redevelopment of the railway land would bring to the city, and the extra population the apartments will bring. I'm surprised and a bit dismayed by the Mayor's suggestion of social housing in the development. Surely, we want this development to be prestigious? Overall, this concept would leave the historic city intact, and no city can stand still and stop progress. This new development enhances the old. It could be a twenty-first century version of La Defense in Paris!'

The Mayor smiles disarmingly at Short.

'Well, Ken, I'm not going to agree with everything the chamber puts forward, you know.'

Chris can hardly believe his ears: was this a political conversion in the offing, or is Muscatelli just being a populist, something at which she is well practised? Short had just returned from a chamber-funded European study tour, which he was now desperately trying to justify, following considerable criticism from a disgruntled membership who were having a hard time making business ends meet in the port city. Short's tour had taken in a number of European cities including Paris, London, Barcelona, Prague and Krakow ostensibly to look at their city centre redevelopment initiatives.

In Paris, Short was particularly taken with La Defense, an area of high-rise offices and apartments built adjacent to Paris's historic core in the 1970s and since expanded to even greater heights. When there, Short heard that critics rate it as soulless and unduly dominating adjacent parts of the historic city centre. But on his return, Short had said he believed the development was economically necessary and took development pressure off the historic parts of central Paris. The same could now be true for Fremantle.

Chris is dying to have a go at Short and comes in with 'La Defense, spectacular thought it may be, is regarded by many as a brave but failed experiment. It's uncomfortable for pedestrians, often unbearably windy, and many of the buildings are faceless. And the whole district lacks vitality. What is proposed in Fremantle has all the hallmarks of another monumental failure!'

'That's a very pessimistic assessment,' Short counters. 'La Defense was positively buzzing when I visited.' He conveniently fails to mention that in large measure this was due to an outdoor music festival, staged there each summer to counter the area's usual dullness. 'But before we get scared off by the naysayers, let's give these redevelopment ideas a fair go.'

After a vigorous debate, Chris's motion to scrap the project lapses for want of a seconder. He fails in an attempt to incorporate a height limit of five levels in Muscatelli's motion.

Short chips in, 'You people are living in the past, always arguing against development!'

Several others agree, but the Mayor indicates she can't support his suggestion of a five-storey limit, so Chris senses his cause is a dead duck.

But all is not lost: to the embarrassment of Chewis, the Mayor's motion calling for a scaled-down development plan and public consultation is adopted by a narrow margin.

Chris supports the motion, knowing that 'scaled down' could mean anything, but justifying it to himself on the notion that he needs whatever support he can get. Deep down, he knows his decision has more to do with his desire for the Mayor than his hope for a political alliance.

As the meeting breaks up, the press is waiting outside. Having put the successful motion on the controversial plan, the Mayor places herself in front of the cameras first and gives a smooth version of events, including some harsh criticism for Chewis. She emphasises the need for public input and a scaled-down development.

That night, the TV news gives as much air-time to her appearance as it does to the proposed development. There's no comment from Chewis who disappears after going into a huddle with Murkitt.

Chris walks away after offering some more critical and angry comments, but they make little air-time later. He now contacts his electorate officer Dean, who finds the outcome bad but predictable.

He's shocked to learn of Chris's support of Paula's motion, given his opposition to the overall concept.

'Chris, you didn't let Paula's charm get the better of you, surely?' he inquires.

Embarrassed at Dean's perspicacity, Chris scoffs, 'of course not, I simply thought her motion was the best we could do in the circumstances. Without the Mayor, the whole project would probably have got the nod!'

Dean points out that the government has the final say in any case, and that Chris needs to be true to his principles on this matter; he's already expressed public opposition to *any* high-rise in the area.

'That's true, Dean, but I did put a motion to oppose the development and then an amendment to limit the height to five stories. But neither got any support.'

After a testy exchange, in which Dean makes it clear he thinks Chris is compromised, they agree to organise a protest rally as soon as possible. Finishing the conversation, Chris is surprised to find Paula at his elbow.

'Perhaps we should put our heads together on this plan?' she purrs, placing her hand on his arm. 'After all, I agree with you that those one-hundred-storey monsters are definitely not on.'

'Mmm, good, but why don't you accept my idea of a height limit?' asks Chris, aware of her body heat and a delicious perfume while still mindful of Dean's critique.

'Chris, you know that the board wouldn't have supported such a low height limit. Any case, we can't just pluck figures out of the air. In the end, it's up to the public to have their say on that issue, surely?' she says, pressing closer to him.

'I agree, but . . .' Chris is finding her proximity increasingly exciting. He knows Paula has a reputation of eating her sex partners for breakfast. But he's attracted to her. Forget Diana, she's too busy; forget Sarah, she's not my type. But Paula?

Paula seems to sense his dilemma.

'No more buts, Chris, how about dinner at my place tonight to talk this plan through?' Paula ensures that now they are out of sight, her body touches his in a particularly erotic way.

'Sure! That sounds great!'

The devil within Chris finally gets the upper hand.

It's obvious to Chris by now that Fremantle's planning will be the last thing on the menu. And that could be just what he needs.

CHAPTER 15

CHANGING SIDES?

And quite a need it becomes. That night, Paula has little to say about building height and yet has Chris rising to all sorts of new heights. His sexual desire is reawakened in a new way. She's sensual and in tune, patient yet greedy, indulgent yet direct in her demands, into lust and yet open to fun and laughter.

By morning, Chris reckons that he has more than met his match in Paula. Over breakfast, he also finds that she's surprisingly open to discussion of Fremantle's redevelopment.

'I'm sick and tired of the develop-at-any-cost line. Fremantle's too good for that. And I decided yesterday to steer clear of the deals offered by Dodge and Short. I can't afford to be captive to their demands simply because they supported my election campaign,' she says with feeling.

'Pity you didn't say that during the campaign, Paula,' Chris jokes. 'But maybe we can do political business as well as the other. How about you speaking against the high-rise at our rally next month?'

'I'll be happy to join you on the platform, but I need to think carefully about what to say . . . I mean we've both got our political futures to consider!'

She smiles while getting up and gently massaging Chris's back and shoulders. This nearly leads them back to the bedroom, but the lounge room Persian rug does just as well in the circumstances.

While a mid-life change of views for such a person as Paula seemed unlikely, Chris later reflects, stranger things have happened. And if that's true, it could be that a fling with Paula would not, after all, compromise his ability to keep faith with the community and run an honest anti-redevelopment campaign.

All this is rationalisation, for however genuine Paula's change of political heart, she has an irresistibly erotic way about her, and this is primarily driving Chris's judgement. But for the moment, he decides it's OK to pursue Paula as a diversion. For the moment, Paula has him by the balls.

She has that sort of reputation. Chasing lovers – of either gender, she's openly bisexual – provides some respite from the world of criminal law in which she specialises and for which she's already made a name, helped on by her studying law at Yale. As a barrister, she succeeded in having many wrongly-accused felons acquittedand, at twenty-nine, was appointed QC, the youngest ever in the State. She's a darling of the media. This not only helps her combat her own family's resentment, but also set her on the path to politics at a time when she was growing restless. Her reputation for winning difficult cases was attracting dodgy crooks as clients. She wanted none of them.

Brought up in Fremantle, in a household where political conversations were frequent, Paula absorbed an interest. She was hurriedly recruited to stand for the Mayor's job after one of the leading candidates, an ex-Mayor who happened to be her cousin, pulled out of the bid with health problems. In his time as Mayor, he had been a populist, but had fostered dubious business and police practices and dodgy developments around the city.

Paula was noticed by the power-brokers as much for her looks and high media profile as for her ability and political views, about which they knew little. As time went on, Paula's backers had reason to question if not regret their choice. Paula had been savvy enough to see that it would be to her advantage to pretend to go along with the aggressive pro-development line of her backers.

She departed from this line during the campaign by questioning the establishment of the FRA and by calling for more balanced development in tune with Fremantle's heritage. This suited many of the city's new residents, wary of the so-called 'hard-line' candidates on the one hand and the develop-at-any-cost nominees on the other. And she always intended to take her own political line once she got the mayoral prize.

During the campaign, she eschewed donations from known standover men, instead privately vowing to beat the criminal element and pouring in considerable funds of her own. By making skilful use of her charm and advocating a new standard of politics in the town, she was elected by a convincing margin.

Since securing the job, Paula had grown increasingly uncomfortable with Dodge and Murkitt's deals, and this sealed her decision to steer clear of them. The brothel application was a narrow call, but she lacked the resolve to raise the matter at the time. Today, as she faces Murkitt to discuss the brothel properties, she vows that it will soon be different.

'Well, Paula, you'll be pleased about yesterday's meeting, what with your win on the high-rise *and* the health farm getting the nod and all that?' smirks Murkitt, while holding the steaming macchiato freshly brewed by the Mayor herself. She made sure her office was fitted with one of the best cappuccino machines in town, and that's saying a lot in a city known widely for its good coffee.

'Yes Bill, but not for the reasons you imagine.'

'Excuse me, Paula?'

'I'm not going to be part of any sleazy deal on this project. The community doesn't want the brothel, it's an outdated industry, and I'm certainly not going to be party to one operating under the cover of a health centre!'

'What gave you that idea? You must be out of your cotton-pickin mind,' Murkitt blusters. 'Don't forget where your real support came from during the campaign. You wouldn't have got anywhere without our assistance, and —'

'That's bullshit, Bill, and you know it. You guys might have fronted up on polling day, but I funded 90 percent of the campaign from my own money. And I warned Dodge when I first heard about this brothel scam.'

Murkitt turns on her with a venom he usually reserves for unfortunate citizens who end up being interviewed in the local police station.

'Right you bitch, you'll live to regret this!'

'Are you threatening me, Murkitt?'

'You'll get yours,' he replies, storming out of her office.

Paula is shaken but takes another deferred action, one that should prove safer. She rings her old school friend, Diana, having run into her at a recent reception and agreed they should get together.

Before that, she hadn't seen Diana for several years; after their school years together and intermittent contact since, their ways had separated.

'Paula, how wonderful!' Diana enthuses. 'I was about to call you, ESP at work?'

'How about drinks at the OBH in a couple of hours?' inquires Paula.

'Great idea, I was going to work on Right's speeches, but I'd much rather speak to my favourite Mayor.'

At six thirty that evening, they renew their lost friendship over cocktails at the Ocean Beach Hotel lounge, taking in the yellow sand and pines of Cottesloe Beach and a glorious sunset beyond. Like its nearby neighbour Fremantle, and despite the resistance of many in the local community, Cottesloe has lost much of its old character as high-rise takes over the streets near the iconic beach.

Paula and Diana reminisce, and by the time their third cocktail arrives, all inhibitions have evaporated. They recall how they had been drawn together at school as rebellious 'twins' and regret drifting apart over the ensuing years. They now recount with pleasure their serious bucking of school rules, indulgence in drugs, and extreme partying.

'Wow, what fun we had!' reflects Paula. 'I know you were cool with my sexual experiments with our classmates, but others weren't!'

'Yeah, remember Irene, she was afraid of sex in any form! But what about your family now you've come out?'

'Oh, they're slowly adjusting to realities. But tell you what, I reckon they'd be proud of my latest skirmish in the bedroom. That Chris Burnside is really something!'

Diana struggles to take this in. She knows that Chris has a fatal flaw when it comes to women; he frequently gets involved with attractive women regardless of his or their circumstances, and that has landed him in all sorts of trouble over the years. Diana reckons that he thinks too much with the 'little head' when it comes to choosing his female partners. But even so, to hear he is on with Paula is not news she was expecting.

'God, Paula, I don't know what to say. Chris and I are old and recently very good friends and . . . are you sure you two aren't just being a bit opportunist here? I'd have to say that you both have a reputation in that department!'

'So they tell me, Diana, but really, I had no idea you and Chris were friends . . . you don't mean . . . hell, I'm sorry, Chris didn't say . . .'

Paula blushes and puts a hand on Diana's. Diana looks directly at her:

'Well, I am a trifle shocked, but I knew Chris was getting restless, and in any case, our sex life has been on hold for a while. We've both become embroiled in our new jobs. To tell you the truth, I was beginning to think it was time we gave up the sex altogether and went back to being the friends that we always have been. It was much less complicated that way, and apparently, Chris is happy to explore new pastures. Always was the bastard! So he's all yours, Paula!'

'Thanks, darling, but I don't want all of him if you know what I mean – just a bit of fun. I don't think it'll last long.' They both break into laughter at this point.

Paula asks, 'did you help Chris during his recent campaign?'

'I was too busy on Right's campaign! Anyhow, just look out for Chris, he could be more trouble than you anticipate. But we were talking about your family before Chris rudely interrupted!'

Paula confirms that her bisexual nature is indeed a source of tension with her family; her socially conservative grandparents were part of the great post-war wave of immigrants from Sicily and her parents shared some of the same attitudes.

Two of her brothers are very straight, which allows them plenty of scope to give Paula a hard time. But Paula has the edge on them intellectually. Only one of her brothers got to university and he's since buried himself in a dull office job. Another has become part of their grandparents' retail empire, Muscatelli's Food Stores.

The third, Emilio, two years younger than Paula, is a non-conformist, into gambling and drugs. Tears come to Paula's eyes as she tells Diana how he disappeared two years ago when his ill-fated hydroponics business went belly up. Paula and he are close; she affectionately calls him 'rebel without a clue'. Emilio has a quick temper, and they often argue, but usually resolve their differences amicably. Paula was especially saddened by a serious argument over his lifestyle that developed prior to his disappearance. They never resolved the matter, and she now misses him even more keenly.

Diana sympathises and tells Paula about some of her own problems that stem from the breakdown of her marriage. In hindsight, she can now see that the experience increased her vulnerability and helped drive her into Cloke's arms.

'Families and relationships, Diana, don't they bring a lot of grief? But tell me how is your job with the *new* Premier? I wouldn't have really thought Right was your cup of tea!' queries Paula, smiling and waving a graceful hand with long fingernails in the air before taking another of the Ceduna oysters they are sharing.

'No, working for Richard is more like drinking a heavy after-dinner port than a cuppa!'

Diana notices her own fingernails needed trimming; she's an inveterate nail-biter and is envious of Paula's immaculate grooming.

'For me, the job's a chance to see how the other half lives, but I suppose that's something you will be all too familiar with from your own recent experiences?' Diana reaches over for the last oyster. 'Wow, they are fantastic! We should have had a dozen each!'

Paula wonders why an otherwise well-turned-out woman like Diana would bite her nails. Paula's manicured fingernails take effort to keep looking good, although they certainly come in handy with lovers like Chris, who told her that running them down his back increased the intensity of his orgasm meteorically.

'Well, yes, the other half,' Paula begins, then throwing caution to the wind, changes tack, 'I've decided to give them the flick you know, partly because of the bloody sleazy, crooked men who control the conservative levers of power down in Fremantle. In any case, I now see that a lot of the bastards are in politics for their own benefit and bugger the community!'

Diana is surprised but favourably impressed.

'Mmm, sounds like the same mob who run Richard's Party. You should hear some of the things I've learnt. If you thought Cloke was corrupt, he's got nothing on this mob! How about you help me form a group to clean up politics at all levels?' suggests Diana, warming to the prospect of a new political adventure.

'Sounds good, but what say we make it women only?'

This raises a question for Diana: What about Chris? Her arrangement with him is to clean up WA politics. But she reflects, the way Chris is behaving – hopping into bed with Paula without any apparent thought to the personal or political consequences – all her arrangements with him should be reviewed.

'Why not indeed? You and I both know that women are the only worthwhile force in WA politics!' proffers Diana with a particularly engaging smile.

'I'll drink to that,' Paula returns the smile, lifting her glass, just served by an unusually attentive waiter.

They tuck into their meals, lemon risotto for Paula and Thai vegetable curry for Diana, and dine in the best of spirits.

CHAPTER 16

MIXED MESSAGES

Later that night, Paula messages Chris asking him to call. Chris is about to go to bed, but despite being tired from a long day in Parliament, he's in touch instantly.

'Paula, great to hear from you, how about a nightcap?'

'Sorry, Chris, I've got too many things on early tomorrow for that. I thought you should know that I met up with Diana tonight.'

Chris is puzzled and senses something awry.

'Well, Diana told me you were friendly with her many years ago, but how come?'

Paula fills him in on the details; he's pleased that the two have met up, but less than delighted when Paula tells him Diana knows the two of them have spent a night together.

'Christ, why did you let her in on that?' he replies irritably. Then, checking himself he says, 'Paula, it was a fabulous night, and I hope there'll be plenty more, but I thought maybe we should keep it quiet for a while.'

'I've never been one for secrecy, except when absolutely necessary – come on, why shouldn't I tell an old friend about a wild fling. Come to think of it, why didn't you tell me you and Diana have been more than just friendly of late?'

Chris is taken aback. He checks himself from asking how Paula elicited this information, realising he's on the back foot. All he can manage is 'Well, Paula, Diana knows me better than you do!'

'It's cool Chris, no need to go on a guilt trip, Diana seems quite relieved that you might be moving on.'

'Oh, really?' Chris feels a mixture of hurt and pleasure. 'But coming back to the point of secrecy, Paula, just imagine what the press would make of our liaison, especially if they knew of the background!'

'Hang on, Chris, Diana's not going to blab, and in any case we're not even in a relationship yet, come on, we slept together last night, and that's it at the moment.'

Chris feels worry overtaking him. On the one hand, he's concerned about the political implications of a relationship with Paula; on the other, he finds her irresistible. But she seems to see things differently. He's a bit miffed that she's playing things coolly and knows he'll have trouble emulating her approach.

'Fair enough, Paula. I see where you're coming from. But I hope you don't mean that's it for us!'

'OK, darling, maybe we can have some more fun together, but I don't think we should be talking about us.'

Chastened, Chris takes another line.

'Right. But even if we are seen together occasionally, the press might make a mountain out of our molehill.'

'I can't see that happening. It might make the gossip columns, but it's not that we're working in the same place or anything,' she says, referring to the 'green-liberal' affair that had brought down one of Chris's predecessors.

Chris has to accept she's right; in truth, he's worried that if their 'thing' is made public, it will make him look like a turncoat, given his opposition to Paula at the recent mayoral election and their apparent divergence of views. Despite the fact that Paula's views are now closer to his, Chris knows he will have a hard time convincing his supporters of this. He decides to be upfront.

'Truth is, Paula, I'm worried about what some of my supporters might think if they hear we're having a fling.'

'Well, Chris, it's not even a fling – yet – and I understand we've both got our political fields to plough, so if you think the risk is too great, why press me for more action?'

'I didn't realise you came with a "meddle at your own risk" warning,' Chris says in a joking tone.

'OK, Chris, I get your point. If and when we do meet again, let's not do it in public! Right?'

'Brilliant,' replies Chris, although sensing Paula is trying to let him down gently, looking for a way out herself, but he's still in her thrall. He presses on.

'Well, let me know when you *are* free for that nightcap!'

'Chris, I hear you' Paula purrs and ends the conversation.

A short while later, Chris's watch rings again; this time, it's Diana. He hesitates but answers the call to hear Diana asking in a mock-angry tone, 'And what the hell are you doing having an affair with the Mayor of Fremantle? She may be my friend, but I thought she was your political enemy!'

'Politics makes for strange bedfellows as someone said!' Chris tries, attempting to make a joke of it.

'C'mon, Chris, just *what* is going on?'

Chris tries to explain.

'In other words, Chris, you let Paula's well-known charms reel you in, is that it?'

'Well, I did think she looked particularly gorgeous yesterday.'

'Right, Chris, thinking with the little head again?'

'Diana, fair go!'

'I know you too well for that, Chris, but it's your funeral and all that . . . more importantly, how are you going to explain it to the Burnside faithful?'

'Yeah, that does worry me a bit, but she and I agreed to keep things quiet at present.'

'Fat chance you've got of that in Fremantle!' Diana, knowing how the gossip-mongering works, replies.

'Well even if word does leak out, I think Paula may be changing her views on Fremantle's development.'

'Hmm, I must say I was impressed with what she told me last night about her going off her supporters like Dodge *and* she mentioned that she might speak at your rally.'

'Well, there you go, wait and see what she says there,' puts in Chris, trying desperately to get off the hook.

'I would have said just be careful, but I know that'd be no use now.'

'That's what I told you before you and Cloke hooked up,' returns Chris.

'Touché!' Diana responds. But then her tone becomes serious again: 'another thing, Chris, I'm not sure how viable our continuing political investigations are going to be if you are going to do the Don Juan number in politics.'

'That's a bit harsh, Diana, surely . . . I mean, I like Paula very much, but I'd say from her call just now that we won't be seeing that much of each other in any case!'

'Ah! She's tossed you aside already?'

'Well, not exactly, but . . .'

'Even if that's true it's not the point, Chris. I'm not prepared to deal with you on this without a guarantee that our secrets are kept under wraps.'

'Alright, I swear I'll keep it all in-house, Diana.'

'Hmm, I wish I could believe that. We'll continue this conversation later.'

Diana rings off, leaving Chris with a lot to think about.

When they meet a few days later, sharing a supper at a late night café near Parliament, Diana is keen to hear where Chris's thinking is at.

'Well, of course this thing with Paula carries danger, but as to our political project, I still can't see why that can't go forward. Look at what we've already achieved,' Chris says, sipping his coffee.

'That was then, now things are very different for both of us.'

Diana pours herself a cup of tea and takes a small chocolate from the dish on the table. She looks at Chris with a challenge in her expression.

'Apart from the risks of our investigations leaking out, I've been reviewing things since we talked. But before I get to that, I should tell you that Paula and I've agreed to start a women's group, with the aim of advancing women's interests in politics.'

'Ah, I see,' replies Chris, not seeing clearly at all.

He wonders if Diana has fallen under Paula's spell too and now wants to follow *her* political path. He reflects that he has never been good at understanding the female psyche.

'Are you sure you're not just throwing me to the wolves here and overreacting to my thing with Paula?'

'Give me some credit, Chris, I am looking out for your best interests. But I also think that it's time we chose our political strategies a bit more carefully, you and I.'

'And end our political project almost as soon as it started?' he asks, feeling increasingly dejected. Diana seems to be slighting him here, and he's not sure of the reason.

'No. Look, Chris, don't be like that . . . we'll still keep in touch, but we've each only got so many spare hours in the day. Meeting up with Paula has made me realise that one of the reasons I am in politics at all is to advance the cause of women in a man's world.'

Diana pauses, looking determined, and Chris realises that she's got a new passion. Before he can reply, she runs on, 'sure I stuffed up with Cloke, and Paula is hardly a role model when it comes to relationships, but I like her energy, her ability to cut through the usual political nonsense. We seem to be on the same political wavelength and all that.'

Chris's mood starts to change. Far from feeling deserted, he realises it could be a good thing, if Diana is going to team up with Paula politically. It could force him to become more self-reliant. And after all, he reflects, delightful though Paula might be, there are plenty of other possibilities out there. His mind turns to Sarah Kingsmill, and he falls into a temporary reverie, contemplating Sarah's friendly demeanour during their recent chat.

'Er, Chris, where are you?' Diana touches his leg with her foot to regain his attention.

'Oh, sorry, just musing,' says Chris unconvincingly, trying not to show embarrassment. But a blush spreads up his neck to his face. He finds a tissue and buries his face for a moment, pretending to blow his nose. He emerges and stumbles to answer Diana. 'Oh. Right you are. I get the message.'

Diana looks at him askance, and he puts up his hands to reassure her, realising that his tone might sound false. He goes on in a more confident manner:

'It's OK, I can actually see that this all makes sense. I've got a good team round me in the office, they can be my behind-the-scenes eyes and ears and I can still get the low-down from you occasionally, n'est ce pas?'

'Exactemant! But from now on, I'll leave the muck-raking and the tall poppy cutting to you.'

They finish their supper, hug, and depart. Chris races to get the last train, and on the journey back, his thoughts return to Paula. *Maybe Diana's right,* he thinks, *maybe I shouldn't be chasing her. After all, she doesn't seem that keen on an encore. Then again,* he ponders, *I can't just drop into a pattern of one night stands. Or can I?* Chris reflects on the messy pattern of his relationships over the years.

He asks himself if he's really driven only by sexual need. No, after all he did fall in love once, but then what a disaster that was, he remembers. And that sets him thinking about his long-lost son. *Perhaps,* he thinks, *I need a new approach. After all, it would be really something if I could find out what my son is all about.* Then he shudders, recalling the terse 'fuck-off' message he had from the boy's mother when he had tracked him down in Melbourne.

Then he had vanished, just like that, and hadn't been heard of since. His thoughts return to Paula, a beautiful contrast, but can a one-night stand lead to a beautiful relationship? *Unlikely,* he again concludes. But the blood coursing through his veins seems to give him a different message. Even the more so as the picture of Sarah Kingsmill reappears in his mind.

As the train rumbles into Fremantle station and he disembarks, he is no closer to solving his delicious dilemma.

CHAPTER 17

RESIDENTS REVOLT

A month later, on a fine Sunday, all eyes are on Paula as she strides confidently, elegantly, to the microphone to address the huge crowd at the anti–high-rise rally in the park opposite Fremantle's railway station. The bus station has been temporarily re-located and nearby roads closed to accommodate the throng, the likes of which hasn't been seen for many a year. The crowd has already been warmed up with stirring anti-FRA songs put together by a local band, the Freo First. TV stations, including TVTV, are well represented.

The first Speaker is the president of Fremantle First, who draws a huge roar of approval as she condemns the FRA and calls for it to be scrapped to rid the city of its nefarious and self-serving plans.

Chris follows. 'Never has Fremantle's history and heritage, its very character, been under greater threat!'

He tells the attentive crowd that he aims to have the FRA plans tabled and debated in Parliament. This would normally not happen, owing to the extraordinary powers given to redevelopment authorities, almost a law unto themselves. Judging from the mixed reactions Chris has so far been met with from politicians on both sides, he'll have trouble mustering the numbers needed to have the plans debated, let alone defeated. But he promises to go down fighting.

As he passes Paula on his way back from the microphone, Chris smiles and touches her gently on the arm. They've met only twice in recent weeks, and that was it; while no word of their liaison appeared in the press, Chris reluctantly agreed with Paula when she told him there was no future for them. Diana continued to question Chris's judgement, and this no doubt helped him acquiesce when the moment came. That and his slowly developing friendship with Sarah.

But today, Paula's mind is on the future of Fremantle and her own future as Mayor. Chris looks back nervously for he is still not sure what she might say.

'People and fans of Fremantle,' she begins confidently, 'one of the reasons I stood as Mayor was to defend this historic city against those who seek to destroy or demean its heritage. The FRA has become an agent of those forces. I am a supporter of good development in Fremantle, but this plan has been sprung on us, it's not good development, it's ridiculously out of scale and character with our city. The plans for Perth's Esplanade are bad enough: this one for Fremantle is more appropriate to New York or Dubai! The whole thing reminds me of the brutalist architecture built by the fascists in the 1930s. We deserve better. We demand something more sensitive and in sync with our city!'

A burst of supporting cheers, wolf-whistles, and shouting follows, but then there's a roar of approaching motorbikes and heavy vehicles on the opposite side of the park, that almost drowns out her rhetorical question:

'But the question is how do we get that result?' Paula stops as a phalanx of burly characters dismount from the bikes and clamber down from trucks, immediately making their purpose clear by giving the hostile crowd the two-fingers up and unfurling banners reading:

BUILDING UNIONS FOR FREMANTLE

Give Railway Development a Chance

The new arrivals are led by two rather ugly balding men with huge potbellies so much out of proportion with the rest of their bodies that they look like some weird set of ageing pregnant twins. Vince Roberts, the thug-like president of the main building union, leads the crew. From his vantage point on stage, Chris is surprised to see with them none other than Wayne Cloke, his own strong build dwarfed by the crowd of even bigger men around him. Chris has heard that Cloke has renewed his alliance with the building union heavies, but Cloke's kept a low profile of late. Now he's apparently served his time on the sidelines and is chumming up to the power-brokers to try and revive JD's temporarily ailing fortunes. Today, Cloke looks slightly dishevelled but menacing nonetheless.

After conferring briefly with Chris, Paula decides to carry on, regardless of the growing melee around Cloke and the union bosses. Police make their way over to check out the new arrivals. Paula now raises the possibility of a lower scale over the railway. This suggestion draws only lukewarm applause, and also a few derisory shouts like 'whose bloody side are you on?'

Reading the mood, Paula changes tack and decides that discretion is the better part of valour. 'OK, I hear you. When the revised plans are published, if the public says no development over the railway, then so be it as far as I'm concerned.' Having made that concession, she now really nails her new colours to the political mast. 'And I can say categorically that whatever pressures are brought to bear, and here she points directly to Cloke and his newly arrived crew, we will not be bludgeoned into accepting what any heavy in the building industry wants. The same goes for the Chamber of Commerce,' she adds pointedly, knowing that Jack Short is also amongst the crowd.

What she doesn't tell the crowd is that earlier in the week she had become embroiled in a heavy argument with Cloke and Roberts, part of a building industry deputation booked in to see her following advice from Murkitt that she was giving trouble. When Paula had made it clear that she wasn't going to dance to their tune, there wasn't much love lost. She came away knowing that she must publically distance herself from the thugs of the building industry as soon as the chance arose. Well, here it was with a vengeance. She concludes, 'this city's development should be controlled by its people, not by neo-fascist governments or building industry thugs!'

She has won back the crowd: a banner-waving, cheering response erupts from all quarters except the one around Cloke, from where shouting and abuse are hurled.

As the shouting dies away, a shot rings out, and Paula slumps to the platform. People run screaming in all directions, some dive for cover, but no more shots are heard. One of the police, in the section of the crowd near Cloke, has been quick to spot the gunman, a bearded man crouching in the lower branches of a tree holding a sawn-off and powerful rifle.

The gunman is grabbed, disarmed, and pulled swiftly to the ground by the alert cop. Murkitt, also on duty, is tempted to tell the young constable to let the guy go but buttons his lip and simply assists him wrestle the gun off the shooter.

Meanwhile, Paula is lying on the dais, writhing in pain as she clutches her upper arm in a vain effort to staunch the flow of blood. The press come running but are barred from the stage by security. A shocked Chris pushes forward and kneels over Paula, trying to comfort her, but he is soon brushed aside by an approaching first-aid officer.

Press attention is temporarily diverted by the apprehension of the gunman, who is bundled roughly into a waiting paddy wagon. An ambulance soon screams in, and officers scoop Paula up after they treat the ugly wound on her upper arm. She's whisked off to hospital, where an emergency team skilfully extracts the bullet and gives her a transfusion to make up for the considerable loss of blood.

TV news bulletins that night are full of stories of the Mayor's 'miraculous' escape from an attempted assassination. The gruesome-looking scenes make compelling viewing. TVTV's cameras have somehow captured the gunman just after he fired the shot, although the footage is fuzzy as they were initially focussing on the mob around Cloke. This scene, along with blood spraying from Paula's arm as the bullet hit and her face contorts with pain, is repeated throughout the night.

Reports make play of Cloke and Robert's presence in the melee near the gunman, and Cloke soon issues a statement fiercely denying any link to the shooting incident. This is eclipsed when the superintendent of police announces that all possibilities have to be investigated in getting to the bottom of what he calls 'this barbaric act'. Privately, however, he agrees with Murkitt's assessment, made just before their press conference, that the Mayor 'had it coming to her'.

The mood in the press and amongst the public is different. Paula is an instant hero and not just in Fremantle. Her change of heart on the redevelopment and her brave performance in the face of danger appeal to locals and others alike. The bullet wound on her upper arm will heal but is likely to leave a scar, which the press predicts will only add to her allure.

Chris is devastated and gets little sleep that night. He tried visiting her, but found an armed police guard stationed at the door to Paula's ward and his entry blocked. Even next morning he finds her hard to get to and is told that police are with her, anxious to get her account of events.

Well-wishers throng the waiting room, but are not encouraged by the protective nursing staff. Eventually, Chris slips through on pretext of urgent political business but is given two minutes only on orders from the ward sister. He finds Paula looking drained and pale, but she manages a weak smile.

'Christ, Paula, you'll do anything to get good press!' he jokes.

'Yeah, I arranged it all!' She grimaces back at him. Chris smiles in a pained manner.

'Seriously though,' Paula confides, 'I had expected the building mob might get nasty after last week, but I didn't factor shooting into the equation!' She gives him a sketchy account of her meeting with the building industry deputation.

'What makes you think it's one of them though? Surely Cloke wouldn't incriminate himself so obviously?'

'Well, you could be right there, the cops tell me the guy arrested isn't a building worker. He seems to have connections to the drug trade rather than the union bosses. And there's something else you'll be interested in, Chris,' she adds, lowering her voice and gesturing him to the bedside so she can't be heard by the duty cop at the door or the ward telescreen,

'Bloody Murkitt threatened me. Now of course he's trying to act the hero, having arrived on the scene conveniently just as the gunman was nabbed!'

'Christ, have you told the cops about that?' he blurts out as Paula puts a hand to his lips in a belated attempt to quieten him. At that moment, the ward sister arrives and bundles him out.

'Talk to you later,' Chris says over his shoulder, a pained look on his face as he is pressed unceremoniously past the puzzled cop at the ward door. Sister waves a dismissive hand at a few hopeful photographers pressing their claim to admission. To Chris's chagrin, they do of course snap his departure while a young reporter flings a question at him, 'Mr. Burnside, d'you have suspicions as to who is behind this?'

'That's a question for the police,' he says, noticing the young policeman who had arrested the gunman approaching behind the press.

All eyes turn in his direction and he says the gunman has been charged with the shooting. His name is Gino Lamazza, formerly of Bruce Rock but lately of Coolbellup, a suburb near Fremantle.

Constable Walters proceeds to Paula's bedside and transmits this information to her. She looks worried and asks if Lamazza has mafia connections. They exchange thoughts on the matter, but neither give much away.

Walters, an athletically built twenty-five year old, is pleased to have a few moments conversation with her before he too has to move on. He remembers to leave his card before he does so, issuing a more than routine invitation for Paula to contact him when she's discharged. The police guard winks at him as he leaves the ward. Paula notices, but she simply smiles disarmingly at the guard. She has plenty of other fish to fry at present.

CHAPTER 18

PARLIAMENT SUCKS

'Order, order, come to order members,' shouts the Speaker, banging his gavel to little effect, as the Parliament erupts in shouts of derision and abuse hurled across the chamber. At times like this, it seems to Chris, still new to the game of being an MP, and a trifle isolated, more like being back at school than in the supposed fount of democracy.

Chris was on the receiving end of similar broadsides when he gave his first speech some weeks back. Contrary to usual custom, he got a boisterous reception. In contrast to his predecessor, Chris is keen to be seen to serve his local constituency first. So after the customary thanks to his election helpers, he sunk the boot into the Rockingham Highway and embarrassed the opposition through an expose of their backsliding on the issue and their part in the imposition of the redevelopment authority.

Today, Chris has entered the debate over the government decision to award the casino operating licence to Kerry Cinnamon. This is potentially embarrassing to Chris since, when still a public servant, his Committee had recommended Cinnamon and the police had given Cinnamon a clean bill of health.

However, Chris is now aware of some damning evidence that has since emerged; he has learnt from contacts in his old department that reliable evidence of Cinnamon's connections to organised crime have come to hand. Both the government and the police have suppressed this. Chris reveals enough to embarrass both.

Right is furious and rises to take a point of order, accusing Chris of misleading Parliament and of being not just a 'naïve idiot', but a 'guttersnipe' and 'a total pretender'.

'There is no point of order. The Premier should himself come to order!' tries the Speaker .

Right glares back at the chair and goes on with his tirade of abuse, knowing the Speaker is floundering. An independent Liberal, the Speaker is also new to the job that he secured only in return for a promise to support the government. The post gives him some prominence, a little prestige and potential power over debate. Throw in a salary hike, a comfortable suite of offices, some clerical assistance, an expense account, access to a generous budget for travel and the package did not look at all bad. Until it came to trying to control unruly MPs.

Showing signs of not knowing what to try next, the Speaker turns to the clerk of the house in frustration. The clerk advises him to rely on time-tested procedures. Just as the shouting match reaches a crescendo with Right hotly disputing Chris's assertions about Cinnamon, the Speaker takes the cue and threatens suspension of parliamentary proceedings. To his relief, the threat is enough to silence Right, who doesn't want this additional embarrassment to mar his first parliamentary session.

Chris resumes his speech, but switches to a different note in conclusion, by speculating on connections between the activities of the FRA and organised thuggery, given the shooting of the Mayor and the proximity of Cloke's mob to the action. He's preparing the ground to have the authority's high-rise plans tabled and debated.

'Get off the grass, Member for Fremantle, that plan will transform your decaying city!' comes the strident yell from an MP on the government benches.

'Yeah, you imbecile, you can't dictate to the FRA!' cries another. And a third: 'the Premier is spot on calling you a naïve fucking idiot. Green by inclination and green by nature!'

The Speaker demands that this remark be withdrawn and berates the Member concerned, telling him that use of 'that f word' was 'unparliamentary', even if the accusation wasn't!

Chris knows his speech has made an impact. Despite Right's earlier bluster, during question time he announces that while the Member for Fremantle's accusations are without foundation, his government will nonetheless undertake further checks on Cinnamon.

Knowing the police and their purple circle, Chris can't help interjecting, 'and a fat lot of good that will do!'

'Not content with slandering Cinnamon, the Member for Fremantle now starts on the police!' the Premier replies indignantly. The house erupts in chaos again while more insults are traded.

Later, in the corridors over a cup of tea with a group of friends and supporters, Chris is surprised when Right approaches and calls him aside.

'Well, Burnside, you've gone too far this time,' he says, his face contorted with anger. 'I thought your first speech was over the top, but this one was scandalous because you're dead wrong about Cinnamon, and you know it.'

'I know differently now, Premier!' counters Chris confidently.

Right's mood seems to suddenly change, for he now smiles at Chris and says without rancour, 'well, that's now a matter for the police. Meantime, I have a proposal for you, how about we meet after dinner tonight to discuss it. Seven in my office suit you?'

Intrigued, Chris agrees.

Later, while waiting in Right's office for him to arrive for their meeting, Chris spots Diana. They say hello, and Diana slips a note into his hand as she hurries past. The note offers to shout him a drink after the night's proceedings. He'll have no problem accepting that one.

Chris is also tempted to accept an unexpected offer from the Premier at the meeting that follows: Chair of a select committee into the building unions. Chris senses that for Right, the committee will be used to give the government a political boost and to put heat on the opposition. But he also knows that the opposition will likely support the committee, as Hipper is keen to distance herself from Cloke and the union heavies. Right explains that while Chris could be a risky choice as Chair, the committee needs an air of independence.

In return for the prize of committee Chair, Right wants Chris to lay off the casino issue, particularly the dealings between the government and Cinnamon. Chris is wary of deals like this: it seems at best inconsistent, at worst, dishonest. And he knows that he's supposed to support a policy of no deals. Yet the idea of the committee excites him, and so he tentatively explores possible committee membership; his suggestions include Sarah Kingsmill.

Right indicates approval and agrees to give Chris until the next day to respond to his offer. Chris leaves the meeting feeling elated, although he knows it will be difficult to give up his pursuit of Cinnamon just when he seems to be getting closer to his quarry.

Chris meets Diana later at Harry's Jazz Club. It's only a ten-minute walk from Parliament, but Chris gets wet in the rain, having been unprepared for the winter storm. He's now using public transport regularly for his journeys to and from Parliament, and drawing some kudos from the local press as a result. Trouble is, today he forgot his raincoat and he doesn't have a car at his disposal. Not much kudos in that, he reflects ruefully as he waits in the foyer for Diana, looking a bit bedraggled even after trying to dry off in the rest rooms. Diana soon comes in, dry as a bone, having been driven the distance. Eyeing Chris's condition, she laughs.

'That'll teach you, you public transport fanatic!'

Chris groans as they enter and head for a table tucked away from prying eyes and ears in a dark corner. They start by reflecting on the last few days' events over a nightcap, Chris choosing single-malt Irish whisky and Diana a hot chocolate. Diana tells Chris how distressed she was to hear of Paula's shooting, she sent flowers and chocolates.

'And talking about Paula, Chris you old devil, where have you and she got to? According to the Press, things might be just hotting up for you two?' She was referring to a recent article in the gossip columns that featured pictures of Chris after visiting Paula during her spell in hospital.

'Well, the affair is over, sad to say.'

'What? When?' Diana is taken aback.

'Paula's shooting may have been traumatic for her, but maybe it helped bring me to my senses. We had a long talk once she was out of hospital and agreed to end our fling and concentrate on our respective political patches.'

'And about time too.'

'Right Diana, you win. And so does Dean in my office, who warned me against an affair to begin with. As you just said, the press was starting to get wise after they saw me visit her in hospital.'

'So you ended it just because the press might have been on to it? You old cynic, you!' Diana teases.

'No, we decided well before anything got into the press, but I'd have to say the constant flash bulbs in my face as I left the hospital each time did unnerve me.'

'Say no more Chris. You're a politician through and through. You and Paula have done a deal on the Fremantle plan I bet!'

Chris ignores the jibe and changes the topic. 'OK, talking of political deals, Right has offered me the Chair of a proposed committee into the unions!'

'He what? He didn't mention that to me, I knew a committee was on the cards, has been since the shooting, but I thought he would put one of his own in charge. He'd have far more control over the outcome that way. So just what does he want in return?' asks Diana, pausing to take a sip of her beverage and looking directly at him with worry in her eyes.

'He wants me to lay off Cinnamon and the casino,' admits Chris a little shame-facedly.

'Whoa, boy! Surely you wouldn't touch that one? After all, you're supposed to be against deals like that, aren't you?

'Well, yes, but this could be the making of me!' Chris says half-jokingly.

'Look, Chris, you've been adamant since you were elected that you couldn't be bought off.'

'All *right*, you've got a point there,' Chris replies testily. After a pause, he offers, a little too breezily, 'so I won't agree to the condition.'

'And if Right then withdraws the offer?'

'Hmm. Well, I don't think he will, he's desperate to make mileage out of the shooting and distract people from the real issues, like cronyism at the FRA.'

'Well maybe, but don't be tempted by the devil and all that.'

'Same could be said for you my dear, you work for the bastard!'

'Hey, come on, that's below the belt and you know it,' returns Diana, kicking him under the table. They both smile as Chris rubs his shin.

Diana goes on, 'let's see what happens there, my friend, but even if Right withdraws the condition, don't forget that union politics is a bloody murky area. I don't think it's a good idea to pitch yourself against the likes of Cloke and the union bosses.'

'Well, you know I'm tempted by risky situations. And I reckon the committee could yield some important leads. And bloody Cloke's activities could do with a bit of airing, don't you think?' asks Chris hopefully.

'Yes, but there could be better and safer ways to achieve that,' counters Diana. 'After all, Elaine Hipper has already hinted to me that she has material that would help expose some of the dodgy operators.'

'Well as far as I'm concerned, if we get one or two of Elaine's allies on the committee, like Yoni McNamara, then we should soon be cooking with gas, surely?'

'Chris, Yoni is a straight operator yes, but come on, aren't you just wanting her on the committee because you fancy her? And next you'll be telling me that you want Sarah Kingsmill on too.'

Chris shrugs and looks awkward, giving the game away and realising it. Not only had he ignored Diana's early warning about Sarah, but he had also recently admitted that he was increasingly attracted to Sarah. More than empathy seemed to be on offer from Sarah: despite being married, she's responding well to Chris's increasingly flirtatious approach.

Not only that, but in the past, Chris had raved to Diana about Yoni's slim body and graceful looks on many occasions. He confessed to Diana that before he set eyes on Sarah, he always had it at the back of his mind to pursue Yoni. Now acutely embarrassed and trying to switch tack, Chris says, 'look I was only giving Yoni as an example of possible members on the committee. There are a few others in the ranks and all of them male, so there you go!'

'I don't believe you for a minute, Chris, and for god's sake, leave Sarah out of it. Having her on the committee would be a disaster given what you've told me about your feelings towards her.'

'But even if you get over all these hurdles successfully, this committee spells danger for you in every way. Apart from anything else, Hipper has still got Cloke and his mates in the Party to deal with. They'll be sure to try and influence the committee members to go easy on Cloke.'

'Ma-aa-aates, there they are again!' says Chris. 'Anyhow, ma-aate,' he adds with a broad grin, 'I'll sleep on that and the deal, OK?'

'OK, ma-aate. Don't say I didn't warn you – a deal like this could really backfire.'

'Food for thought,' Chris says as they part with a hug, and he heads for the nearby station to catch the train to Fremantle, with more storm clouds gathering on the horizon.

Diana's words of warning have made a mark, and he starts to feel unhappy. One of the few passengers sharing the train at this hour tries to engage Chris in conversation about the storm coming in, but Chris is in no mood for small talk and buries himself in some unfinished paperwork. Or tries to.

As he alights at Fremantle and heads for his pad, a biting wind is blowing in from the ocean, bringing dark clouds in its wake. This makes it particularly difficult for Chris to light his last cigarette of the day, and in the end, he gives up when it starts raining. He gets drenched on the walk home. This only dampens his mood further.

Next morning, Chris feels little better after a restless night. He couldn't get the committee, or Sarah Brunswick, out of his mind, and Diana's warnings kept coming back to him. He's still in two minds as he heads for his ritual coffee.

At the other end of town, Diana is contemplating the women in politics project. Checking her diary before leaving home, she is delighted to find that she and Paula have a meeting later that day. Their agenda? Possibilities for political detective work and consideration of like-minded women to approach.

Now this could be the start of something really good! Diana muses. Her morning muse turns out to be exceptionally well-informed.

CHAPTER 19

CHICK POWER

Paula also has a big day ahead of her. She's almost recovered from the shooting and is now back to work with a vengeance. Apart from the meeting with Diana and several pressing matters of council business, she also has to pay a visit to the police to follow up the case against her assailant, Gino Lamazza.

Lamazza has been portrayed in the press as evil personified. While Paula finds this rather bemusing, not to say prejudicial to the trial, friends point out that the dramatic shooting of a woman, especially an attractive one who is a popular figure, adds grist to the press's emotional mill. Of more interest to Paula are the hacks' efforts to explore the connections between Lamazza, Cloke and the union militants.

This prompted a typical reaction from Roberts and Cloke, the threat of defamation writs. Both regularly use these 'stop-writs' as they are known in the trade, since once served, they prevent any further public statements until the matter is heard in court. Paula knows that such matters rarely get as far as court or are settled out of court. She sees these writs as a way of silencing critics, a product of weak defamation laws, which she regards as protecting the rich and powerful to a far greater degree than anyone else.

Having had this avenue of speculation closed, the press concentrate on rumours of mafia involvement in the shooting, pointing out that

Paula's cousin, the previous Mayor, was rumoured to have mafia connections. There follows a series of articles on organised crime, full of dramatic incidents and accusations that have Lamazza in regular company with city crime bosses such as Sizall and Lilliano.

This morning, Paula arrives at Fremantle Police station in some trepidation. She has to get past the menacing Murkitt at the front office, something she isn't happy about, given their recent falling out. Murkitt called her after the incident, protesting that whatever their differences, there was no way he would get involved in a shooting. Paula found this insincere to say the least. She suspects he might have a link to the shooting, but in any case, knowing Murkitt's influence, she's wary of relaying her suspicions to the investigating police, or even informing them of her confrontation with him.

As it turns out, Murkitt is all smiles this morning. They exchange strained, perfunctory greetings before she hurries on to talk to the detectives. She is being called on to identify Lamazza, given that he was surrounded by people unwilling to testify as witnesses and that the fuzzy TV footage won't be acceptable in court. She isn't looking forward to this, realising it will bring back all the trauma of the shooting. Even now, some weeks later, she's having trouble sleeping.

At the line-up of figures that follows, she has some trouble identifying the bearded and gaunt-looking Lamazza, explaining that she only saw the gunman in the split second after she was shot and she was falling to the stage.

But as she finally gives the nod to the relieved and irrepressible constable Walters, she notices something eerily familiar in Lamazza's demeanour and particularly in his shuffling walk as the line-up makes an exit.

Instinctively, she covers her mouth and lets out, 'oh my god, it can't be!'

'What do you mean?' Walters asks, solicitously putting a hand on her shoulder.

'Are you sure that guy's name is Lamazza?' she asks, shaking herself free from Walters's hand.

'Well, his paperwork checks out, but why d'you ask?' comes the response from a puzzled Walters.

'It's just that I could swear from his eyes and what I can see of his face beneath the beard that he's Emilio, my kid brother, who's been missing for the last two years!' says Paula, struggling to come to terms with her instinctive certainty. 'Otherwise, he's a double,' she adds vehemently.

'What? I mean that's got to be a weird coincidence, because nothing in this guy's background links him to the Muscatelli clan. Any rate, why the hell would your brother want to shoot you?' asks Walters, scoffing.

'You don't know my family! Emilio disappeared after a big row with me,' says Paula passionately, recalling the traumatic events.

She explains to Walters and Senior Detective Schilz, who's joined them in a nearby interview room, that the row blew up in response to Emilio's antagonism over Paula's flamboyant liaison with a fellow barrister in her chambers. Add to this Paula's success at the bar and her appointment as a QC, while Emilio was struggling to fend off fraud and drug charges following the collapse of his business, amid stories of company cash funding Emilio's drug and gambling habits and you had a volatile recipe.

'That's as may be, but how can you be sure this is Emilio?' asks Schilz, preferring to believe the identity of Lamazza the investigating police have been constructing.

'Well, of course I'm not sure, his beard and hair make it really difficult to tell, but his other features are familiar, and the way he shuffles as he walks is exactly like Emilio. I want this checked out further, detective!'

'Of course, Madame Mayor,' Schilz responds disdainfully, 'but you will appreciate the serious nature of this whole matter.'

'And you will appreciate, Officer, that if this guy does turn out to be Emilio, I want him released,' responds Paula, still struggling with the implications. 'He may have shot me, but I don't want him in court.'

'I think you'll find the police have the final say in cases like this,' says Schilz drily.

'I guess you're right legally there,' admits Paula, thinking with her QC's brain for a moment, 'but this looks like a family matter to me, and I wouldn't be happy about the idea of testifying in court against my own brother!'

'Well, that's not a decision for us, it'll have to go to the Public Prosecutor,' cuts in Constable Walters, appearing to make an effort to stay on-side with this enigmatic Mayor.

He then turns to his colleague. 'But first we need to check this Lamazza character out further and talk to our missing persons bureau.'

'Sure,' agrees Schilz, relaxing a bit now as it appears they have the upper hand again.

'Thanks, officers, maybe I can help by talking to Lamazza myself?' Paula offers.

'That could be useful later,' Schilz allows, 'but first, it would help if you could give us a few more details about this missing brother of yours.'

Paula does so and then hastily leaves for an urgent appointment. But not before pressing the police to fast-track their investigations and to contact her immediately they have any leads.

On the way back to the nearby council chambers, Paula calls her mother to pass on details of the morning's unusual scenes. Her mother will be delighted if Lamazza turns out to be Emilio, for despite Paula's talents and Emilio's life on the edge, he remains her favourite.

The blow of his disappearance hit his mother really hard; she's been fretting ever since. Her much-loved husband died recently after years of ill health, another tragedy for the family. Paula had been distraught at the time, but now reflects that this incident wouldn't have been good for her father's declining health.

Her father had been so disgusted with Emilio's down-market lifestyle that he had virtually disowned him. To have him accused of shooting his beautiful daughter would have been the last straw. As it was, her father had not wanted him found, but the rest of the family had tried everything from private detectives to the internet, all to no avail. He had sunk without a trace. *What a bizarre way to reappear,* she thinks.

Paula has trouble concentrating on her official duties during the day, her thoughts keep returning to Emilio and the difficulties she encountered dealing with him over the years. Would that really explain why he would want to shoot her? It was at once a worrying and an exciting prospect to maybe have him back after all this time.

Later in the day when she meets Diana, Paula seems needy, and Diana hugs her warmly. Paula is grateful to have a friend to share the pain with; indeed, she feels a growing attraction to Diana. Politics is initially put aside for another long discussion about family matters.

As they savour a bottle of fine Italian chianti from Paula's cellar and sit in the fading sun on her apartment veranda overlooking the ocean, Paula brings Diana up-to-date and shares her story about Emilio. Diana is intrigued; she missed the publicity when Emilio disappeared two years previously, having been on an extended holiday overseas. Diana empathises and tells Paula of the torrid time she's recently experienced with her own family over Cloke.

Their conversation finally drifts back to politics, and they decide that candidates for their honesty in politics group should be representative of different parties and interest groups. They divide the task of contacting these people, set a date for their next meeting, and move on to discuss a charter. Just as they get to some tentative wording, Paula's watch rings shrilly.

'Oh hello Detective,' she says, motioning Diana to stay put. Paula listens to Detective Schilz for a few minutes and then says, 'really he said that? I'd better get down there right away.'

'You're off to the Fremantle police station again?' divines Diana.

'Yes, two times in one day is a worry, but the police are a bit stumped. The guy has admitted that Lamazza is not his real name, he assumed the identity as his bosses knew what the cops didn't. Lamazza was rubbed out in the course of ongoing gang reprisals. Our man and Lamazza have similarities, you know, height and build, their faces are a bit different, but the look-alike beard and hair style did the rest. But the guy is refusing to confirm that he is Emilio, has clammed up, and says he will now only talk to me!'

'Well, that seems to seal the issue. It must be him?' asks Diana.

'Certainly sounds like it, god, how weird!'

They part shortly afterwards, Diana dropping Paula at the police station on her way back through the city. Before Paula gets out of the car, she kisses Diana firmly on the lips. They both savour the prospect of meeting again soon.

At the police station, Paula is taken straight to a guarded interview room where the mystery figure sits, handcuffed and rather bedraggled, but now beardless. Schilz looks up at Paula with a guarded expression. He motions the flanking officers out of the room and melts into the background, leaving Lamazza opposite Paula.

'Emilio?' Paula looks him straight in the eye, now certain that this is her brother.

At first he looks away, but then breaks down and weeps, whining in a thin voice, 'Paula, my sister, I'm so sorry!'

He struggles to reach across the table to her, but the handcuffs prevented such intimacy.

'Oh, thankyou Emilio.' A million questions race through her mind, but she doesn't want to ask them in this situation.

'Can't you get the handcuffs off him?' Paula asks desperately, turning to Schilz.

'Well, ok,' says Schilz warily, still not convinced. Before removing the cuffs, and glancing in the direction of the observation window into the room, Shilz discreetly checks under his coat, making sure his gun is at the ready and that the prisoner stays on his side of the table.

Immediately his cuffs are removed, the prisoner reaches across and grabs Paula, repeating amid tears

'my sister, my sister'.

Shilz allows the prisoner to move around the table while keeping him under close scrutiny.

Tears come to Paula's eyes too, and she moves closer to Emilio. They hug. They stay this way for several seconds, until Paula asks, choking back more tears, 'Emilio, why did you shoot me?'

'Paula, I only meant to frighten you! The bullet wasn't meant to hit.' His voice fades away until he says softly, looking at her wildly, 'It was meant as a warning! But they're out to get you, Paula!' Emilio says, looking at her with a strange intensity.

Paula is taken aback; this isn't how she remembers her favourite brother.

'Who's *they*, Emilio?'

'Dark forces, sister, dark forces,' he whispers.

Paula fears her brother is obsessed; she doesn't know what he's been through, suspects he's trapped in some sort of twisted psychological space. By this time, it's clear even to the cynical Schilz that they have a very unusual family reunion on their hands, and so he temporarily leaves them to their odd conversation.

Half an hour later, Paula emerges looking worried. She tells Schilz that she wants her brother bailed. Emilio had started to tell her of his disappearance, but then became extremely agitated, had broken down again and become incoherent, ranting about the dark forces. Paula could sense there was something important driving him, but is worried about his mental state more than anything.

Schilz said he would have to get on to his superiors, muttering about charges he still had to face. But Paula tells him that if the police or the DPP insist on bringing Emilio to trial, she will be there as his defence lawyer and not as a witness for the prosecution. Schilz grimaces, reluctantly promising to set the wheels in motion for a bail application. Paula leaves and makes for her mother's house, to pass on the good and bad news.

CHAPTER 20

EASTERN AFFAIRS

Chris grips the armrest tightly as the jet tilts upwards and thrusts into the air. It's a smooth take-off, but he's always been a nervous flyer. Right from the first time he flew to London many years back. Then, he found a good joint helped before boarding. Today, he decided against that old remedy, thinking the airport sniffer dogs might detect the remnants. He thought he would have a whisky on the plane, but now he wasn't sure he could stomach it.

From the seat next to him, Francine smiles to herself and says almost solicitously, 'you ok there Chris?'

'No!'

Chris is tetchy, looking distinctly green as the plane rises rapidly over the coastal plain, banks, and affords a fabulous view of the city's office towers huddled ever closer to the river.

Francine, who loves the landscape from the air, takes it in greedily, but refrains from drawing Chris's attention to it, lest he become airsick. Instead, she concentrates on the sprawling suburbs that eventually peter out into long tentacles of development spearing into the metallic green bush and the sparsely covered ranges behind the city.

As the plane continues its climb, Chris is having regrets, and not just about the parlous state of his stomach. To his staff's surprise and much critical comment, Chris accepted the deal with Right and so was now Chair of the select committee.

Right had been insistent on the terms of Chris laying off Cinnamon. Chris didn't spread the word about this, knowing he was in breach of his own policy. He told his staff to stay mum on the deal too, something they aren't happy about.

Diana was horrified and told him so. Chris argued that there were plenty of other ways in which Cinnamon could still come to grief. Diana isn't convinced.

Now, Chris wonders, *is this the beginning of the political slippery slope for me? Surely not, after all aren't deals just part of politics? Perhaps,* he muses, *but not when you claim publicly* – as he had in the inaugural speech – *that you are above all that. Ah well,* he reflects, as Diana wisely said, 'you've made your bed, now you're just going to have to lie in it!'

This turns Chris's thoughts to the members of his committee also on this flight: Sarah Kingsmill and Yoni McNamara are among them. When it came to crunch and ignoring Diana's prescient advice, Chris secured both for the committee. While Yoni showed no particular interest in Chris, that wasn't the case with Sarah.

The committee had been in session for a few weeks before this trip, investigating politics and corruption in the industry. Melbourne is notorious as one of the centres for this activity. The payoff for his researcher, Francine, is that she can accompany Chris and do some supplementary research on one of her favourite topics, crime and corruption. Francine is planning to concentrate her research on the murky parallels between underworld crime, politics, and corruption in Victoria and WA.

The flight is pretty routine, although Chris feels a tinge of fear each time the plane strikes turbulence. Eventually, he falls into a fitful sleep. Earlier, after the taxi picked Francine up for the early morning journey to the airport, Chris pointedly told her that he only had a few hours sleep. His hangover drew little sympathy from Francine who, at the age of twenty-four, can stand a few more boozy late nights than her boss, almost twenty years her senior.

Chris wakes in a funk half an hour before they reach Melbourne, and Francine asks how he's feeling.

'A bit better. Ask me again when the flight is over,' he says cryptically, with a grimace. 'But this committee is starting to give me the shits!'

'Really? I'm surprised, since this trip could be fun if only you'd relax, *and* you've got Cloke to look forward to when you get back!' she reminds him.

She's referring to moves for Roberts and Cloke to appear before the committee in a few weeks. But it's still far from certain if they will show, and even if they do, that their appearance will help Chris's cause. The committee has already been inundated with submissions full of hubris from the big employers and the unions.

The companies are anxious for revenge on the unions, and in their turn, the unions are keen to play down the militant and project an unlikely image of being reasonable. Much of this amounts to a power struggle. And there are sweetheart deals, whereby unions guarantee no strikes in return for special loadings. Dodgy company officials frequently resort to arrangements with unsavoury union bosses, who feather their own nests far more generously than those of their members.

But when it comes to analysis and recommendations, discussions on the topic have already turned into set-pieces, dividing along Party lines. Attacks on the unions from the conservative members and on the companies from the others. Or simply attacks on each other. All of this was more or less as Diana had predicted and so is doubly galling for Chris. And so far, the committee has turned up little in the way of specific evidence of shonky practices.

Francine now suggests to Chris that her best contacts in Melbourne are likely to be informal ones, off-the-record people who didn't want or need a committee. Chris frowns at this, but then leans over in her direction and to avoid being heard by others says, *sotto voce,* 'I've been mulling over complaints from some of our committee. They don't like my ruling, which limits travel and provides economy seats only. I reckon politicians get enough perks at the taxpayers' expense already. Did you know that backbenchers can access $100,000 in a parliamentary term for research-related travel? To get the approval stamp, the trip has to be relevant to the Member's political job, but what isn't relevant to politics?'

'Chris I get the point, you can get off your high horse now! Let's just hope *this* trip doesn't get labelled a junket,' Francine quips.

They part company at the airport, with Francine heading for a suburban university campus, where she has contacts. She's arranged a de-briefing with Chris for later in the week.

Chris heads for the taxi rank, and the party of other committee members and staff take three vehicles to the city. As Chris's taxi snakes its way along the bleak Tullamarine Freeway, he discovers to his disappointment that Sarah, one of two back seat passengers, has opted not to stay in the city, but instead near relatives she wants to visit in South Yarra. She takes the taxi on from the hotel, located near Swanston Street railway station.

The week in marvellous Melbourne evaporates quickly as, after the formal business of each day, members pursue their own agendas. Chris takes the opportunity to catch up with some old friends and contacts. He's delighted when one of his old mates offers him a spare ticket to a Coldplay concert, the band preceded by the evergreen Paul Kelly. Two of Chris's favourites on one night, a rare treat these days, he reflects.

The hearings provide valuable insights into bribery in the local building industry, bribes offered by the new wave of Asian investors keen to get their development projects through the approval system. Cases where the bribes have been offered to or asked for by council members and officers to speed approvals, building union officials to keep peace on building construction sites, and building companies to secure their usual contracts.

Following the last day of hearings, dinner has been scheduled at a restaurant in Carlton. It's a warm and busy night in the city, and having decided to walk the short distance, Chris has some difficulty making his way along the crowded pavements. He notes the huge variety of cultures and faces in the crowd; it makes Perth seem very Anglo-Saxon by comparison. Chris makes his way up Lygon Street, the spruikers are out in force, all promising the culinary experience of a lifetime.

This afternoon, Chris chaired a successful final committee session: a likely link to Roberts emerged through the evidence of a union dissident. He's in buoyant mood taking in the sights, sounds, and aromas of this lively inner city district with extra gusto.

Once he finds the restaurant and is shown to a table in a private room, Chris's mood is heightened at the sight of Sarah, for she'd said she might have to miss the occasion, as she was going upcountry with her relatives.

'Arrangements for the country fallen through?' Chris asks her across the table.

'No, but we're not leaving until tomorrow morning, so I thought I'd join you cosmopolitans,' Sarah replies ironically while moving her head invitingly and winking in his direction. Chris takes this as an understanding of what might follow later.

Sarah then turns to the politician next to her and engages in animated conversation so as not to overdo her interaction with Chris, who takes the hint and pays her no special attention during the meal. A few of the party linger for extra coffee and liqueurs while others head off.

Chris decides to join the lingering party as Sarah is among their number. After some lively interchange of views on the weeks' proceedings, Chris and Sarah contrive to be last to leave, and they hook up down the street.

'Fancy a nightcap at my hotel?' Chris asks, his hand brushing her cheek.

'Sure, but my hotel will be safer from any prying eyes,' Sarah offers, squeezing his arm. Chris takes the point, and they grab a taxi and head for her hotel apartment in South Yarra.

As it's a warm night, they take their room service drinks onto the balcony overlooking Albert Park. They sit and contemplate the view and the prospects before them. Despite his desire, Chris is nervous and is glad when Sarah broaches the next move.

'Don't be nervous, Chris, no one knows we're here.'

'I'm not so much nervous about that as about the risks of us getting involved. For a start, what about your husband?'

'What he doesn't know won't hurt him,' she says emphatically. 'Besides, the marriage has been running out of steam since I got into politics.'

'Happens all too often.'

Chris moves over to Sarah, puts his arm around her shoulders, his nerves calmer after the exchange and the whisky. Sarah turns her head to his, and they kiss. After a few minutes of ever more passionate kissing, they move inside, Sarah through to the bathroom. Chris strips off and hops into the large bed. Sarah returns, her long reddish hair now loosened, draping her trim body in an inviting manner.

'Botticelli's *Birth of Venus* has got nothing on you!' Chris exclaims, entranced.

'Why, thank you, kind sir!' Sarah returns mockingly with an inviting smile, her ample breasts bouncing as she joins Chris in bed. Their hot bodies meet in a long and passionate embrace. Chris moves his hands over her smooth skin, kisses her breasts. Her nipples become firm as he moves his attention to her stomach and her shaven mount of Venus.

Sarah's fingernails are biting deep into his back. His tongue soon finds her secret place, and Sarah starts to moan with pleasure. She pulls him up to meet her kiss, and as his rock-hard penis encounters her clitoris, they both cry out.

She wraps her legs firmly around his ecstatic body. With her encouragement, they try several different positions before she reaches the first high orgasm of many for the night. After his own orgasm, Chris doesn't need much recovery time before they make love again and again.

They sleep briefly until dawn when Sarah suggests Chris should take his leave, she needs to pack to join her relatives on their planned weekend trip to the country. They kiss and the passion returns, but before things get too steamy, Sarah gently guides Chris to the door. They promise to meet as soon as they can back in Perth.

On his way back to the city, Chris reflects that she is really something this Sarah, an erotic and emotional charge he hasn't felt the likes of for many years. Paula was fun, she was erotic, but there was no real passion in their lovemaking. This promises to be a very different experience. The difference in their political outlook and the possible consequences of the liaison are far from his thoughts as he makes his way back to the hotel on an early tram.

CHAPTER 21

FAMILY CONNECTIONS

It turns out to be a day for trams, for after a refreshing shower and a large breakfast, Chris decides to head for St. Kilda, one of his favourite Melbourne haunts. The sun's out, but there are storm clouds on the southern horizon. Chris turns away from the café windows bedecked with tempting cakes and pastries and strolls down to the pier and the beach. The sea looks brittle, ruffled by an early breeze, but the sun is warm enough to enjoy. The night of excess catching up with him, Chris stops at an al fresco café, orders a double espresso, and sits contentedly enjoying the view and the passing parade.

A group of shrouded Muslim women disembark from a bus marked Day Trip and walk past laughing and chattering energetically in their native tongue, but from their smiles and pointing, Chris gathers they are impressed by the unseasonally warm weather as well as the location. After finishing his coffee, he strolls past them with a nod and walks out on the pier where he sits near the meticulously reconstructed pavilion, destroyed by fire some decades back. He relishes the sun and rolls a cigarette. He lights up and sucks in the smoke with undue pleasure as he goes over the night with Sarah. He finds himself in danger of being smitten.

Ah, the vegetarian's tobacco! he thinks self-indulgently, as he coughs to clear his throat of the deadly tars and tries to clear his mind of Sarah.

On resuming tobacco smoking recently, job pressures the explanation he offered, he decided against e-cigarettes and tailor-made, preferring rolling tobacco, rationalising that this is less harmful than the more processed variety. But at the end of a day, his throat tells him otherwise.

As he ambles back down the pier, taking in the distant view of the city skyline, he sees closer at hand a group of students filming some contrived action on the pier. There is a statuesque woman nearby, apparently directing proceedings. She looks more than familiar to Chris, who does a double take.

'God, that's my ex, Jenny!'

He hasn't seen her for years now since she and their baby, George, disappeared from his life. Chris hesitates, knowing that he is likely to get a hostile reception. The last time they'd met, she didn't want to know him. She was no doubt still angry from his cancelling the phone meeting that had been planned and that Chris had cancelled at the last minute.

Well, I really would like to find out more about George, Chris thinks.

Jenny calls, 'fifteen-minute break.' and the students down their equipment, most head off for the nearby kiosk, but a few stick around talking. Chris seizes his chance and moves forward, Jenny chatting breezily to her students. As the students disperse, she sees Chris, and her demeanour changes.

'What the fuck are you doing here?' she hisses.

'In Melbourne on business, my day off.'

'Not sure if I believe that line, but how did you find me?' she says, her anger barely under control.

'Pure chance, I've always liked St. Kilda, so here I am.'

'Just my bloody luck. Anyhow, I don't want to talk to you, Chris, you can see I'm in the middle of filming.'

'Understood, but I do need to know about George.'

'Oh, come on, you cancelled our last conversation. And then you run into me by chance and suddenly show interest in your son?'

'Come on Jenny, you know I've tried to find him, and you've blocked my efforts. You return my letters, and then change address . . .'

'That was years ago, and I've moved a few times since then too. But why would I want anything to do with you, you prick, after the way you treated me?'

'Jenny, come on, let's not go over all this, just tell me about George. Please,' he pleads.

Jenny seems to soften and offers, 'Look, I can't now, but in any case, it's all difficult.'

'What do you mean?'

'Christ, Chris, give over, you can see I'm under pressure here,' she says as the students reassemble, some looking on curiously. 'Meet me later on if you really want to know.'

Reluctantly, Chris agrees. A few hours later, he locates their designated meeting place, a nearby pub. Having time to kill as he's half an hour early, he orders a whisky and a counter meal. He speculates on why Jenny had used the word *difficult* to explain what had happened to their son.

As he finishes the meal, washed down with another whisky and a beer chaser, he realises that the designated meeting time is well past and that it looks increasingly like he's been stood up. Annoyed and wondering vaguely if he has time to track her down before he leaves Melbourne, he drifts to the pool table and joins a game.

When Bill, one of the old regular players, hears Chris is an MP from the West, a ribbing follows.

'Fuckin' pollie, is ya? How d'you lie straight in bed at night? I reckon that Premier of yours, what's his name, er . . . Crockett?' says Bill, scratching his head in an effort to jog his addled brain.

'You probably mean the last one, Wayne Cloke,' says Chris. 'Well, he's not in Parliament any longer.'

'Yeah, well, they all cut and run when they're caught out, and whatever his bloody name is, I reckon he should be on trial for defrauding the public!'

'No argument from me on that one, and I can tell you quite a bit else about him,' returns Chris.

'But the guy that took over as Premier has been bloody slow getting around to prosecuting Cloke and his mob.'

He explains how the Corruption Commission has not concluded hearings on the Cloke scandal and has lately procrastinated. He tells Bill it's an issue he intends pursuing.

'Typical,' says a cynical Bill, 'this new geezer is probably up to his neck in his own scams. They're all as bad as each other I reckon, not to mention those fuckin' building companies!'

'Funny you should say that, it's because of building industry scams that I'm in Melbourne.'

When Chris tells of his mission, Bill turns serious, telling Chris he has long experience of the building trade in both Western Australia and Victoria. In the rambling conversation that follows, Chris learns far more about corruption in the building industry than he has in hours of hearings. He carefully notes details of a personal building project that Vince Roberts has on the go in a nearby coastal resort.

Careful notes are not on Chris's mind later that night when he ends up at a party in the vicinity. Bill invites him along when the pub closes, and there are drugs aplenty to keep Chris going during the night. He doesn't find out any more about the machinations of the city's criminals, but he gets a double dose of its party machine.

Chis eventually gets a taxi as the sun is just lighting the new day, but he's oblivious to the spectacular sunrise as he dozes and then collapses into bed. It takes a sleep in and a slow start to get over the night's indulgences and those of the night before, come to that. He achieves partial recovery with the help of water, fruit and juice. This combination gradually pumps enough vitamins into his system to get him back to a semblance of health.

He's late for his debriefing with Francine, and he has some trouble taking in her gangland scenarios and other information she has collected. Through her contacts, she's met informants who've given her a chilling rundown of the crossovers between the law, politics, and organised crime in Melbourne.

After a recent further spate of gangland killings, Francine was learning how Melbourne qualifies as the nation's crime capital. She's about to expound on this scenario when she sees Chris dropping off. She digs him in the ribs and asks good-humouredly, 'is this the MP for Fremantle or Rip Van Winkle?'

Chris jolts awake, embarrassed, and is about to give Francine a suitably edited version of last night's action, when a figure arrives at their table and says, 'this'll be Chris Burnside and Francine Burt, I reckon. I'm Bob Stanecich, pleased to meet you both.' A tall figure stoops to extend a hand to Chris.

'They said I'd find you here,' he offers by way of explanation.

Chris is non-plussed until Francine cuts in, 'oh sorry Chris, I forgot to tell you in all the buzz that my host at Latrobe said he might send us another informer. Yeah, hi Bob, sit down I've heard a lot about you!'

Over tea and another double-strength coffee for the tired Chris, Bob, former detective turned academic and whistle-blower, explains that he's putting together a book on his research into the country's criminal under-belly.

'You would probably have come across the names Sizall, Lilliano and Roberts then?' asks Francine.

'Have I what!' said Paul, and with obvious relish, he outlines some of the many connections he has uncovered between the organised crime scene in Victoria and WA.

Sizall and Lilliano head rival gangs, each cultivating links with mafia and gangland bosses as well as elements in the building unions and the federal police, headquartered in Melbourne. Roberts tries to play both sides against the middle. Dangerous game.

Stanecich also tells them about some potentially explosive evidence involving Cloke's connections to all of this. Chris is intrigued, but disappointed that Stanecich is having difficulty getting hold of the documentation. As they leave a few hours later, Chris reflects that the jigsaw facing them now has fewer missing pieces.

He would start to fit some of the new pieces together on the journey back, but he's painfully aware that the key pieces are still out of reach.

As, he reminds himself, is Sarah Kingsmill. She won't be back in Perth for a week or so, as she has more socialising lined up in Melbourne.

Chris gathers from what she told him that her Melbourne connections are pretty well-off, living as they do in and around South Yarra and Toorak, two of the city's poshest suburbs. *Come to think of it, Sarah herself is pretty affluent,* thinks Chris, having made a fortune in business before she stepped into politics. This aspect was given a fair bit of attention when, at the election, she swept into a seat long-held by the opposition.

Her pronouncements in Parliament on the 'evils of socialism' in relation to low-income housing policies further marked her out as no friend of the left. This was confirmed at recent committee deliberations, where she scoffed at some 'straight' union suggestions – strongly backed by Chris – that the builders should be more generous in their payments to building workers left outside the cosy deals between the 'insider' employers and their union compatriots. To Chris, this was one way of making things fairer in the industry; to Sarah, it was political heresy.

Chris now smiles to himself at these ideological differences and, in his state of high fever over his new conquest, dismisses any thought of problems, were the world to find out about their liaison. However, he instinctively realises that the affair should remain under wraps and his staff not told. He knows that they would be horrified.

CHAPTER 22

FAMILY MATTERS

The extended family would have made a baker's dozen had all gone according to plan that Sunday at Villa Muscatelli, the family home occupied by Paula's mother and grandmother. Sunday was ritual family gathering day, especially for Paula and her brother Peter, where they could recall a happy childhood in the house, built in the 1950s. From where it stands, as if brooding, just below the brow of Monument hill behind Fremantle, Villa Muscatelli takes in magnificent views over Cockburn Sound and the Indian Ocean.

Today, Mama has called whole family together over a traditional Sunday lunch, to face the crisis caused by Emilio's reappearance. The meal has been meticulously prepared over hours, days in fact, by Nona, and the one thing they can all agree is just how good it is.

Paula, always conscious of her waistline, savours a small portion of the entrée, Nona's ravioli filled with garden-grown spinach and local ricotta, followed by a few slices of lamb roast infused with garlic and rosemary, served with green beans, all but the roast from the garden. But Paula finds she cannot so easily resist a generous serve of the Villa's weekend harvest of potatoes, roasted to perfection, partly because she is keenly aware of Emilio's absence.

After prolonged sessions during his compulsory psychiatric assessment, Emilio overcame the shock of being outed. Paula and he rebuilt their trust, and Emilio gradually told the horrific story of his past two years. Misadventures centred around heroin addiction, forced deals, and orders he could not fulfil. The experience broke his spirit by taking charge of his mind and body.

Despite his absence today, Paula is comforted by the knowledge that Emilio is not far away. His views from the nearby hospital's secure psychiatric wing almost match those from the Villa, but he doesn't appreciate that.

He is still depressed, showing signs of lapsing back into chronic instability. His possible court appearance has been deferred due to further assessment. Depending on the result, he could be bailed out, but he will still likely face charges over the shooting. The deferral of the trial had only been achieved after some strong lobbying, with Paula using connections from her days as a QC. One of them is working on the family's behalf to oil the many squeaky wheels in the State's legal system.

After the meal, the kids take off to enjoy the warm and sunny spring day outside. Nona fusses until everyone else is settled, and Mama turns to Paula.

'Paula, now tell us the news, yes?'

'Well, Emilio was very down when I saw him this morning, but the thing is, I think he was pressured into the shooting.' As she speaks, she deliberately makes eye contact with her brothers.

'Si? Come on, Paula, he's conning you again! Why should we believe anything from that lying bastard?' throws in her elder brother, Paul.

Throughout the period Emilio had been missing and much to Paula and her Mama's distress, Paul had only made perfunctory enquiries about him. Her younger brother Peter at least helped in the attempts to track him down.

Paula frowns and decides not to take Paul's bait.

'Paul, I don't expect you to believe me or Emilio, but I'm sure he was in with drug dealers who have close connections to the big crime bosses.'

'Yeah well, if that's true, it's bloody typical of the idiot!' came Paul's reaction.

'Shh, Paul please, let's just hear the story,' says Mama brusquely. For once, Paula is glad of her mother's authority, as it is the one thing that silences Paul.

But attention now turns to Peter as he chimes in with 'if Emilio's story *is* true, it'll be bloody dangerous for him to dob his bosses in, he'll need police protection.'

Paula nods her agreement as Peter asks, 'who are we talking about here in the boss department?'

'I don't know that yet,' says Paula, 'but a few big names could go down for this'.

Paul can no longer contain his anger. This is the only time he's been in the same room as Paula for many moons; more often than not, he claims to be too busy to get to family dinner.

'Yeah, sister, that's all very well, but what are we up to here? Trying to put the big boys behind bars? I thought that was the police's job. God, Paula, all of this mess is down to you. I mean, you said some outrageous things up there on the platform.'

'So, Paul, even if Emilio wasn't there, you say I deserved to get shot for speaking out? Is that your idea of democracy?'

'OK, Paula. I'm sorry, but I thought you were on-side with the developers in Fremantle.'

'Not this damned lot. They're just a bunch of desperadoes.'

'Huh, well you sound like a fucking commie to me, maybe that's the influence of your new boyfriend, that bloody idiot MP Burnside? Talk about sleeping with the enemy, girl!' tried Paul, knowing he was treading on dangerous ground.

'That's none of your bloody business, you prick. I'm allowed to have some fun in my life. In any case that relationship is over,' returns Paula sharply.

'Well, another one down. At least it wasn't a woman this time, you bloody tramp. You're blushing!'

'Oh, shut up!' Paula is embarrassed by the thought that she might be heading for some 'fun' with Diana, but refrains from saying anything.

'Enough, you two! Maybe you do have too much fun, Paula, when you gonna get married?' cuts in Mama, trying to defuse the tension, but adding more fuel to the fire.

'Mama, come on, how many times do I have to tell you that's not in my thinking!'

Soon afterwards, Paula leaves for her flash apartment in the city's west end. She decides to walk down the hill via the main square, adjacent to the town hall and council chambers where she spends so much time these days. As she rounds the building, Paula is almost knocked over by a man walking fast in the opposite direction.

'Christ, sorry,' he says, turning to pick up some dropped papers. Paula recovers and is about to go on, but they get into one of those dance-this-way/dance-that-way passing routines Paula sees that it is none other than Bill Murkitt.

'Oh, you again,' Paula comes out with, almost involuntarily, the image of his mocking look when she was at the police station coming back to her.

'Well, I hear this morning's meeting went well. Real kind-hearted brother you've got there!' returns Murkitt with a smirk.

'Watch it, Bill. And don't look so bloody smug. This is no laughing matter for me or my family.'

Murkitt looks at her sceptically, about to respond, when a fast-thinking Paula changes tack.

'And I'll tell you what, Bill, you're headed for trouble if you help Doug Dodge with this brothel scam.'

'Scam? That's bullshit and you know it,' tries Murkitt, but the quick colouring of his face gives him away. He struggles for words and then fires back, 'Hang on a minute, you referred Dodge to me in the first place.'

'Only to get him off my back, Murkitt – and I thought you'd discourage him.'

'You bloody politicians are all the same! As soon as there's trouble, you blame someone else.'

'Is that right?' counters Paula. 'Well, in this case, your number's up!'

'We'll see about that. Christ, I just reckon it's a pity your brother didn't have better aim!'

'I'll take that as another threat, Murkitt, don't get too cocky, you're going to have some problems if Emilio comes to trial.'

Paula walks off, leaving a seething Murkitt glaring after her and wondering what she meant.

Chris arrives home from Melbourne to find a message from Diana suggesting they meet soon. Chris leaps at the opportunity. A few hours later, they meet for supper at a local watering hole.

'Chris what will you have?' Diana asks as they scrutinise the menu.

'What's this tapas thing?' inquires Chris with a puzzled look. Despite his supposed worldliness, Chris still has a narrow range of food experience, in situations like this usually sticking to hot chips or a toasted sandwich.

'Spanish-style sort of entrees, I think you'd enjoy them.'

'Well, some of them and a wine would be good.'

Diana signals the waiter, orders, and then says, 'Hey, did you hear that I've quit working for the Premier?'

Chris is thrilled.

'No, good for you, when did that happen?'

'Just the other day. I've had my fill of that bloody conservative environment,' Diana lets on, 'and I reckon I've got enough inside information to cause Right a lot of embarrassment. Elaine's office looks far more interesting. I start there in a couple of days.'

'Well, your decision to quit will certainly make life more difficult for Right,' suggests Chris. 'How did he take it?'

'He's not exactly delighted, wanted me to sign a confidentiality agreement that'd gag me from talking about anything I worked on with him!' Diana answers with a gesture of desperation.

'The bastard!' chimes in Chris.

'Just so, but I told him I was already bound by the silencing clauses of the Public Service Act and that I was really just going back to my former job. That seemed to bite!'

'And so do these chilli prawns,' says Chris, helping himself to the last on the plate, while suggesting they order another serving.

'Well, good luck with it all, mate, any other news?'

'I'm in danger of getting into a serious relationship with Paula Muscatelli,' Diana replies without hesitation.

'You what?' he almost shouts from shock. A few inquisitive heads turn, Diana gestures to the telescreen behind him, and Chris quickly lowers his voice.

'God, Diana, how could you? You warned me off her to start with, and now, this?'

'Don't tell me you two are still an item? You've both told me it's over!'

'No. Christ, no, Paula is an attractive woman, but emotionally, she's not my type.'

'And Sarah is?' Diana teases, not knowing, but suspecting Chris is up to his old games.

'How the hell did you find that out? We only just started?' Chris splutters, then realises he's said far more than he needed to. He puts his head in his hands, suddenly feeling weary; it's after midnight on his biological clock, two hours ahead of WA time.

'God's sake, Chris, I think you've got problems ahead if you're really into Sarah.'

'Oh, give over, any case, it's you we're talking about here. What the hell are you up to with Paula?' Chris replies, looking increasingly forlorn.

'Does this mean you're turning into a lesbian for Christ's sake?'

'No, but you just said that Paula's got a lot going for her. That counts for a lot, and we are re-establishing a lost friendship.'

'Some way to do it. You didn't have to jump into bed with her!' he says emphatically. Chris finds himself feeling protective of Diana in a way he hadn't expected.

'No, we didn't have to go to bed, we just felt like it, and it was fantastic. We've had some truly erotic times together, and we're re-establishing our close friendship.'

'Maybe you should just work out how serious you are going to be with Paula?'

'Well there's no need to hector me, you've hardly got a great record in the relationship department to boast about. And if you take anything further with Sarah, I'd suggest your political career will suffer dramatically,' Diana retorts.

Taking this in and trying not to lose his cool, Chris says, 'look, Diana, fair call, I do understand your attraction to Paula, but crossing the gender divide seems a bit drastic!'

'Oh, come on, Chris, you're sounding really old-fashioned for a so-called progressive thinker!'

'Am I? Hmmm, maybe gender is irrelevant here. I'm just looking out for you, is all.'

'That's sweet of you, and of course, the same applies to me with your latest gambit in Sarah. Gender is certainly not an issue there, but political differences are. I don't think your voters will be impressed with you fraternising with the enemy.'

'Funny, that's sort of what one of my colleagues said to me.'

'What, they know about you and Sarah too?'

'Well no, this was a few weeks back when I was spotted having a few drinks with Sarah. Nothing was going on then, but –'

'Forewarned should have been forearmed and all that, Chris, don't you listen to anyone's advice?'

Diana sighs, signals the waiter, and orders some more tapas. As they munch through the marinated anchovies, Diana tells Chris he should end the thing with Sarah before it's too late.

But as far as Chris is concerned, it's too late already. He tells Diana enough to show her that he's smitten and driven.

'You are in trouble then, Chris. You need to recognise what this could do to your ambitions.'

'Oh, come on, a few moralists aren't going to stop me, why I'm single after all. I know what I'm doing here.'

'You could have fooled me, Chris. Look, she's married, she's shown herself to be a wealthy status-quo, type *and* she's likely to be in Cabinet before the year's out. Well, that's providing you two don't become front-page news. You couldn't be asking for more obstacles in the way of a relationship or successful political trajectory for either of you if you tried!'

Chris suddenly flares up, 'Jesus Diana, why don't you just bloody well mind your own business. I've had enough of your moralising. You're always trying to run my love life. Just look at your own backyard first . . .' He trails off, embarrassed by his outburst.

Diana is taken aback and wanting to avoid a confrontation, gets up, and tells Chris, 'look you grumpy prick, if that's the way you feel, I'm off.'

She leaves him to ponder. Chris stays and orders another bottle of red and drinks it all while trying to think through his situation. He leaves as the bar closes, his judgement even more clouded. However, he realises he overreacted with Diana, even thinks she struck a raw nerve, but he's not ready to admit that to himself yet. For now, he had Sarah where he had always wanted her. Or so he deludes himself.

CHAPTER 23

FAMILY TIES

A month later, there's an unusually large crowd waiting outside the court house on what turns out to be a fine spring morning. A preliminary hearing of the case against Emilio Muscatelli is scheduled. A decision is also expected on whether he should be allowed bail until the full trial.

It has become public knowledge that the accused is the Mayor's brother. This, together with the news that Emilio has undergone psychiatric assessment, had caused a public sensation, heightened when word of Emilio's possible connection to the underworld was leaked by some unscrupulous cop. The media are having a field day, fanning the public's prurience. This morning, the press are here in force, jostling for position as people arrive.

The courtroom fills quickly until there's standing room only, leaving many either queuing for a place or milling around outside watching the telescreen for authorised court highlights and hoping to see more significant arrivals and departures. An excited hubbub fills the air. An escorted police van comes into view; someone shouts, 'That'll be Muscatelli.'

Cameras start whirring, although little can be seen except the vehicle and its motorcycle escorts. The van is heavily barred and has menacing opaque windows, as if to say it holds a really dangerous criminal. People crowd around as it approaches and then sigh as it disappears through a security gate to a back entrance. Reporters jabber into watches and mikes, making gratuitous judgements relating to Emilio, or Paula, or both.

A moment later, Paula almost gets mobbed as she approaches the courthouse with her brother Peter amid excited cries.

'There she is!'

'On ya, Paula!'

'Here's to the Mayor!'

'Why the hell did your brother shoot you, Paula?'

Paula smiles but makes no attempt to engage the crowd. Peter shepherds her through to the court entrance with the spectators kept at bay by security guards. Paula is immaculately manicured and elegantly dressed, wearing a long black number that clings to her like that of a film star arriving at the Oscars. But her face, now fully revealed by her pulled-back hairstyle, betrays the stress she's under. Since news of Emilio has hit the press, Paula has refused comment, beyond saying how glad the family is to have him back and how they hope the charges will be dropped.

The throng of reporters surrounds her, thrusting microphones and asking, 'is it true your brother is mad?' 'We hear you are going to speak on your brother's behalf. Do you think that will dent your popularity?' 'Why shouldn't your brother be jailed? He's a violent criminal, a danger to society.'

Paula looks preoccupied and tense while Peter fends the questions off with an indication that she's anxious to get in to the court, but will answer questions afterwards. Once inside, Paula makes for the seats reserved for family, amid much pointing, stares, and smiles, and even the odd wolf whistle from the packed gallery.

Peter takes the seat next to her, looking a bit disconsolate, and their QC, the eminent Darlene Pocket, well-known for clever court tactics, approaches for a last-minute briefing. She remains confident, even as Paula suggests that court tactics will count for little against a prosecution determined to extract their pound of flesh.

A few minutes later, court officials have trouble quietening the crowd as Emilio is led in, handcuffed and surrounded by guards. Paula winces at the sight, having only visited him the night before, and having been able to enjoy some almost intimate moments, since although the room they were assigned was heavily guarded and observed, there had been no one else with them.

Before that, she had seen Emilio regularly in prison and in the psychiatric ward and had gradually gained his full confidence. He slowly regained his strength and stability, the methadone treatment programme he's been prescribed helping him manage the drug habit. Paula's improving dialogue with Emilio also enabled her to get a lot closer to the truth behind the shooting.

Emilio looks around the courtroom like a startled animal, eyes betraying fright. A tentative smile spread across his face when he sees Paula and Peter on the nearby benches. Paula smiles back in as reassuring a gesture as she can muster.

'All rise in the court!' comes the command from the court registrar. As the wigged Judge comes in sombrely, the public rise in a shambles, many unused to court procedure. A few catcalls can be heard and laughter erupts.

The Judge glares at the public gallery, beckoning to a court official on the bench below him. When the official announces in stern tones that any more interruptions will see offending members of the public ejected, the crowd quietens.

That quiet is kept during most of the opening proceedings, but expressions of surprise or exultation are heard as the charges of 'attempted murder' and 'malicious assault causing grievous bodily harm' are read out. The prosecution indicates they will argue for attempted murder, given a public figure and a very public setting are involved. They foreshadow reports that will show the accused's psychiatric condition was not relevant at the time of the shooting.

Finally, they indicate that Emilio will, in due course, also face charges of drug dealing. For all these reasons, bail is out of the question. Paula's heart sinks, but she comforts herself by recalling her lawyer's confidence. Darlene Pocket rises to her feet to answer to the familiar courtroom question from the Judge, 'and how will the accused plead to the charge of attempted murder?'

'Not guilty, Your Honour. And we plan to establish that on grounds of diminished responsibility.'

Several members of the gallery gasp, and the Judge observes drily, 'diminished responsibility, hmmm . . . and just how would you plan to establish *that* for your client?' he asks, turning to QC Pocket. 'We've already heard from the prosecution that psychiatric reports to be tendered at the trial will show the accused to be sufficiently in command of his faculties for diminished responsibility to be rejected as a plea.'

'If it pleases Your Honour, the burden of evidence will be submitted at the main trial, but today I'd like to indicate that we have psychiatric reports that are before the court and that disagree with those to be tabled by the Crown. We also have a statement from the accused's victim, his sister Paula Muscatelli, that may affect Your Honour's view of the case and the grounds for bail. I seek your permission to call her to the stand.'

To a smattering of applause from the gallery, the Judge gives his approval to this move, after some consultation with his clerks and the prosecution legal team. Paula is guided by a clerk to the witness box, putting a brave face on it, but feeling nervous and strained. After further preliminaries, during which she establishes her bona fides, her QC comes to the nub of the matter.

'Madame Mayor, do you believe your brother shot you in a deliberate and calculated manner as the prosecution claims?'

Paula leans forward, aware of the spotlight now on her, gradually re-discovering her confident public persona. She looks directly at the Judge.

'Yes, I agree that the act was calculated, but in a different way from what the prosecution claim. My brother was pressured by others to shoot me. He learnt to shoot when he was in the army, and he was always a good shot. But at the rally, he never intended the bullet he fired to hit me. He was in a very disturbed state, he had decided to try and warn me, to shoot across me, but his arm was pushed as he took the shot, causing the bullet to hit me.'

Murmurs, oohs and aahs, come from the public gallery, causing the Judge again to order quiet. As she surveys the gallery, Paula notices a small group of men in suits remain inscrutable behind dark glasses.

The prosecution lawyer jumps to his feet, saying in an incredulous tone, Your Honour, objection, there is absolutely no evidence of the accused having been pushed. That is a ridiculous proposition and I submit that not only is this out of order at this preliminary hearing, but also that it's a complete fabrication!'

Before the Judge can respond, Pocket shoots back, 'Your Honour, I'm aware that the prosecution won't accept this version of events, but at the trial, we will be able to establish three important facts: one, Mr. Muscatelli was in an unstable mental condition and under extreme duress when he agreed to shoot his sister; two, the accused hatched a plan at the last minute that involved shooting not at but across his sister; and three, this plan was foiled as he was literally pushed off course. This is the basis of his plea of diminished responsibility.'

The Judge decides to take back charge of proceedings, banging his gavel with force and saying forcefully, 'order in the court! I remind both the prosecution and the defence that this is only a preliminary hearing, not a trial. When and if that trial does proceed, there will be ample time for the defence to substantiate what do sound like rather wild claims. But, Ms. Pocket, we digress. Your witness has not finished her contribution, I believe. Proceed with less of the histrionics if you please.'

Pocket turns back to Paula.

'Ms. Muscatelli, perhaps you can help us clarify this matter by telling us why you think your brother would have changed his mind, having agreed to shoot at you?'

'Emilio was under great duress when he made that agreement. I know this from my long discussions with him over the last few weeks. Ties are strong in our family, and despite what has happened, I still have a good relationship with my brother. He is truly sorry for what happened.' Paula smiles in Emilio's direction and he returns the smile.

'I love my brother and he loves me,' she adds dramatically.

Some laughter is heard from the gallery. Paula frowns, but goes on to explain how she paid many visits to Emilio in recent weeks and found his story amazing but tragically believable. She hopes she has helped him through his life's worst crisis. Paula's plea does not sway the prosecution, however, with their lawyer immediately rising and saying, Your Honour I object to the court being subjected to this sentimental clap-trap about sibling love. With respect, I submit that the court cannot rely on this testimony, as Ms. Muscatelli clearly has an emotional attachment to the accused which must diminish the strength of her submissions. She is hardly in a position to offer objective judgments as to the motives of the accused!'

'Mr. Prosecutor, that is a matter for me to decide. I do not accept your description of the witness' statement, and I would remind you that Ms. Muscatelli has been through a very traumatic shooting, allegedly carried out by the accused, her brother. For her to be now making a plea on his behalf seems a very unusual act to me. However, at the same time, I agree that the court should not be swayed by undue sentimentality from witnesses. I suggest to Ms. Muscatelli that she shy away from the emotive language she has just used.'

'Certainly Your Honour,' Paula agrees, her confidence temporarily dented.

'Please resume, Ms. Pocket, but stick to the point and encourage your client to do the same!'

Pocket is annoyed but coolly refuses to let it show as she turns back to Paula.

'Ms. Muscatelli, you say your brother refused to identify those who pressured him to shoot you. This surely puts doubt on his story.'

'No,' Paula's voice quavers, 'I've talked to Emilio on this matter, and he's afraid of these people, with good reason, for unlike him, they're hardened criminals. He also distrusts the police assigned to the case.'

More murmurs.

'The criminals concerned are what my brother calls dark forces. They deal in hard drugs in huge quantities. They get their dealers hooked. Emilio was a dealer for a large gang. He was taking heroin at the time, they had him under their thumb.'

'But Emilio has given no names to the investigating police, so how can we have any confidence in his accusations?'

Paula brandishes an official-looking document in front of her and says evenly, 'I have here a Statutory Declaration from Emilio containing a description of events related to the duress and naming several people connected to the shooting.'

'Your Honour, we seek to tender this document to the Court,' says Pocket, knowing she is drawing a long bow.

'Objection, Your Honour! We have had no prior notice of this, nothing supplied in the discovered documents. It's out of order,' complains the prosecution.

'Yes, Ms. Pocket, how *do* you justify this request? It is certainly out of order as far as regular court procedure is concerned,' intones the Judge impassively.

The public gallery breaks out in animated conversation before being quietened by the Judge's gavel. Pocket then explains, 'my apologies, Your Honour, but we only came into possession of this document this morning.'

'I don't regard that as sufficient reason to try and breach established court procedure, which as you know requires you to lodge copies with my office and with the prosecution *before* and not during the hearing,' the Judge says in an offended tone.

'Granted, Your Honour, but if you were to see the document, you would I think agree that it does contain matters which are highly relevant to my client's case,' offers Pocket, in as ingratiating a manner as she can muster.

To Paula's great relief, the Judge decides to adjourn the court to allow himself and the prosecution to sight the document and discuss it in private. The courtroom suddenly fills with loud chatter; Pocket goes into a brief huddle with Paula and her brother, trying to assure them that things are not as bad as they could be. Pocket then speeds off to private discussions with the Judge and prosecution on the controversial document, leaving Peter and Paula to nervously mull over proceedings.

After a tense quarter hour, the Judge returns to the courtroom and rules that the declaration is not admissible as evidence, but could affect the trial to follow and so should be tabled at that time.

However, he regards the declaration with some scepticism given the state of mind of the accused and the last-minute appearance of the document. Should the document be used at the trial, he would order the names contained in the declaration be suppressed until the matter has been fully investigated. He went on to explain that such an investigation could conceivably alter the course of events and lead to different charges or other people being charged.

The Judge adjusts his wig, glares at the group of sun-glassed members of the gallery who had started to volubly exchange views on his statement, orders quiet, and then asks the prosecution for its view.

'Whatever the ultimate fate of the Declaration, Your Honour, we have grave doubts as to its authenticity and are very disturbed that it might be used in evidence.'

Pocket QC springs to her feet.

'Objection, Your Honour, this document was drawn up by none other than Paula Muscatelli, herself a QC, and she certainly stands by its authenticity.'

The Judge is about to uphold the objection, when the prosecution lawyer, who rarely makes mistakes, blushes and explains, 'What I meant to say, Your Honour, was that we have grave doubts about the authenticity of the contents of the Statutory Declaration, not the method of its composition. We have little faith in the testimony of the accused, particularly when it surfaces in this unusual way.' He glares in Emilio's direction.

'I will bear those views in mind when I make my decision as to the fate of the declaration,' snaps the Judge. 'Now, instead of your gratuitous judgements, Mr. Prosecutor, please let me hear your arguments against bailing the accused.'

'As you please Your Honour' says the Prosecutor, disturbed by the Judge's changed demeanour. He goes on in an agitated manner, 'The Prosecution is adamant that this man should remain behind bars until the trial since we believe his behaviour has clearly demonstrated that he is capable of extreme violence. He is therefore considered a danger to the community.'

He then reads out a document from a police psychiatrist who agrees with this judgment, albeit in more sober tones.

'Thank you for your views, Mr. King,' says the Judge rather coolly. He then turns to Pocket and asks if he agrees with the Prosecutor.

'Well, no, Your Honour, we submit that the accused was in a temporarily disturbed state at the time of the shooting, from which he is now slowly recovering. His distorted state of mind at the time was partially due to drugs he was taking. He is now extremely remorseful. He has gone onto a treatment programme for drugs and has had a complete rapprochement with his sister, his unintended victim.

'He understands he will have to face trial on this matter in the near future. But he is convinced that given the chance to explain to the court exactly what happened and how he was pressured into agreeing to shoot at Mayor Muscatelli, we will be able to show that was not his intention at the time. The real criminals are those named in his Declaration. We submit that these names should be investigated by police, and that these men should be brought to book.'

'As I've already told you, Ms. Pocket, that is a matter for the police, the DPP, and the scheduled trial. As Judge here, I will not have those matters canvassed further. I am more interested in what you have to say about the danger your client might pose to the community.'

'Well, Your Honour, in the circumstances, we don't think Emilio Muscatelli is a danger to the public. His family is prepared to house him in the period leading up to the trial, and in fact, we submit that it is not the general public who need protection from Emilio, but Emilio who may need protection from those who arranged this crime.'

'Objection, Your Honour, the court has still no evidence before it which links anyone other than the accused to this crime,' the increasingly perturbed Mr. King says forcefully.

'Objection sustained,' rules the Judge and, raising his hand as Pocket is about to protest, says, 'Before we go any further, I want to say that the arguments of the defence have not convinced me that this prisoner should be released. The accused will therefore *not* be granted bail. In my view, he is still in need of further psychiatric treatment and is potentially a danger to the public, however much he protests his innocence and no matter what his eminent sister may think. After all, as we have heard, Mr. Muscatelli admits firing a shot at his sister, intentionally or otherwise. At the least, he seems unstable and should therefore be kept in protective custody until his trial.'

Paula is shocked and breaks down, openly weeping as Emilio is led away, looking extremely downcast. As Paula is comforted by Peter and Darlene Pocket, they notice the group of sunglass-wearing types in the court gallery have melted away.

Outside the court, Peter steers a grief-stricken Paula away from the waiting media pack to their waiting car, which speeds away as reporters try unsuccessfully to thrust their microphones and cameras through the fast-closing doors and windows.

While Emilio's bid for bail has failed, his declaration has more impact. Although the names of the accused have been kept under wraps as ordered by the court, the weeks that follow are uncomfortable for several of those named. The ACC investigators are bemused but intrigued by Emilio's story of duress from a circle that includes Murkitt; he claims that the shooting has been plotted by these characters and delegated to Emilio.

Emilio says he reluctantly agreed, after being warned that otherwise he would be handed over to police in connection with a recent amphetamine haul. As in the past, Emilio was to have been the recipient of the drugs, and while this theoretically meant that he could have made money by dispersing the cache to street users, in practice, his addiction meant he needed it all for himself. To break this nexus, Emilio claims to have hatched his own modification of the shooting plan to foil his sister's would-be assassins.

Under close questioning, Murkitt denies being a party to any of this. He imagines he has got away with it, for he knows the others involved will also be in denial mode. With no corroborating evidence, it's simply Emilio's word against his, and he's confident he can cover up well enough in court to satisfy the jury of his innocence. After all, he had plenty of practice over the years.

CHAPTER 24

EXHIBITIONISM

Everyone who wants to be seen is at the Fremantle Arts Centre for the opening of one of the year's glamour exhibitions. While relishing the content and the big audience, Chris is a little uneasy to be associated with an event that draws so many of the glitterati.

Francine reminds him that this is always the case in the world of the arts, even in relatively egalitarian Fremantle. And photography is no exception. Even if, as in this case, the photographs on display are all born of protest against the urban status quo. In fact, Chris observes, that gives many of the conservatives in attendance a sense of daring, for protest is not something they are not normally comfortable with.

But this is art after all, darling! Indeed, 'hello, darling!' greetings and air kisses hang thick in the air as the guests arrive.

Chris's feelings are soon swept away as his friends and constituents start to roll in. The exhibition 'Urban Protest, Global Disquiet' has been put together by his old friend, Viola, who has spent many years roaming the globe in search of the ultimate photo. Her stark black-and-white photos document people and scenes from community struggles around the world, and in the exhibition are accompanied by equally stark images from other photographers.

In curating the exhibition, Viola has used massive mounting boards, some strung from the ceiling on gently rotating globes, others against backdrops of enlarged images of particularly violent or poignant moments of protest.

The centrepiece of the Perth motifs is very recent, a dramatic enlarged two-shot of Paula, one of her addressing the crowd at the rally, the second of her slumping to the stage after being shot. Paula herself was reluctant to have these photos so prominently displayed and had insisted that one of Emilio being arrested not be shown, particularly given recent events in court and the impending trial. But when the purpose of the exhibition was fully explained to her, she relented on the two-shot.

Paula is in the crowd tonight; she has enjoyed the exhibition. It helps put behind her the trauma and pain of Emilio's failure to gain freedom. Diana is also amongst the crowd, with her new boss Elaine Hipper and a clutch of other MPs.

Premier Right arrives late and barely hides his displeasure at the distinct anti-conservative message in numerous exhibition photos. To Chris's delight, he is accompanied by Sarah, who sashays in wearing an off-the-shoulder dress with a plunging neckline. Press photographers cluster around her, but Chris, despite his growing excitement, keeps a respectable distance. Such is the press interest in Sarah that the Premier is made to look the less important guest.

Chris takes particular pleasure in Sarah's appearance tonight. Despite Diana's warnings, they've had several assignations since Melbourne, though they've been careful to meet at locations well outside their regular stamping grounds and at hours where they've not had to account to staff or spouse for their absence. Hot sex was high on their agenda at the meetings, that both agreed should be brief, not for emotional but for strategic reasons.

The Premier doesn't stay long, pointedly walking out during Viola's opening speech when she draws parallels between her photographic record of resistance to an urban redevelopment project in Barcelona and the montage of the attack on Paula in Fremantle. Viola doesn't miss a beat, but takes her cue from Right, saying in her distinctive Spanish accent, 'And vinally I vant to say I am delighted zat your Premier 'as evidently been offended by these images and 'as left. Zat pays much greater tribute to ze activists and artists involved in zis exhibition than my vords ever can!' to a crescendo of delighted applause and approving laughter.

At this point, Sarah Kingsmill approaches the speakers' microphone and steps in front of an astounded Chris who – as MC for the night – was about to close the formal proceedings. Chris looks on with a mixture of horror and admiration as Sarah starts addressing the crowd, 'you're wrong on several counts, curator.'

'Get off, you weren't down to speak!' from an angry interjector in the crowd.

Chris realises he should intervene and makes to move Sarah away from the microphone. But as he puts his hand on her shoulder, she looks around at him pleadingly and shakes his hand off. Chris feels powerless to stop her as she continues, 'in case, you don't know, I am Sarah Kingsmill, the Member for Wanneroo, and I accompanied the Premier here tonight.' This to loud jeering from some sections of the crowd, calls of 'shut up and let her speak' from others. 'The Premier said he was impressed by the high quality of the work in this exhibition. Furthermore, there was no meaning to his leaving early, other than an urgent but unscheduled meeting.'

Some murmurs of apparent disbelief emerge from the crowd, but Sarah ploughs on, 'however while I have the microphone, *I* would like to say, as a proud member of the government and as one with a great interest in the future of our city, I think our developers and builders do a marvellous job. Whatever this exhibition urges, there is simply no need for activism here, certainly not in Fremantle. The recent rally was stirred up by certain leaders.' Here, she looks accusingly at a shocked Paula. 'Including your Mayor, not to mention your local member,' she says, pointedly turning around to glare at a bemused Chris. 'If the redevelopment authority goes ahead with its plans for central Fremantle, the city will benefit greatly.'

There are many boos and jeers at these pronouncements, and Chris, reddening partly because of her references to him and his cause, but more because of her physical proximity, finally steps back to the microphone and tries to restore order. Sarah deliberately brushes past him as she steps back, disarming Chris further. He splutters, 'hrrmmm! thank you Member for Wanneroo, for that unexpected contribution, all I can say is that many people support our calls for drastic revisions to the FRA plans for this city. As far as I'm concerned, the FRA should get out of Fremantle and go to Wanneroo where they will be more welcome, at least by their MP.'

The crowd applauds, several interjections follow, others press forward wanting to speak, but to avoid a shambles, Chris closes the formal proceedings and invites the special guests to supper. He turns to Viola, who has been nonplussed by Sarah's speech.

'Well, who vood believe 'er?'

'Not sure, Viola, but you old politico, you certainly got things going, even if it wasn't quite in the way you intended!' says Chris, hugging her by way of congratulations.

Paula's not far behind, but as she passes Sarah, still standing nearby, she glares. Paula is determined not to be fazed by Sarah, a woman who might match her in glamour, but who is clearly out of her usual political context tonight.

Paula takes Viola's hand and expresses her appreciation for the special reference she made to her: 'I am believing ze only Maya in Vestern Australia ever to 'ave been shot for 'er trouble!'

'Vy, zank you, Paula, whatever zis Sarah says about ze Premier.' She waves a hand dismissively in Sarah's direction. 'Ze man vill regret his action ven he sees ze news tomorrow. He gets, 'ow you say, 'is justice desert?'

'You mean his just desserts' Chris corrects with a laugh. 'I certainly hope so. And talking of food, it's nearly 10, come on let's find supper.'

'So ve eat at ze right dime! notes Viola approvingly, used to Spanish habits.

As the crowd disperses, the exhibition lights are dimmed. As the guests move towards the supper room, Chris again finds Sarah next to him.

'Sorry about that intervention, Chris, but your friend Viola left me with little choice. All this is bloody revolutionary clap-trap if you ask me!' she says to him forcefully. 'I would have left when Richard did, but then . . .' Her voice trails off, and she leans in, grabs Chris's arm out of view, and whispers in his ear, 'then I thought, you sexy bastard, Chris, and well, my husband's away this weekend.'

They separate from the crowd, and feigning anger, Chris steers Sarah back towards the display, saying loudly for the benefit of bystanders, 'now, Member for Wanneroo, I think you need to revisit this exhibition and maybe your views of it!'

As they step into the dimly lit room, there's no one else around and rather than turn up the lights, Chris whispers, 'you may be a damn conservative, but god, I find you exciting.'

'Likewise, you bloody communist!'

They kiss, hands groping each other eagerly in the semi-darkness. They are in danger of getting to a more compromising stage before Sarah draws away with 'we'll have plenty of time later, darling, let me know when you finish here, but meantime shouldn't we be joining the others?'

Chris reluctantly agrees and they recover to rearrange dishevelled clothing. Looking more like the couple of disagreeing political colleagues they are trying to emulate, they head back to the supper room.

Later in the evening, the supper drawing to an end, Francine returns to the exhibition room to lock up. She is shocked to see the outline of a figure poised with a torch and spray can in front of the two-shot of Paula. He seems too preoccupied with his task to notice her. She freezes as the figure stands back from the photomontage to admire his handiwork.

'Right you bastard!' Francine screams as she flicks on some lights to see the words

COMMUNIST

STOOGES

DESERVE

TO BE SHOT

sprayed in red lettering on the enlargement. To her horror, she sees that the photo has been slashed several times right across the image of Paula's face.

And that the figure responsible for all of this is none other than Councillor Doug Dodge, who gives her a startled look, pockets what looks like a knife and tries to beat a retreat.

But Chris, alerted by Francine's cry, foils Dodge as he heads for the main door. A by-now panicking Dodge throws the spray can in Francine's direction and pushes past Chris, swinging a wild punch.

Fortunately for Chris, Dodge is wide of the mark and his fist lands on the windowsill behind. He swears loudly and rushes off. But others have been attracted by the commotion, and in response to a cry of 'get the fucker', Dodge finds himself tackled and brought down heavily by a fast-approaching supper guest, momentarily re-living his glorious footy days.

He pins Dodge to the ground while the others collect around exclaiming and laughing, and a shocked Francine tells them what was behind the bizarre scene. Chris finds it hard to believe that Dodge would have gone to these lengths to show his dislike for the Mayor, but he knows Dodge has been angry with her since she nailed her colours so dramatically to the mast.

'Christ, Dodge,' says Chris as he takes a closer look at the struggling figure held down by the tackler.

'Hey great tackle mate, you'll be applying for the Dockers next!' quips Chris, who in the 1980s had often watched the very same man play Australian Rules football for local team South Fremantle in the days before WA joined the national league. But that was over three decades ago.

The tackler just grins, signalling victory and moving to hold a swearing and embarrassed Dodge in an arm lock. Francine alerts him to the knife and he quickly moves to disarm the struggling culprit.

'Leave my private property alone, you prick. Get off me, let me go!' pleads Dodge.

'No way, Dodge, not after your behaviour. We'll just wait for the cops to arrive, shall we?' Chris barks back. 'Francine, can you contact them?'

'I have already, Chris, they're on their way.'

Ah come on fellas, it was harmless really, just a bit of fun – an urban protest!' from Dodge, trying desperately to turn the tables.

'Yeah, well, you've done a lot of damage to that brilliant photo of Paula and to our exhibition. We don't see that as fun, and anyway, you've always said that protestors should be dealt with by the full force of the law!' chips in his tackler while tightening the armlock.

Paula comes in to the gallery to examine the scene and is visibly shaken, seeing that she is again the target of violence. She decides it's time she retreated. Diana, anxious to get away, offers to run her home and, as she drops Paula, promises to call in later on her own way home.

At the Arts Centre about fifteen minutes later, none other than Bill Murkitt arrives at the crime scene with a young off-sider. Murkitt has cursed his luck to be the only senior Fremantle officer on duty tonight. Given his 'working relations' with Dodge, Murkitt was disinclined to believe the story Francine relayed, but agreed the police should come and see for themselves. By the time Murkitt arrives, Dodge has been allowed to get up, but is still firmly held.

'What's this, citizen's arrest?' growls Murkitt. 'What right do you have to be treating an elected Councillor of the City of Fremantle like that?'

'I told you what happened,' says Francine. 'Come in here and have a look at the damage.' Murkitt follows Francine and Chris tardily into the exhibition room while his off-sider takes charge of Dodge.

'Dodge did *this?*' Murkitt asks, trying to stop himself from smiling, only too glad to see Paula under further attack. After some procrastination, Murkitt reluctantly agrees to arrest Dodge. Dodge fumes and splutters, but his anger diminishes as it comes home to him that he has literally been caught red-handed.

He still holds out a vague hope that Murkitt will be able to smooth the rocky legal path ahead, perhaps shield him from some of the consequences of his ill-timed attack. But any such thoughts are put to the back of his mind when Murkitt whispers with some venom into his ear, as he pushes him towards the police car:

'You silly prick, this was never a good idea. You realise this could totally stuff up our brothel deal?'

'Oh, fuck off, Murkitt,' returns Dodge accusingly, 'that deal's already stuffed, and that's down to you.'

Murkitt guesses that Dodge is referring to hitches struck in getting police approvals. He remains quiet but twists Dodge's arm further to stop him giving anything away to others in earshot. Further exchange is cut short as a news reporter approaches and tries to interview Dodge. Murkitt orders her away. Dodge reflects gloomily on his situation as he is unceremoniously pushed into the back seat of the police car.

At the station, Dodge calls a lawyer and in later interview claims that he had not intended to do any damage, a claim not easily squared with the spray can and knife he had been carrying. He then claims he had intended to graffiti outside and leave it at that. But once he found he could get inside, he had been carried away by a sudden impulse that he now profoundly regrets.

His lawyer grimaces at the unlikely story and tells Dodge afterwards that he expects a difficult time ahead in the courts. Not to mention how it might affect his political career. After Murkitt contacts a mutual supporter to arrange bail, Dodge heads for home completely humiliated for the first time in his adult life.

When Chris meets Sarah a few hours later at a city hotel under cover of darkness, they are hungry for each other. Chris finds he is excited more than usual by the frisson of their earlier encounter.

They talk of this as they lie back in the warm afterglow of their lovemaking. Chris tells Sarah he feels annoyed that he didn't wrestle the microphone from her, but pleased that he stated his case clearly after she spoke.

For her part, Sarah admits to Chris she was unexpectedly jangled by the hostility of the crowd. She half-jokingly suggests – in response to his earlier suggestion that the FRA look to Wanneroo rather than Fremantle – that Chris come and address a public meeting she has organised at Wanneroo. This is where ambitious development plans – that include high-rise apartments around the shores of Lake Joondalup and along the coast – will be under discussion.

While Sarah has a few reservations about the plans and is under pressure from electors who like the place the way it is, she isn't sure how to handle the matter, given her government's likely support of the development plans and her own clear political ambitions.

Chris might be just the man for the job. In his eroticised state, he tells her he might well take up the suggestion. They fall into a deep sleep after this exchange, and Chris leaves reluctantly when the morning sky starts to show signs of light. Rather than risk being spotted on the first train out of the city, Chris opts for a taxi to ferry him home. Once there, he abandons the idea of more sleep and starts the day with his usual coffee on the strip.

CHAPTER 25

UNUSUAL BUSINESS

A few hours later, Chris and Paula are examining plans on Paula's office desk, a respectable distance kept between them. Despite last night's meeting with Sarah and the blossoming of his new affair, Chris finds this proximity to his previous lover difficult to handle. As an unwilling party to the end of the brief affair with Paula, his erotic memories linger and are fired up when he encounters her. This morning, he finds Paula's magnetism is increased by her classic but fashionable Zampatti-designed outfit.

Paula herself is in skittish mood, resulting from the press coverage of last night's vandalism, featuring large photos of the damage to her photo-montage. She realises that this will not only be good for her own political image and increase the popularity of the exhibition, but it might also help her in her quest to have Emilio exonerated. Then there was the added satisfaction of hearing reports of Dodge's arrest on the morning news bulletins.

Chris notes her upbeat mood, moves around behind her, and is about to put his arm around her, but at the last second, thinks better of it. She's oblivious of his move and says, 'you know, these revised FRA plans don't look promising to me: I told Chewis recently that there was no way I would support a development of more than five stories.'

'Great, you said you were going to do that when we were at that fabulous little hotel on the river. Remember that night?' Chris asks in an uncalled for reference to their last and very intimate time together.

'Just goes to show I'm a woman of my word!' says Paula lightly, ignoring Chris's other references, and adding, 'Chewis made it obvious he doesn't need my support. Maybe I should've voted for your motion calling for a five-storey limit at the last meeting after all? Then the pro-development maniacs might have got the message.'

Their differing perspectives had moved closer together during the affair, as if symbolic of their short-lived physical fusion. And as the public meeting had so dramatically illustrated, Paula was finding new voice in defence of Fremantle.

'Mmm, now you tell me,' Chris jokes, 'I mean you were probably right that it wouldn't have got through, Paula. But shit, these towers of fifty to seventy-five stories on the plan are almost as bad as the one-hundred-storey version.'

'This looks like the old ambit claim trick to me: ask for one hundred, then seventy-five stories and you might well get forty or fifty, which was what they wanted in the first place!' suggests Paula. 'It certainly doesn't conform to my motion's requirement for substantial scaling down.'

'Yeah, I agree, but I'm not sure that other members of the board will see it that way. Whatever, the community certainly won't like this version of La De-bloody-fense any more than the last!' says Chris with feeling, again edging closer to Paula

'True,' replies Paula, now aware of Chris's advances and trying to keep her distance, 'but I don't think the FRA or the government are worried about public opinion right now. Chewis tells me he's confident of getting support for the revised plans, which means someone has been leaning on the government reps who voted with us last time around.'

Outside the office, an approaching Francine, also invited to the meeting, is annoyed to see Paula and Chris in close proximity through the open office door and coughs and knocks loudly.' Paula spins around, realising the situation could have looked compromising.

'Oh hi,' she offers, blushing slightly. 'We're just looking at these awful plans, and I don't think they're much better than the first ones.'

Francine takes the plans in while giving Chris a quick scowl, then says to them both, 'agreed, but as expected, I guess.'

She keeps her cool. Francine has kept a watching brief on the redevelopment plans and senses the FRA would not give up lightly, picking up her cue from the failure of the opposition to support debate on Chris's motion calling for abandonment of the whole project. The problem for opposition leader Hipper is that while she didn't support the FRA high-rise scheme, there's a small but powerful faction amongst her own MPs, allied to Cloke, who are in favour. Until her Party has a united stand, Elaine's not prepared to let the matter go further.

'Well, where to from here?' asks Paula as they sit in the comfortable chairs grouped around a coffee table next to the desk.

'A coffee would help the decision,' suggests Francine. Chris agrees enthusiastically as he missed out on his regular caffeine dose this morning.

Paula calls in her personal assistant, who busied himself in the adjoining room while the gang of three exchange views on the current unexpectedly hot and humid late spring weather. Then Paula's desk phone rang and as she took the call, Chris and Francine overhear her saying, 'Diana, darling, hello!'

When she comes back to the circle a few minutes later, Chris smiles broadly at her. Paula returns the smile but picking up the mood, quickly changes the subject as her assistant brings in three steaming cups of coffee, cappuccino for Francine, espresso for Chris, and a latte for the Mayor.

'Now, according to the motion we got through at the FRA, Chris, these plans have to go out for public consultation, so that gives us a bit of breathing space. Time to build up opposition,' Paula suggests.

'Sure, but I don't know about another public rally, there's got to be a safer way of mobilising the public!'

'Indeed.' Paula rubs the scar on her shapely upper arm. 'At least the shooting reunited me with my missing brother,' she quips. 'Seriously, I think we could organise something even bigger this time. After all, they say that lightning never strikes in the same place twice.'

'Paula, that's sounds unnecessarily like tempting fate to me,' offers Francine, 'but I was thinking on the way over this morning that we've got David Suzuki coming to town soon. He's the star turn at that big conference on rising sea levels, which threaten to engulf Fremantle itself before too long.'

'That's a great idea, Francine,' returns Paula. Chris nods his agreement.

The Mayor goes on, 'I've been talking to the federal government on sea level rises just this week as it happens. They still don't want to know about it. But do go on, Francine.'

'Over to you, Chris. After all, weren't you talking to Suzuki recently?'

'That's right, and when I told him of the redevelopment plans, he was very sceptical about the whole deal. He was appalled to hear about you getting shot, by the way, Paula.'

Paula smiles appreciatively.

'How about an old-fashioned protest meeting organised around him speaking at the Freo Town Hall?' she suggests. 'There we could keep a closer eye on things, and since we're bound to draw a huge overflow crowd, we could have the speeches televised on to the big screens in the Square outside. Compete with the new Telescreens that are so overpowering there.'

'Sounds good to me,' agrees Chris. 'And we could have some good hot music in the Square leading up to the meeting to keep the crowd interested.'

'TVTV would love to do the telecast I bet,' Francine suggests.

Meanwhile, Chewis is summoned to see the Premier. Before the meeting, Right had told his staff that he was embarrassed over Chewis's lack of protocol over the high-rise plan's leaking. He would carpet Chewis and chastise him over his failure to consult the board.

But when Chewis walks into the meeting with Right, there's a wicked grin on his face. Right returns his smile once the office door is closed and then loudly pretends to remonstrate.

'You stupid bastard, why didn't you let me know what was going on? People need to be kept in the loop.'

'Indeed they do, Premier, please accept my humble apologies,' Chewis smirks. That smirk was the only clue to the deal they had done.

Chewis is happy with the revised plans, even though he knows there will still be plenty of opposition in and around Fremantle.

A few days later, the board meets again. Chewis unexpectedly opens the meeting with a fulsome apology for his failure to refer the initial high-rise plans to the board. He notes that the revised plans have been circulated to members a few days previously so they had time to consider them before the meeting. He asks for their sympathetic consideration, suggesting the best of both worlds.

'Members will see that these plans offer high-rise apartments of modest scale, with extensive views and a handsome return. The lower height of these towers will blend more easily with the historic core of Fremantle and yet provide a bold statement of the city's new direction as a place to live and work.' Several members nod their agreement with Chewis who, looking gratified, continues, 'and I know some of you are worried about my future role in all of this. After all, I have undertaken several private developments in recent years. Members, I will not re-contest the position of Chair when my initial one-year term expires in a few months.'

All faces turn to him at this point and there are a few polite murmurs of 'oh no' and 'what a pity, Mr. Chairman' from around the table. A brief round of regrets and thanks to Chewis follows from the more obsequious members. Difficult as this is for Paula to listen to, she's more concerned about the revised plans.

She looks over at Chris, who mouths, 'I told you so.' Paula frowns, knowing that her charm and appeal are likely to be less effective today. After expressing her own less than enthusiastic thanks to the Chair, she says, 'I think that support for the revised plans reflects an unwarranted interpretation of my motion calling for a substantially scaled down development. A reduction from one hundred to seventy-five stories is not a substantial scaling down, and fifty stories is far from modest, still far too high for Fremantle.'

'It's certainly modest in comparison to the previous plan,' chimes in Ken Short. 'This compromise the chamber will support.'

'That's hardly the point, Mr. Short.' Paula glares hard at him.

'Members, please let's have orderly debate,' from Chewis, now smiling.

'I move that the height limit on the towers be five stories,' tries Chris.

Paula seconds the motion, but the only other member to support the motion is, to Chris and Paula's amazement, Murkitt.

The rest of the board put their votes enthusiastically behind the revised plans. Not only that, but they also agree with a rider, to the effect that whatever the public consultation period produced, the board recommend the current plan to government.

Paula is surprisingly unruffled at the outcome, and as Chris catches up with her after the meeting, he asks her why.

'Just wait and see, all will be revealed,' comes the cryptic reply

'Oh, come on, Paula, don't be so bloody mysterious,' replies Chris indignantly.

But he quickly softens his attitude when she gently touches his arm. Paula knows Chris is still captive to her charms and figures she can use this to her own advantage.

'Sorry, but I can't tell you just yet. I promise the outcome will be in our favour. This time you're just going to have to be patient.'

As they leave the meeting, Paula tells the hovering journalists that she believes the board has made a gross error, public reaction will not be favourable, and that the redevelopment can still be stopped. She doesn't say how this will be achieved, beyond telling the press about the planned appearance of Suzuki, and quoting the old saying that there are many ways to skin the proverbial cat.

CHAPTER 26

LOCAL CONNECTIONS

As he sits in his parliamentary office, Chris is agitated. He's already consumed four scones with jam and cream, followed by an equal number of sausage rolls with tomato sauce, washed down with several cups of tea. Health food it isn't, but Chris has gotten to like the traditional morning tea served to MPs and their visitors. Having skipped breakfast due to another morning hangover, he needed something to soothe his nerves and couldn't resist ordering a whole tray for himself.

His tension rises further as he ponders today's committee hearings. He's particularly apprehensive about Wayne Cloke and Union Boss Vince Roberts, finally pinned down for an appearance. Only the threat of a formal summons has forced their hand. But Cloke is a wily operator, and Chris is nervous about tackling the ex-Premier. Worse, the detailed information on Cloke and Roberts, as promised by Stanecich in Melbourne, has still not arrived, despite repeated assurances. This is threatening to undermine his plans altogether.

Chris has been briefed by Francine, but he still feels distinctly underprepared as he collects his papers. Francine goes to the mailroom in search of the promised file, only to be told there was no package from Melbourne, even in the second delivery of the morning. This puzzles her, as Stanecich confirmed yesterday that the file was belatedly dispatched by courier from Melbourne. They do have an electronic copy of the draft, but the final hasn't come through, and in any case, originals are needed if they are to be tabled as evidence. Francine tries to contact Stanecich, but he can't be reached.

Meanwhile, as he makes his way to the committee room, Chris's head aches and he feels distinctly queasy. As he enters the room with a few minutes to spare, he notices an unusually large number of spectators in attendance.

The morning goes agonisingly slowly, with witnesses and routine questions bogging down proceedings into what Chris regards as a boring spectacle, but the public seats remain at capacity in anticipation of Cloke. There's still no sign of either Francine or the Melbourne file. All Chris has is a cryptic message from her, saying she's working on it.

He groans and tries to think through the possibility of cancelling Cloke's scheduled appearance. But even in his foggily minded state, he realises he couldn't easily explain away such a course since he needs to keep knowledge of the file secret. So in the end, well after midday, he summons Cloke and mentally resigns himself to the spectre of his old adversary getting the upper hand.

The tension in the room is palpable. People crane their necks or stand to get a better view, and the press seats suddenly fill as Cloke, tall and solid, strides confidently to the witness seat. Elaine Hipper and Diana also come in with a clutch of other politicians and staffers, all keen to see Cloke back in official action. Diana notices Chris is looking drawn, but isn't aware of the drama going on behind the scenes. On the other hand, Sarah Kingsmill, who has also been looking at Chris solicitously, has an idea of what's likely to happen, following their pillow talk during their tryst a few days previously. But like others in the room, Sarah's attention is now clearly focussed on Cloke.

Cloke smiles superciliously as he takes the oath, swearing to tell the truth, the whole truth and nothing but. During delivery of his submission, Cloke impresses the assembled throng with his coherence and confident manner. Chris's political wit is further dimmed by this adept performance, and his headache is developing into a debilitating migraine. Circles swirl before his eyes while his digestive system continues to battle with the heavy morning tea.

The clock on the wall ticks its way towards 1:00 p.m., the end of the time allocated to Cloke. A hush falls as attention now switches to Chris, who as Chair has the right to open the questions. Chris is still shuffling through his papers, now desperate about the file and trying to delay the inevitable. He rubs his head in an effort to salve the throbs pulsing though his cranium, but to no effect.

'Fuck,' he says under his breath, 'this could be curtains for my political career.'

'So much for the Member for Fremantle.'

'He looks washed up already,' comes a comment from a Cloke sympathiser in the audience.

Mild laughter breaks out as Chris tries to cover his embarrassment by calling for order. But that feeling is short-lived as Francine suddenly appears in the room with a file clutched under her arm. Chris glares in her direction, annoyed that she hasn't kept him fully posted, but summons her in an agitated manner. She hands him the file while bending down to whisper excitedly in his ear, 'calm down Chris, look you'll never believe it, they found this in the wrong pigeon-hole after the final morning delivery. Some idiot at work there! Anyway, this is like manna from heaven and I've written out the questions for you on the first page.'

'OK, thanks, that's fantastic!' Chris manages, his anger dissipating as he looks anxiously at the clock and sees that there are still a few minutes left. He opens the file, skims the contents and finally asks in an unusually subdued voice, 'Mr. Cloke, can you please tell the committee whether during your time as Premier you were on a retainer from the building industry? If so, this would mean that you were not only working for the building industry and the unions, but also the government, and all at the same time.'

Murmurs and exclamations break out from the audience as Cloke darkens and retorts sharply, 'I deny that accusation absolutely. There is no substance in the Chairman's allegations. I invite him to repeat it outside, and he will need to be wary of the legal ramifications.'

'Ah, the old threaten-to-sue trick,' responds Chris, at last warming to his task, his headache still pressing, but his eyes becoming clearer. 'Well, Mr. Cloke,' he goes on more confidently, 'I'd like to draw your attention to this file, submitted to me as Chair from a source who is in a position to know. This information has been corroborated, and I am confident it proves conclusively that you were in receipt of a retainer of no less than $1 million per annum. This amount paid to you by the major construction companies over three years of your government. I'm going to hand you this summary of the information which will be distributed to the press later.'

The document is handed to Cloke by an orderly, and as he takes it in, animated conversation breaks out in the room. Chris waits a few moments, motions for silence, and asks, 'just how do you explain *that*, Mr. Cloke?'

Cloke rises in anger, waving the offending document above his head as he shouts, 'This is pure fabrication. You're out to frame me and are using information from people with an axe to grind.'

'You deny the receipt of any such commissions?'

'Totally and absolutely!'

'Well, you may regret that in due course. Session adjourned!' from Chris, mightily relieved, but still feeling seedy.

He knows he's landed a heavy blow. Chaos breaks out as Cloke attempts to leave, only to be surrounded by reporters thrusting microphones into his face and throwing questions. He has by now regained control of his anger and squeezes out smiling at the growing crowd of reporters around him.

'These accusations are completely false and malicious. They've been brought to the committee by an MP whose previous charges against me have yet to be tested in a democratic court as opposed to this star chamber.'

Chris is taken aback by the strength of the counter-attack, hoping that the political damage has already been done and instead of responding, seeks to restore some semblance of order. He grabs his microphone and reminds reporters that they cannot demand answers of MPs in the committee rooms or indeed anywhere in Parliament house. Cloke looks almost grateful for this intervention as Vince Roberts and a few other supporters gather around and escort him away.

Most of the press follow the small group outside but soon discover that Cloke has a getaway car at the ready. The press are left to snap and film the car speeding away into the blue yonder.

The reporters return to the committee room, where Chris is now the centre of attention. Chris has been swapping notes with some of his committee, who, depending on their political affiliations, express delight, surprise and outrage at Chris's unannounced attack on Cloke.

Sarah Kingsmill smiles broadly and loudly congratulates him on bringing another Labor icon to justice. Chris winces, but she hugs him and slips a note into his hand, suggesting he read it later. Chris pockets the note, trying not to give his feelings away.

His attention is then taken by Mike Chesterfield, an MP still loyal to Cloke who secured a place on the committee by threatening leader Elaine Hipper with more trouble than she needed. Wily and long-serving, he has already proved a thorn in the side of committee deliberations on several occasions, especially when there's any suggestion of Cloke being under the hammer. His small but influential faction is known as the Clokeites. Chesterfield has a habit of telling the committee that the former Premier is a misunderstood genius.

In response to his use of the same words today, Chris simply replies, 'Mike, have you not heard that geniuses often turn out to be flawed?'

Chesterfield glares and walks off, muttering darkly something about bloody moralistic independents always out to damage the ALP. Chris lets this one go and announces that he'll make a statement before the afternoon's proceedings get under way. This helps to clear the room. He then seeks out Francine and says, *sotto voce*, 'brilliant work Francine, you saved the day! Thanks for that well-timed delivery. I'm sorry I was a bit grumpy, but I thought you'd never make it and my head and stomach were giving me merry hell.'

Seeing several others approaching, Francine figures now's not the time to go over the morning's events. She shrugs, saying in a business-like manner, 'how about I catch you soon for a de-briefing?'

'Good, I'll meet you on the front steps in about fifteen minutes.'

Francine heads out for some much needed fresh air. Chris is keen to get clear too, but he wants to talk to others in the room. At that moment, someone gives him a bear-hug from behind and says, 'another big catch today, I see. On ya, Chris!'

Recognising Diana's voice and touch, Chris turns and grabs her hands.

'Diana,' he says somewhat shame-facedly, but smiling nonetheless.

'Hell, Chris, you didn't look too well today, but I had no idea you were waiting on that file. Why didn't you tell me?' she asks, looking a trifle hurt.

'I would've done, but circumstances *have* been against us lately. Look,' he says, lowering his voice, 'I still feel bad about my tantrum at supper.'

Before he can go on, Diana cuts him off, 'forget that, mate.' Diana is buoyed by the political drama of the morning. 'Although you did behave like a prick! Any case, I know you ignored my advice. I can see Sarah is on *very* friendly terms with you. Let her get any closer in public and all the world will know as well.'

Chris looks worried and is about to suggest a tête-à-tête, but their exchange is cut short as Elaine Hipper approaches. He turns his attention to her, recalling his exchange with Chesterfield.

'Elaine, I hope this morning doesn't prove an embarrassment for you up here.'

'That's never stopped you before, Chris,' she retorts reprovingly, but with a solicitous smile. She leans closer to him to be out of earshot of the people still milling around.

'Cloke's had that coming for years! Good on you, I'd love to know more about the information you used.'

Chris raises a quizzical eyebrow at this, for although he knows of Hipper's ongoing battle with the Clokeites in the Party, and her desire to out dishonesty in politics, he hadn't expected a direct approach so soon. This can only be to his advantage, so he says quietly, as Diana looks on approvingly, 'great, I'd love to discuss it with you.'

'Diana'll arrange a time with you to suit us all,' Hipper says conspiratorially.

Diana and Elaine make their exit, and Chris soon follows. As he comes out of the building, he spots Francine just below the front steps, deep in conversation with his electorate officer Mike Dean, who's here to help Chris deal with the press. An hour later, Chris's headache has finally cleared and his stomach settled by an unaccustomed healthy lunch of lightly braised vegetables, rice, and ginger tea that Francine insisted on ordering for him at a nearby eatery.

They head back to Parliament house, where Chris is able to deal confidently with the large band of press hounds that have gathered. After reading Mike's pithy statement, he takes a few questions.

'Mr. Burnside, what do you think the information you tabled will lead to?' the first reporter asks from among the clamour.

'I'm hopeful,' says Chris with a smile, 'that the statutory declarations included will lead to investigations by the ACC, we've sent them certified copies of the originals, and personally, I reckon that criminal charges against Cloke should result.'

'Hang on,' a young journalist asks aggressively, 'as ex-Premier Cloke pointed out this morning, no charges have followed on the casino allegations against him. Why should they this time, surely you're being reckless with *these* charges?'

'I don't think so. I've already said in Parliament that the government is dragging its feet on the casino scandal. That's a cause for concern, and I again call on the government to live up to its promises and have Cloke and the other culprits charged immediately.'

'Why haven't you named your sources, and how can the declarations be believed by the public otherwise?' a sceptical old-timer asks.

'Well, good question,' says Chris warily, 'I'm confident that the information in the declarations is true. And Jack as an experienced journalist you'll be aware of the importance of protecting sources. So in the interests of the people who supplied this information, I won't name them. But with their agreement, I have passed on their names to the ACC, so their statements can be verified.'

The afternoon hearings turn out to be far shorter than anticipated due to the failure of the other key witness, union boss Vince Roberts, to show. He had last been seen in the company of Cloke, speeding away to some safe haven.

Chris decides against tabling the damaging sheaf of information he has on Roberts. This links Roberts to organised crime figures in Melbourne. Chris surmises that fear of such revelations has kept Roberts away, and he figures that the right time will soon come. For the moment, Roberts's absence speaks for itself.

CHAPTER 27

MOUNTEBANKS AND ILLYWHACKERS

As they share a bottle of Frankland River Chardonnay in the cool of the early evening, Chris is relishing his time with Elaine Hipper. It's a Thursday, Parliament over for the week, and they relax on wicker in the private outdoor courtyard that adjoins the leader's rooms. Most of Elaine's staff have left, although Diana is still working away, hoping to join them later.

Chris and Elaine are having an exchange over diseases infecting the Western Australian body politic, in particular Chris's recent near-nemesis, Wayne Cloke.

'D'you know, Elaine, I reckon Cloke qualifies as a mountebank.'

'I've heard Cloke called many things in my time, but never that.' Elaine's memory is searching for the meaning of the word.

'Isn't a mountebank a quack who used to sell wares at country fair and the like, you know, the sort who spring up all over the place in Peter Carey's *Illywhacker*. I seem to remember Carey used the word as his title for that very reason. Doesn't illywhacker mean quack too?'

'I think you're right. Wow, I hadn't thought of illywhacker! Great book wasn't it, by the way?'

'Loved it.' Elaine nods in agreement as she ducks into her adjacent office. She's back in a flash, tablet in hand.

'Right you wordsmith, mountebank is one thing, but what about illywhacker?' She finds the word on her tablet and expounds, 'well, according to this source, illywhacker means a confidence man or trickster. And mountebank can mean either a quack or a charlatan, so there you go!'

'Maybe it's time we revived these words just for Cloke?' reflects Chris, laughing. 'And when you think about it, Cloke qualifies under all headings, mountebank, illywhacker, charlatan, confidence trickster, quack, even a good old snake oil salesman.'

Elaine recharges their glasses from a second bottle. Chris lights a cigarette – parliamentarian breaking own rules again – draws heavily and coughs, attempting to exhale over his shoulder so as not to blow smoke over Elaine. He drifts off into a reverie.

Since she took over the reins from Cloke, Elaine explains, she's been dogged by his supporters in the Parliamentary Party, particularly Mike Chesterfield. Some lost their seats at the election, but many remain and operate as a faction that makes things difficult whenever they get the opportunity.

The harder she presses matters relating to Cloke, like the casino scam, the more trouble the faction causes. Elaine senses Chris's attention is not all there. So she stops and waves the bottle in front of him.

'Another glass? Will that bring you back to the present?'

'Oh, er, sorry, Elaine, Chris replies, blushing. 'Mmm, thanks, another glass is definitely called for!' Covering slightly, he says, 'I was just thinking that none of this spells a very bright picture for you.'

'You could be right there, but the more immediate question is what the hell can be done about the FRA scheme given these troublemakers in my ranks? I think you should pursue your motion calling for abandonment of the FRA scheme. I can't guarantee you Labor's support at this stage, but the more I think of it, the more I reckon that debate is crucial to my plans to get back into government. And I think it will put pressure on the rats in the ranks.'

'That sounds promising, but of course, I need not just your support, but also that of the independents to get the motion through,' muses Chris.

'That's something *you'll* have to work on. Your call, but surely it's better to risk defeat on the motion than not have it debated at all?'

'Oh, and just what motion is that?' inquires Diana as she walks in to join Chris and Elaine, holding up another bottle of wine alluringly.

'Good timing, Diana, we've just finished the last one!' says Elaine, slurring slightly.

Elaine hands Diana her fancy new electronic bottle opener, a gift from the caucus on her election, and then brings Diana up-to-date on the motion they're discussing.

Before the conversation continues, Diana reminds her boss to call her allocated government car so she can get home without being caught by the latest drink-driving blitz. Even being caught in your own driverless car is considered a drink-driving offence.

Diana offers to accompany Chris on the train – she was headed for Fremantle in any event – knowing this would not just avoid the cops but give her the chance for a personal chat.

A few hours later, as the train buzzes down the line to Fremantle, they're joined by a growing crowd of revellers. The atmosphere is merry, Chris is feeling mellow and enjoying his chat with Diana, although he feels miffed when he learns she's meeting up with Paula later in the night.

At their destination, Chris suggests a coffee and they end up at Chris's favourite haunt on the strip. Diana's attention is momentarily distracted as a message comes in on her watch. She looks perplexed as she takes its content in.

'Damn,' she says, turning to Chris, 'Paula has a family emergency and can't meet up till tomorrow morning. Now I'm stuck here with nowhere to go.'

'Come on, Diana, you can crash at my place, even sleep in my bed.'

Diana casts a sceptical look in Chris's direction as if to say, 'Chris, not that all over again.' Chris realises his error.

'I mean I'll take the couch.'

'Just as well you got that right! Thanks.'

Once they reach Chris's pad, it's not long before Diana is installed in Chris's bedroom, while he promptly falls into a booze-induced sleep on the couch. His slumber doesn't last for long.

Despite or perhaps because of Chris's somnolence, Diana finds it difficult to get to sleep, so she turns to her latest crime thriller. She always carries some fiction with her to fill the few idle moments she encounters between appointments or when on the train. She finds such fare a welcome antidote to the endless grind of the political round.

Diana eventually falls asleep, but is woken before five by the searing early summer sunlight filtering though the rickety contraptions that pass for window blinds. She isn't due at Paula's until seven, but decides to shower and get going. On her way out, she finds Chris still sprawled on the couch, snoring unevenly. She creeps out, leaving a note of thanks addressed to the 'untidy member for Fremantle'.

It's still only five thirty, but it's already warm and Diana decides on a walk. Walks are a habit of which she's fond, and this morning she has the chance to reacquaint herself with Fremantle. She takes in the proposed site for the high-rise station development and the dominant FRA headquarters nearby and reflects on the shenanigans of that body.

This very subject dominated the conversation that she had with Chris and Elaine the previous night over that third bottle. It had been sufficient to remind her of the strong possibility of those shenanigans soon taking an unexpected turn.

This was something she was planning to discuss further with Paula over breakfast. But by the time she reached Paula's unit, an hour later, other needs took over. To Diana's pleasure, Paula appeared at the door dressed in a very sexy apron and high heels, with no other clothing in evidence.

'Diana. How wonderful. Do come in, darling.'

'Why, you look stunning!'

Paula closes the door behind them, and they embrace and kiss hungrily. Diana and Paula spend more than a few minutes enjoying the finery of the silk Paula is wearing as their bodies entwine on the linen of Paula's bed.

'Cool in more ways than one, Paula!' whispers Diana.

Paula is not just cool, but positively sparkling the following weekend when she speaks at the Fremantle Town Hall meeting. With David Suzuki as the star turn, Paula's given the job of lead-in Speaker . A massive crowd of over ten thousand is in attendance and those unable to squeeze into the hall watch proceedings on huge screens set up in Kings Square outside. This is all part of TVTV's direct broadcast of the event, using their outside broadcast van purchased with their newfound funds.

Lively local band music helps create a carnival atmosphere leading up to the meeting. A bank of anti–high-rise banners drape the square and the hall. As Paula approaches the dais to speak, she gets a rousing reception that temporarily brings proceedings to a halt. She starts unexpectedly by playing a video featuring her still-imprisoned brother Emilio.

She persuaded prison authorities to allow the video to be made – with the assistance of TVTV – on her most recent visit to see him. The video shows Emilio apologising for Paula's shooting, and going on to express his support for Paula's campaign. It concludes with Emilio embracing Paula, as if to underline his innocence and the total contrast to the circumstances of the first rally. The film has the crowd cheering wildly, except for one dissident who shouted out, 'so the Mayor is fraternising with criminals now!'

He's soon answered by supportive interjections and Paula smiles, waits for the hubbub to die down and goes on to make a brief and impassioned speech against the FRA project, finishing with the declaration, 'community opposition to this scheme is so deep that if the government continues to ignore it, it'll be dumped at the next election.'

Cheers nearly drown out her next words, which advise a watch on the results of the upcoming parliamentary motion sponsored by Chris, designed to stop the FRA scheme. She goes on to tell them that while

Chris isn't speaking today, he'll lead this debate in Parliament next week. In response to Paula's request, Chris identifies himself in the crowd, and to their delight, she blows him a kiss for good measure.

Suzuki follows with an inspirational address, during which he describes the FRA scheme as akin to a dinosaur and headed for the same fate and likely to cause an ecological disaster in the city, especially when combined with rising sea levels.

He professes that he can't understand why the government supports reckless over-the-top development in an age when sustainable buildings are desperately needed. A standing ovation follows and the meeting is wound up after an overwhelming vote against the scheme. Thousands more express their support electronically on a specially set-up computer hotline, with TVTV streaming the progressive results live on the internet.

The meeting and follow-up prove a major embarrassment to the Premier and his friends at the FRA, the more so given recent articles in the press on the murky links between the building industry and government, articles sparked off by Chris's committee coup against Cloke. Collectively, these events have undermined the government propaganda supporting the scheme, which it is belatedly putting out through TV, telescreen, and press advertisements.

CHAPTER 28

A BALANCING ACT

A few days later, as the last light is fading from a warm early summer sky, Chris and his team are working late in his parliamentary office. It's the eve of the day Chris will answer Elaine Hipper's challenge and again attempt to have the FRA matter debated. Diana contacted him earlier to say that Elaine was confident of securing caucus support for the motion at their regular meeting tomorrow, although she was still worried about what the Cloke faction would do in this event.

Chris has worries of his own after a further unpromising conversation with independent MP Jill Woodall. Jill says she's broadly sympathetic to the case against the redevelopment but she and the other independents are all conservative at heart and don't want to see the government defeated over a development scheme which might be unpopular with the public, but widely supported in the commercial and development world.

Francine bursts into his room, an excited look on her face.

'Chris, you'll never believe what has just been delivered,' she exclaims, waving a small disk in the air.

'Well, it'd better be good because those bloody independents are still equivocating,' Chris says, gesturing to the intercom on his desk. 'Jill Woodall says they won't necessarily be voting together and she still can't decide whether to support us.'

'Yes, well what's new? We knew that after this afternoon's meeting,' Francine says impatiently. 'But look Chris, this DVD has just arrived from a mysterious source in the Premier's Department. Let's put it on, it could change everything! Dean, come in here and get this damned machine working for us.'

Dean does his handiwork. The three sit down to look at the DVD and, an hour or so later, leave still talking about the explosive material they've seen. They seriously consider taking it straight to TVTV so it could be broadcast before tomorrow's debate. But they finally decide that it's best to keep it under wraps, as they don't want their opponents pre-warned.

Instead, they'll attempt to use the material in the Parliament itself. For this, they need a ruling on whether Chris could show it during debate, and so Dean makes a copy and delivers it to the Speaker's office with a note requesting he keep it strictly confidential and give them an urgent ruling on its use. Meantime, Francine rings the press to give them a veiled tip-off, and Francine and Chris then make contingency plans in case the speakers' ruling goes against them.

The next morning is steamy, with the mercury already at 35 degrees by ten o'clock as Chris struggles up the hill from the station to Parliament house. As he approaches, the importance of the day looms larger in his mind, simultaneously accentuating his excitement and tension. Once inside the building, he finds the air stifling.

As he makes his way to his office, he carefully avoids the knots of MPs and advisers standing around in the corridors, sipping tea or coffee and talking animatedly. But as Chris passes, one MP steps away from a huddle of senior government types and taps at the copy of the morning news-sheet he's holding, bearing the headline:

RIGHT FACES DEFEAT OVER FREMANTLE
HIGH-RISE SCHEME
Burnside promises explosive revelations to sway vote

'More grandstanding, I see, Burnside. You and your revelations . . . what bullshit! I s'pose you reckon you can bring another government down?' he growls sarcastically.

A few others in the group laugh and utter desultory support for their colleague. Chris merely nods, reckoning that despite his bravado, the MP senses trouble ahead. Despite being fired up over the DVD containing the explosive revelations, Chris is nervous, still unsure which way the vote will go. Jill Burnside was in touch earlier after reading the report in the morning paper, but even after Chris gave her some broad hints about the revelations, she gives the impression she's still undecided.

As he comes into the legislative chamber where proceedings will soon get under way, Chris's attention is drawn to a buzz of activity in the galleries above. Reporters are milling around, exchanging views, and a crowd of spectators is building up. The throng becomes noisy until warned by an officious orderly that quiet is the rule for observers of the democratic process, even when the house was not yet open for business.

Chris looks up again at this admonition as he dumps some files on his spacious leather seat and sees Diana coming in to the gallery with a large contingent of supporters. He grins distractedly and waves as she makes an aside to her flock. The flock peer down at the chamber below where MPs are drifting in.

Diana returns Chris's wave and points him out with relish. But the visitors only catch a glimpse, for by this time, he's turned on his heel and repaired to the small gallery at the rear of the chamber, the place reserved for MPs' personal visitors and staffers. Here he speaks to Francine, only to learn that the ruling they had asked the Speaker for has not yet been made. Getting up with a scowl, Chris says with obvious anxiety, 'keep me posted on the contingency.'

'Sure, but stay calm if you can, Chris,' says Francine with a smirk.

Chris grimaces, thinking, *get fucked*. He stops short of vocalising the feeling, instead clutching his forehead in an effort to quell his irritability as he returns to his seat in the chamber.

As he sits down, the irritability slowly subsides, but he's nonetheless preoccupied with worry. He thinks for a moment of simply skipping and escaping the heat by heading for the beach. But the thought soon dissipates as the Sergeant-at-Arms enters to announce, 'Members, Mr. Speaker.'

As Chris stands with other members to acknowledge the Speaker sweeping in in full regalia, he thinks, *This is our last chance to get this bloody FRA scheme off the books,* mindful that Parliament is about to go into its long summer recess.

After the preliminaries of the day, Chris catches the watchful eye of the Speaker and nervously moves for debate to be brought forward on his motion. He has done this many times before, always failing to gain a seconder, and this time seems likely to be no exception, as government members jeer and interject, 'boring!' 'Give us a break, you bloody megalomaniac.' 'You sound like a cracked record!'

The interjectors assume that Chris's motion will again fall on deaf ears, since whatever the press says, Right still has the numbers and thus is surely able to control the agenda. And the government backbenchers also reckon that the opposition is hopelessly divided and won't want to be drawn into the debate.

So there's consternation when opposition leader Elaine Hipper rises and says assertively, 'Mr. Speaker, I second the motion moved by the Member for Fremantle.'

Shockwaves make their way around the chamber, and several interjections erupt.

'You bloody turncoat!' yells one government backbencher.

A few derisive cries also emanate from the opposition benches behind their leader, from the diehard Clokeites. As Elaine explained to Chris at their meeting, the group has been furious ever since Chris had again outed their hero.

But this morning, their fury has turned to bitterness following their decisive defeat in caucus debate, twenty votes to a mere four. Were any of the remaining four brave or foolish enough to defy the caucus vote, they risk losing backing from the Party.

'You can't count on our votes, Hipper!' dares Mike Chesterfield nonetheless.

'Resign!' shouts one of the others.

'Sour grapes!' from a Hipper supporter.

'Order, members, please!' from an exasperated and somewhat bemused Speaker who goes on, 'I have a motion before the Chair and that is to approve debate on the Member for Fremantle's motion calling on the FRA to abandon its high-rise plans. I understand that the Leader of the Opposition has seconded the motion. Did I hear correctly, Member for Subiaco?'

'You did indeed, Mr. Speaker,' affirms Elaine. 'I can inform the house that this morning the Labor caucus resolved overwhelmingly to oppose this appalling and environmentally disastrous high-rise development.'

'You what?' interjects the Premier, his worst fears now confirmed. 'Your Party is becoming even more populist, you're opposed to good development. Suzuki comes riding into town, bulldozes a motion through a stacked public meeting, and you jump on the bandwagon!'

'This scheme is not a *good* development, and you know it, Premier!' responds Elaine evenly.

'And there is massive corruption involved which you will pay heavily for,' Chris could not help adding, although as he does so, he looks around anxiously to the gallery behind him. Francine meets his glance with upturned hands and shrugs her shoulders, as if to say no word from the Speaker as yet.

Right yells at Chris confidently, 'you self-righteous idiot, show us the evidence.'

Chris shoots back, 'I will if and when the Speaker allows its admission.'

A few sarcastic oohs and aahs come from MPs as the Speaker intervenes angrily, 'Member for Fremantle, that's more than enough of your grandstanding, you'll hear my ruling on the material you have given me when I have fully considered the matter, I'll not be rushed. Meantime, I'll allow no more comments along those lines. It's my job to make the ruling, yours to convince your colleagues to bring on the debate.'

Government and Clokeite MPs are delighted to see Chris put in his place so decisively.

Mildly embarrassed by this ticking-off, and worried that the Speaker will rule out use of the DVD if he pushes the point, Chris moves on. He argues that as the FRA is about to make its final decision on the scheme, and as Parliament will soon be in recess, today's the only chance the Parliament has to influence the course of the controversial development.

Elaine Hipper follows, outlining frankly the role of the Cloke faction in disrupting any move on her part to oppose the FRA development. The Clokeites had convinced a majority of unions on which the Party is still heavily dependent to withdraw support unless the Party endorsed the FRA development. This threat was justified on grounds of the jobs that would be created by the development.

'However, Mr. Speaker,' Elaine continues to a now hushed house, 'the position of the majority of unions affiliated to our Party changed following the recent scandalous revelations about ex-Premier Cloke, a result of the investigations of the Burnside committee.' Here Elaine turns to acknowledge Chris, who nods in response.

An interjector from the government benches takes advantage of this exchange.

'Hipper, you're no better than Cloke, and your Party's still full of his supporters!'

'True!' pipes up Mike Chesterfield to much laughter.

Hipper glances disdainfully at Chesterfield and responds calmly. 'Members will know that under my leadership we are committed to open and honest processes. Today's caucus vote establishes once and for all that former Premier Cloke now has no real influence on the Parliamentary Party.'

Right rises to deride these comments and indicate that the government will let the debate go ahead in any case, confident they can carry the day.

'Unlike the Labor Party, my government is all in favour of open debate and democratic practice and . . .'

The rest is drowned out by jeers and interjections as the vote is resolved in favour of the debate proceeding.

So far, so good, Chris thinks.

But as he now has to open the debate on the FRA scheme itself, he again asks the Speaker to rule on the admissibility of his material which Chris considers vital to the debate. The Speaker declines his request, further admonishing Chris for being impatient and warning him not to raise matters contained in the material he's due to rule on.

This infuriates Chris since in the absence of the material, he's on shaky ground. Familiar with the case and full of passion against the FRA plan, he's able to mount a convincing case against the development. But he isn't able to produce any tangible evidence to support corruption charges except against Cloke, which in this instance doesn't help his case. This allows government speakers room to exploit Chris's position.

But with the possibility of defeating the government in the air, Chris receives support in debate from most opposition speakers, and this heartens him considerably. But all this seems in vain when Mike Chesterfield announces, to much consternation and derision from his colleagues, that his group of four MPs will be abstaining from the vote.

They can't support the motion since whatever the caucus vote and, Chesterfield adds sanctimoniously, risks to their own futures, they believe the FRA scheme is vital to the city's development and indeed the State's economy. On the other hand, they are not prepared to vote with the government.

The fate of Chris's motion now lies with the independents, who so far have given little indication that they'll support him. *And still, the Speaker hasn't ruled on his material, clearly wanting to prolong his agony,* Chris thinks angrily.

He's becoming an emotional wreck, but then Jill Woodall, the independent Member for Melville, takes Chris by surprise when she speaks in support of the motion. She sits down amid much clamour. Chris, who sits just across the narrow passage leading to the rear gallery, can't resist coming over, squeezing her hand, and giving her a peck on the cheek. Jill, a modest woman, smiles but flushes as cat-calls and risqué interjections fill the air.

'Watch out Jill, Burnside's got a shocking reputation with women!'

'I've heard the rumours too,' Jill laughingly responds.

'What did he offer you to get your vote?'

'No comment,' says Jill, to Chris's chagrin.

'Order, order, members. The Member for Fremantle will return to his seat and desist from such unparliamentary behaviour!' intones the Speaker.

A barrage of laughter and more badinage greet him.

Chris returns to his seat, blushing but smiling and now more confident that he can win the vote. However, his tension and doubt soon return when he hears the other three independents indicate that for various reasons, they will either be abstaining from the vote or supporting the government.

Chris is due to give his closing speech, the right of reply reserved for the mover of a motion. After consulting with Elaine, he's done the numbers again and confirmed that the only chance they now have of winning the vote is to convince the wavering independents to come on side.

If they did this, it would likely mean that the Speaker would have the casting vote. The question then, was which way would he use it? And more importantly, surely he would have to rule on Chris's material beforehand?

So as he rises to speak, he dares to ask, for the third time, if the Speaker would rule on whether his material can be used in debate.

The Speaker looks severe and Chris anticipates further criticism.

However, the Speaker asks for quiet while he leans down to talk to the clerks. After a few moments of intense interchange, which seem like hours to Chris, the Speaker finally responds, 'Member for Fremantle, I am now ready to rule. Before I do and for your elucidation members, I'll explain that the Member for Fremantle last night submitted to me a video recording of some conversation that he wanted to play during his speech. There are some delicate legal and procedural points to consider in playing such tapes in the House, especially since they are evidently recordings of conversation held in the office of an MP who has considerable influence in this chamber,' he says, looking directly at the Premier.

A worried expression comes over the Premier, and he quickly consults with his deputy next to him. They both look up warily as the Speaker continues, 'I've fully considered these points and am satisfied that playing the tapes would not breach our standing orders directly. However, I am not keen to turn this place into a de facto TV viewing room or cinema, and so I won't allow the Member for Fremantle to show the DVD as requested.'

Government members cheer while Chris groans and is about to protest, when to his surprise, the Speaker goes on, 'but members I *will* allow the showing of a particular part of the recording, which I've identified, and which I will now set up for viewing. As is the practice with documents tabled, the entire DVD will then be considered to be in the public domain.'

The Speaker beckons Chris to the Chair amid uproar in the Chamber. He explains the part he's sanctioned for viewing, and Chris is happy with the outcome. Even if it'll prevent him showing the full version of what he judges to be the most interesting political footage he's ever seen.

Chris senses things might be going his way and reckons he'll use delay to effect. He begins the right of reply routinely, rebutting points made during the debate. After several minutes, during which MPs make known their impatience for the film-show to proceed, he comes to the point.

'Members, many of you have given me a hard time this morning for labelling the FRA and government deal on this development as corrupt and apparently having no evidence for such an accusation. The Premier challenged me earlier to produce the evidence. Well, here it is,' he says, flourishing the second copy of the DVD above his head. 'This is a video of a meeting held between you and a number of prominent characters in your very own office, Mr. Premier, and the extract you will see is incontrovertible evidence of extraordinary chicanery surrounding this FRA scheme.'

Exclamations filled the chamber as the Premier, who has turned pale at Chris's words, leaps to his feet.

'Point of order, Mr. Speaker!

The Speaker turns to the Premier, asking him to elaborate.

Right loses no time, looking extremely agitated.

'Mr. Speaker, the Member for Fremantle should *not* have a video-recording of any meetings held in my office. That is illegal, and it would therefore contravene privacy to show illegal recordings in this place. In any case, how do we know this video is authentic? Knowing the Member for Fremantle, I would hazard a guess that the whole thing is a fabrication!'

'I assure you that this is ridgy-didge, just wait until you see it. It has the Premier's office logo on every frame,' Chris returns tantalisingly. 'And, Mr. Speaker, the DVD was not obtained illegally. In fact, it arrived unsolicited in my parliamentary mail!'

Guffaws resound around the chamber, but the Speaker remains serious and turns to the Premier, who's fuming to his colleagues.

'Mr. Premier, am I to understand that you make a practice of video-taping all meetings held in your office?'

The Premier struggles to his feet, rapidly turning a shade of scarlet, and in a shaky and embarrassed voice admits, 'well yes, Mr. Speaker, that's true, so that we can gain an accurate record of history in the making.'

'Sounds like *you* might be history, Premier!' comes an interjection from the opposition benches, amid much laughter.

'A post-modern Richard Nixon!' says another.

'Order members, the Premier is addressing me!' from an exasperated Speaker.

'Mr. Speaker, even if this video should be authentic, I still ask you to rule against it, since it was obtained without my permission. And while the disclosure of its contents may not compromise me (laughter all around, even from government benches), it could embarrass the others involved in the meeting,' says the Premier nervously.

The Speaker asks if the people taped at these meetings were aware of the practice. The Premier, even more embarrassed, replies that no, they weren't but it was never his intention that the recordings reach the public arena until all parties involved had agreed to their release. He argues that this was another reason for preventing the DVD being shown.

The Speaker consults the clerk again before ruling, 'Mr. Premier, this DVD appears to be a certified copy, and I am told that there is in fact no rule preventing the showing of items such as this, however they were obtained. The Chair recognises the Member for Fremantle.'

The Premier, who still doesn't know which meeting is on the DVD, has thought in panic of several possibilities.

Why, oh why, he now reflects, *had he let his own ego get the better of him and started taping meetings in his office?*

Right was tempted to move against the ruling, but he's alert enough to see that he might lose that vote, and that it's only a matter of time before the DVD finds its way to the press and the public arena. That sounds like a political disaster, but it would look even worse if he tried to block Chris's manoeuvre.

Chris asks for the DVD extract to be shown, first explaining that the people in the meeting are Premier Right, John Dick of Flexible Constructions, Ken Thumper of ABC Building Co., Fred Chewis, head of the FRA, and former Premier Wayne Cloke. This in itself causes consternation, but the video rolls on in an unusually quiet chamber. Chris calls out the names of the participants as they speak.

Right, leaning over conspiratorially to Ken Thumper and John Dick, who are seated next to him.
Well, John, Ken, have your companies got the capacity for the scale of this Fremantle high-rise project?
Dick, seriously: *Sure, we think so. Ken and I agree that there should be no problems if Flexible is able to share the work with non-union builders like ABC without causing a major industrial upset. It'll need a watertight deal with the fucking building unions to implement this idea.*
Thumper, smiling broadly: *That's it, Richard. We can work together, but only if those bloody unions don't cause us their usual grief.*

Cloke, looking uncomfortable, but smirking: *Well, I don't think that'll be a problem if they get the rates you've mentioned, and of course, if I get my slice of the deal!*

Right, breezily, as if addressing a picnic gathering: *No problem there, Wayne. Like the rest of us, you're in for 1 percent of the contract price, which we conservatively estimate at $2 billion.*

Chewis, glumly: *That includes me, of course?*

Right, laughing nervously: *Yes Fred, trust me!*

This nearly brings the house down, and for a few moments, Chris stays quiet so the words can sink in. The Premier tries to make himself inconspicuous and mumbles something about a forgery. A frenzy builds in the press gallery as reporters rush to start making calls to their offices to break the headline-grabber of the session. As some MPs missed parts of the exchange because of the excited hubbub, Chris asks for it to be repeated and points out that there are several more juicy exchanges on other parts of the DVD. He concludes triumphantly, 'and that, Mr. Premier, is all the proof anyone needs to show that not just is this project completely ill-conceived, but that you and the FRA are in it up to your necks! Not only that, you have been planning a scam of massive proportions in league with a former corrupt Premier who is is headed for jail. It certainly looks like he'll have a lot of political company when he gets there!'

When the vote on Chris's motion comes on, the Speaker calls the vote in favour of the government on the voices. But Chris immediately calls out 'division required!'

'Ring the bells,' intones the Speaker.

The bells summon absent members before the doors are locked and the votes are recorded and counted. Chris is amazed but extremely pleased to see that all the independents follow Jill Woodall and vote on his side. The Speaker announces the result to a hushed house, 'the result of the division is Ayes 26, Noes 26, with 4 abstentions. A tied vote, which means I have the casting vote.'

All eyes are now on the Speaker who goes on 'members, as you know, I would normally support the government in the event of a tied vote. But given the extraordinary scenes we have just witnessed indicating extensive government corruption, I have no choice but to cast my vote in favour of this particular motion.'

A near riot breaks out, with the realisation that not only has the government been defeated in a vote on the floor of the house, but also that they are in deep political trouble. This and the telling video footage have grave implications for Right's future as Premier. He retreats from the chamber, followed by several senior colleagues gesturing angrily at him.

Others mill about on the floor, with many opposition MPs and even a few from the government rushing to congratulate Chris and Elaine Hipper. The two are locked arm-in-arm, smiling delightedly at the unexpected result. Cheers come from one section of the public gallery, boos from another. A fist-fight almost breaks out until orderlies separate two figures from opposing sides, men who decided to take out their differences there and then. The two are escorted from the gallery as the house is adjourned early for the day.

As Chris leaves the chamber with Elaine Hipper and Jill Woodall, Diana rushes up to give the group a wild hug and shouts 'three cheers for the leaders of the bloodless coup!'

A few cameras, rapidly drawn from the bags of onlookers, click and flash as Elaine cautions, 'hang on Diana, we're not there yet!' Curious glances come in as people in the public gallery crane their necks in an effort to follow the action of the disappearing happy knot of MPs and excited staffers. As they head towards Elaine's office, Chris and Diana hug. The intimacy of the moment sparks memories for both of them.

'Don't get any ideas!' says Diana in a low voice, squeezing Chris's arm tightly in a knowing way. But both have ideas aplenty as they rejoin the group going into Elaine's office for what promises to be a long celebration.

During which Diana lets it slip that she'd been tipped off about the DVD and its contents well before it arrived. So she and the HIP group half-anticipated the events leading to the vote. This was behind Paula's comment a while back about there being more than one way to skin the proverbial.

'Well, Diana, you might have let me in on it,' says a miffed Chris.

'Knowledge for women only, not something a man could be trusted with!'

'Hrmmph, what it's a case of women ruling the world then, is it?'

'It's on the cards, buddy.'

CHAPTER 29

CHICK POWER PLUS

The group of three women are clearly having fun. They spill out of the café, talking loudly and laughing as they make their way to a waiting taxi at the foot of the stairs. They had been enjoying a private celebration amongst women who were collectively the core of the 'honesty in politics' group, which had become known as HIP. HIP had now secured its first win.

With a little help from their friends, that is. During lunch, Elaine, Diana, and Paula toast all of them. Their only regret is that the toasts aren't alcoholic, all have business to attend to in the afternoon. But the lack of alcohol is hardly noticed as they're all in high spirits to start with. They drink first to the woman who supplied them with the vital information that had been fed to Chris before the crucial debate.

'Here's to our deep throat!' Elaine proposes, and conversation briefly turns to the DVD which had produced the scenes that turned the vote.

The vital recording had been clandestinely forwarded by a former colleague of Diana's in the Premier's office, a person who acted with the aplomb of a secret service agent. A difficult job since the video-recordings were closely guarded. But not closely enough to prevent the officer who worked on the transcripts from getting a pirate copy to Diana. A pirate copy that went undetected on the computer records for which the officer was responsible. Deep throat had kept her distance from Diana for the past few months. Meanwhile, the coup had been arranged through messages sent between mobile communicators, records of which they'd instantly erased.

'But here's to Diana, too, who kept the secret under her lid. How did you do it, kid, given your recent record?' smirks Paula, a gentle dig at Diana, who'd been keen to tell all her friends about their relationship, well before Paula was expecting it.

'Relationships are one thing, politics quite another! And in that department, I boast years of training darling, in both political parties!' returns Diana with a grin, before turning to Elaine.

'And anyway, Elaine, we should be toasting you, for your decisive move in breaking away from Chesterfield and his mob.'

'And don't forget who galvanized them down in Freo and beyond, especially that QC of yours eh Paula?' adds Elaine wickedly.

'Well, she's not a patch on Diana!' responds Paula with passion, pressing her leg against Diana's under the table.

Diana responds immediately by pressing back warmly, but as she does so, she feels a slight nervousness over her pending unfinished business with Chris.

As it happened, Chris Burnside was the only man to come in for the group's special attention. Elaine said while they were enjoying their toast to Chris, 'you know, we could make Chris an offer of honorary membership of our group!'

'Do you think he'd like to undergo a sex change?' Paula jokes.

'I have a better idea than that!' offers Diana brightly.

All three laugh uproariously once Diana had spelt the idea out. They agreed that Diana would have to use all her skills to get Chris to go along with this one.

Meantime, each had more serious business to attend to. Elaine and Diana head back to the leader's office for a meeting requested by Mike Chesterfield. When he agitatedly booked the meeting earlier, he told Diana he wanted to talk to Elaine urgently about the future of the Parliamentary Party.

When the taxi reached the side entrance of Parliament House, Paula and Diana embrace passionately before they hop out of the vehicle.

They scurry just ahead of the waiting press ruck into the sanctuary of the building.

Not before the photographers get a few long-distance shots of Paula and Diana's parting intimacies. Paula smiles and waves good-humouredly to the paparazzi as she takes the taxi on to her own afternoon business, a meeting with Darlene Pocket, QC.

Elaine is both distressed and relieved at the outcome of her meeting, during which Chesterfield vents his accumulated anger at the events of the last few days. Shouting repeatedly, the staff hear his accusations that they'd all been taken in by a forged DVD. So they're not that surprised when Chesterfield sweeps angrily out of the office. Following, Elaine dolefully turns to Diana, looking shaken.

'Well, that's him gone forever!'

'How do you mean?' Diana is busy at the computer, breaking off to talk to Elaine.

She picks up her now ever present ebony to manicure her nails. To chiacking from her friends and colleagues, Diana pays more attention to her appearance since taking up with Paula.

'The silly prick is resigning from the Party and threatening to take his three acolytes with him,' responds Elaine, her face marked with frustration.

'Well, good riddance to the bastard I say, hells bells, you should be celebrating . . . I mean with Chesterfield gone, your dream of a Party without Clokeites is starting to come true,' observes Diana. 'But I guess it's not good for our numbers?'

'My thoughts exactly. It means that we're at least one down for the vote of no confidence in the government, which should come on next week, and this time, we may not get the support of the independents,' replies Elaine. 'Jill Woodall was in touch earlier to say that despite her support yesterday, she's wavering on a no-confidence motion in the government. She doesn't necessarily want to force another election.'

'That's a worry, we need to meet the independents ourselves,' suggests Diana. Elaine nods her agreement.

Their attention turns to a document that's emerging noisily from the printer next to Diana's desk.

'But listen, we'd better get on with this press release on Chesterfield's latest manoeuvre.' Diana hands Elaine the document. Elaine peruses the draft.

'That's great Diana, just add a few sentences about Chesterfield's threats. Unless we move fast, it's going to be difficult to stave off the press. I'm sure Chesterfield is out there talking to them right now!'

Sure enough, the press are soon wanting comment; Chesterfied has spilled his decision to resign from the Party and re-badge himself as True Labor. And what is Elaine going to do about it?

Elaine is caustic about Chesterfield's new label and says she's considering her position. She'd wait on a caucus meeting before announcing her Party's next move.

The press release says the same in fancier terms but makes great play of the fact that as opposition leader, Elaine had never gained any real support from Chesterfield, who must be totally gullible to fall for Right's line on the forged DVD.

'Either that or they're being bribed!' jokes Diana as they check through the release.

'Diana, re-ally!' says Elaine in mock horror at a suggestion they both knew could well be true but best left unmentioned.

The scene is chaotic at Elaine's house in nearby Subiaco later that day. Politicians and staffers scurry about the old bungalow. The house has an air of shabby dignity with peeling ceilings and crumbling brickwork increasingly evident in the absence of renovations which Elaine just hasn't gotten around to. The antediluvian feel is emphasised by the piles of books which spill from shelves and onto tables and floors in search of a resting place.

Elaine has no time to contemplate the state of her house or consider whether its condition is a metaphor for her own life, as a friend had unkindly suggested. She's in the midst of a series of meetings that she and Diana had decided were best undertaken away from the poisoned atmosphere of Parliament House. The main focus of the late afternoon business is the attitude of the Independents to the developing political crisis. Each has been invited to talk, Elaine desperately hoping they will see things her way.

She was a bit closer to realising her hopes when the last of the four, Jill Woodall, left the house a couple of hours later. Jill had come around to the idea of supporting a no-confidence motion, especially after Elaine had promised her a Cabinet spot if she formed the next government.

The other Independents remained equivocal. This was despite Elaine and Diana supplying details of other dodgy behaviour within government, namely the carving up of lucrative government contracts between Party benefactors, such as Ken Thumper and John Tough.

The Independents still find it hard to believe that a conservative government could be so corrupt. This challenges their deep faith in the fundamental integrity of the political system, Laborites apart of course.

All of this was potential manna from heaven for the press, who had not taken long to suss out where Elaine was conducting business. A bevy of journalists arrive demanding entry and interviews. Having been refused both, they cluster on the road verge outside, cameras and recording devices at the ready to quiz the retinue of politicians as they arrive and leave.

Knowing the sensitivity of the whole business, the politicians don't give much away, and neither does Elaine when she finally emerges. But between them, the politicians contribute sufficiently tantalizing tidbits to keep the evening news reports in a frenzy of speculation over the fate of the government.

The highlight of the evening news bulletins is a frantic scene that developed while Jill Woodall was being interviewed. The background quickly became the focus of the report as an angry James Ambognas confronted Gabor Soraszem of TVTV. The two had arrived separately, but simultaneously. Ambognas, smarting from a massive fine that had just been imposed for his attempted knife attack on Soraszem, swore and gesticulated angrily at Gabor as they converged.

The earlier incident is in danger of a sequel until the assembled press intervene, but only after they were able to film a vitriolic verbal and punch-swinging battle between the two. Parallels are drawn between the battles of the TV producers and those preoccupying the politicians.

CHAPTER 30

WHERE HAVE ALL THE POWERS GONE?

The change of political style is unmistakeable, for women *are* now in charge. The fall of Right's government had come in December and was followed by the cobbling together of a temporary new alliance in government. Women dominated the senior posts and the Independents, headed by Jill Woodall and Chris Burnside, are key parts of the team. The government was commissioned on an agreement that it would go to the polls at the slightest hint of parliamentary defeat. At the moment, this suited all players.

Whatever the future held, on opening day at Parliament House the following February, everyone noticed the marked change. The stalwarts, the loyal and efficient staff of orderlies and clerks, still quietly shocked at the female ascendancy, nonetheless remarked that the atmosphere was calmer, more considered, and less confrontational. Gone is the atmosphere of an old boys club or the boys' playground at school.

It's been replaced by a more subtle ambience, which comes from an attempt to govern not by the strident exercise of power, but by more gentle means, more zen than hierarchical. Female energy seeking to replace the outdated male confrontational style. But the women are soon to realise *that prize* is not yet within reach, as even if women are in charge of government, men are still the majority in Parliament.

The no-confidence motion laid the foundation for the new government. In the end, it only scraped through by one vote, even with three of the four Liberal-leaning independents voting with the opposition. This, and the abstention of the other independent, was just sufficient to cancel out the defection of Chesterfield to Right's side. Chesterfield's 'True Labor' faction had thus proved to be ineffective, and he soon announced his intention to resign from Parliament altogether.

Resignations were in the air. Right's government resigned following the passing of the no-confidence motion. During debate, Right blustered about how his government was in no sense really corrupt, that it had been fitted up, framed, condemned without trial. The Speaker was heard to mutter 'here, here' at various points during Right's speech, further fuelling Elaine and Diana's suspicions that the government held something over him, given his vote against Right only a week or so earlier.

A desperate Premier defied belief by claiming that in terms of honesty, his government was streets ahead of the Cloke government. This brought howls of derision from the public gallery and a yelp from Mike Chesterfield who interjected that he was sick of Cloke being used as a whipping boy. Right soon laid off this line since he could not afford to alienate his unlikely new ally.

Chris pointed out in a fiery speech that Right was clearly trying it on over comparisons with Cloke. First and very suspiciously, Cloke had still not been charged, and second, Right had been caught red-handed in dodgy deals involving Cloke himself. Chris speculated on the reasons for this unlikely alliance, the true nature of which, he predicted, would soon be revealed. Chris also showed that Right's claims that the DVD was a forgery looked increasingly hollow, using statements vouching the DVD's authenticity that had come forward from several political commentators.

To general consternation, Elaine Hipper had then documented several other cases of outright cronyism and corruption in the Right government. Elaine made extensive use of files that the HIP group had accumulated. This included the leading role of the ex-police Minister in the brothel industry, the embarrassment of these revelations causing him to quietly resign his seat over the Christmas break.

Hipper decided to keep her powder dry on further material she possessed, material that pointed to more-than-cosy links between police, drug barons, builders, unions, bikies and senior Ministers. With more research, this could prove of great advantage at the next election, which was bound to come on early. In the meantime, some would in any case be covered by the report of Chris's committee, which had been overtaken by events, but which was still due to be completed and tabled within the next few months.

But on opening day, elections are far from the minds of most who come to see the new government in action. Excitement fills the air as the politicians file in to take their new places. There was the Premier-designate Elaine Hipper, looking a little nervous, but confident. She and her new Cabinet would be sworn in once they formally had the confidence of the Parliament. Her new deputy, proposed Treasurer Yoni McNamara, and the irrepressible Judy Doorknock, designated Minister for Health and Police, flanked Elaine. Women comprised half of the other twelve Ministerial positions, which would give them a total 9 of 15 Cabinet positions, or 60 percent, a figure seen as critical to creating a more caring and even approach to decision-making.

Opening time for the special session of Parliament approaches in the crowded chamber, which is today housing a joint session of both houses to be presided over by the Governor. Members of the upper house are crammed in temporary seating, while some share the capacious leather chamber seats with colleagues. The more relaxed MPs find this cosy, but others look distinctly uncomfortable at being so physically close to their colleagues, and so end up perching on their haunches or on the wide armrests between the seats.

One front-bench seat is conspicuously vacant. Unlike most of those surrounding, this seat is to be occupied by a male, none other than Chris Burnside, who is to be Minister for Planning, Transport and the Environment. This powerful post was one Chris only accepted reluctantly, and after a lot of soul-searching, since his anarchistic instincts made him loath to become such a key part of the government machinery.

During discussions with Mike, Dean, and Francine over the offer, Chris was initially equivocal.

'Look, you guys know I really respect Elaine and her new team, which after all, we helped her form. And since I've been elected, I've often dreamed of being a Minister, even though that appeared to be totally out of my reach. Now, here's not just a chance, but a huge one! But maybe my personal ambition is overtaking my political agenda?'

'Chris, everyone knows you're politically ambitious. That's not a crime, you know!' replied Mike emphatically. 'Personally, I would see it as more of a crime if you rejected the offer because that's just another key post occupied by Labor. Hipper has already said she won't have more than three Independents in the Cabinet. And however good *this* Labor government turns out to be, there are still huge grey areas in their policies from our point of view.'

'Chris, don't forget our ideas on railways. And we need to do something about Rockingham Highway since Labor is still undecided despite the exit of Chesterfield,' urged Francine. 'Hey, and by the way, getting you off the backbench might also curb your increasing grumpiness. Mike and I both reckon that's not been helped by the frustration of not really getting our agenda advanced fast enough.'

Chris reddened slightly at this admonition, but then smiled and said, 'good point Francine. You're both spot on about the issues, but if I don't take the position, we could still negotiate from outside the Cabinet. Remember that Hipper will still be dependent on the four other independents for general support in the Parliament. And the Greens are negotiating in the upper house and say they will only join the alliance if the government agrees to come up with some more green goodies. And there's no Cabinet posts on offer to them!

'But, Chris, think of the possibilities. And I don't just mean policy matters, I'm thinking of my own future here too,' said Francine in a jocular way, although Chris knew that there was a hint of ambition about her too.

'Francine, if you get a key job in the ministry, you'll never finish your book on the Mad Roads Department,' countered Chris.

'Oh bugger the book Chris and in any case, you're wrong,' Francine shot back. 'I've been talking to a guy in planning who's keen as mustard to help me produce the book whatever happens in government. You know, he's the one who has been trying to subvert MRD road plans from within the Ministry for decades – he helped provide a shit-load of inside information for the thesis!'

'Yeah, that'll be bloody red George, I bet?' Francine nodded.

'Well, you win on that point Francine, but I still need to think over this whole Cabinet business.'

'You've only got another couple of days, Chris, remember the special session of Parliament is on soon, and Elaine wants a decision by the end of this week,' Mike reminds him.

A harried constituent had arrived in the office and the discussion was put on hold. But even as Chris talked to his constituent, he knew which way his decision would go. He can't resist the lure of power. All the things we could do with it – all good of course – he enumerated to himself even as his constituent babbled on about irregular rubbish bin collections.

Over a coffee with Diana later in the day, the matter was sealed. Chris explained his reservations about taking the job. Diana listened patiently but then cut across him, 'come on Chris I know you've been hankering for a place in Cabinet ever since you got into Parliament.'

'Yes, but I don't want to become detached from my electorate as happens with so many Ministers.'

'Pull the other one mate.'

'We-ell, you're right. I've run out of reasons for not taking the post. I'll do it!'

'On ya man, but be warned: keep your hands off the women!'

'Who, me?' Chris replies tongue in cheek, taking it further by asking, 'Why, are you after one of them?'

'Sure, I've always wanted to make love to another Cabinet Minister, but an honest one this time,' Diana jokes while grimacing at the memory of the affair with Cloke. 'No way, man, and don't think that opens the door to my bed for you, my friend.'

'Hmm, pity, I thought you might say that.' Paula wins again. '*I'll* just have to go for a Minister myself,' retorts Chris impishly.

'Excuse me, but what are you bloody well saying?'

'Well, you know I've always fancied Yoni McNamara.'

'I know that, you bastard, you got her on your committee as a 'reserve' in case you couldn't get it on with that bloody Sarah.'

'That bloody Sarah is right,' says Chris, 'she's taken compassionate leave since Right's defeat, hasn't been in touch with me and is not to be found anywhere.'

'Is that so? Serve you right, buster!'

'That's a bit unfair.'

'As you sow, so shall ye reap, Chris.'

'Don't get biblical on me!'

'Ha! This place could easily become like Sodom and Gomorrah with you around, you randy bastard. Any case, I wondered why I hadn't seen Sarah in the corridors lately. She's probably gone to visit her conservative friends in London, now that her mob is back in power there. With any luck, she'll move there!'

'You're just being cruel now,' Chris objects.

'Am I indeed?' Diana is determined to underline her point. 'Well, Chris, coming back to who *is* here, I'm telling you, if you move on Yoni, I'll recommend to Elaine she withdraw your Ministry immediately!'

And so Chris has been warned again. He knows Diana is serious and starts to think of ways he might conceal any affair. His political ambitions may be almost fulfilled, but his desire is another matter entirely.

Chris's seat is still vacant as the final bells ring. People in the know wonder if he's had second thoughts. Just before the Speaker enters the chamber, there's a flurry of interest as a flamboyantly dressed female figure approaches the government benches. She pushes past colleagues in a rather ungainly fashion and determinedly sits in Chris's seat. MPs in nearby seats begin to protest.

Soon, however, laughter and wolf-whistles break out and several MPs do a double take as they realise the person who's in the seat is Chris in drag. He's responded with enthusiasm to Diana's suggestion that he become an honorary woman! He's decked out in a long flowing red dress, baubles, and cheap jewellery : a necklace and large rings on both hands, which also feature red lacquered fingernails. He wears distinctive makeup, including violet eyeshadow and a gorgeous bouffant hairdo.

Some MPs are scandalised at the extraordinary – for Parliament – sight. Richard Right, who is having trouble adjusting to the reality of being on the opposition benches again, immediately starts yelling scathing criticisms across the chamber. Chris smiles, blowing kisses and waving cheekily in response. This fuels more wolf-whistles and dodgy jokes from all parts of the chamber, including the fascinated public gallery.

As the mood develops, there's more good humour than rancour and a light-hearted atmosphere dominates as the Governor's approach is awaited. Elaine had worried that Chris's stunt would engender criticism and fatally flaw her new government. The atmosphere assuages her doubts, and she now thinks that if this is symptomatic of a new approach, politics could actually become fun.

But some did not want to join in the fun. Indeed they see the whole incident as an affront not just to Parliament, but also to the community generally. Right and a few other stodgy colleagues mutter indignantly about disrespect to Parliament. A couple of uptight family value MPs go further, indicating they would walk out were it not for the Governor officiating.

Yet the Governor is not exactly your usual conservative establishment figure. Cloke's predecessor had appointed him in a move that was controversial at the time, since while he was well qualified for the job, he was also openly gay. Right had been tempted to sack him, but the Governor had become a popular figure by dint of his natural good humour, charisma, and his whole-hearted support of humanitarian causes.

His good humour is on full display today. During the opening ceremony there were guffaws as Chris struck a few provocative poses in his roomy front-bench seat. As the Governor exits the chamber, he comes over to the government benches, leans over to Chris, and kisses him.

This delights most, although a few shout 'shame' across the chamber. But their cries largely fall on deaf ears. Most onlookers see good humour rather than bad taste. 'A belated and real-life sequel to the popular Australian movie *Priscilla Queen of the Desert*,' as one news report later described it. Another waxes lyrical about the new Burnside and Sullivan Opera in the making. As the chamber empties, Chris is surrounded by a bevy of MPs keen to show their appreciation of his antics.

CHAPTER 31

TEMPTING OFFERS

Paula is especially chuffed when Elaine Hipper is restored as Premier, even if the pundits suggest Elaine's second gig could be as short-lived as her first. There's a theory that the male-dominated world of politics only allows women to occupy leadership positions when they have little prospect of keeping them.

So far this could certainly be true of Hipper, who was first given a poisoned chalice when she took over from Cloke, and who now heads a potentially unstable alliance. But Paula's among those who think things could be different this time around, since for the first time in the State's political history, there's a majority of women in charge of the government machine.

Long may it last, thinks Paula as she stretches and leans back in her comfortable mayoral office chair. She's here on this bright and hot Sunday morning to catch up on the week's paperwork. She's one of the few people in the building, and as she sips her café latte and indulgently dips one of Nona's legendary biscotti in her glass, she finds it hard to concentrate on the turgid report in front of her.

Hell, she thinks, *even the title 'The future of WA's rubbish collection system: a discrete modelling of waste streams and an evaluation of feasible disposal alternatives in Southern Metropolitan Perth' is boring! Is this why I became Mayor?*

For relief, Paula turns her mind to the torrid events of the last few months. While certainly not an avid supporter of the Labor Party, Paula is now more aware of its potential role in protecting the city from unwanted development. She admires the courageous way Elaine addressed the issue during parliamentary debates. While some cynics are suggesting that Hipper had simply used the issue to propel herself into power, Paula knows better, mainly as a result of many exchanges they enjoyed in the HIP group.

She now knows that Elaine is a woman of her political word. Politically ambitious yes, but there for reasons of principle. Paula admires Elaine's consistency, something that she aspires to but finds harder to achieve. In her short and so far spectacular time as Mayor, Paula has been seen as an opportunist. She'd also been diverted from the main game by temptations in the form of sexual partners, such as Chris.

Ah, the gorgeous Chris, I'm certainly glad I seduced him! But should I have indulged my desires so much? He was devastated when our affair finished, despite what he said, she muses as she savours her biscuit. The sensuality of the moment and the memory combined to send a pleasurable shock of energy through her languid body. *Hmm, well I guess the affair helped change my views on the FRA development, but then, I didn't really have to go to bed with him for that,* she thinks with a tinge of self-criticism.

The predatory aspect of her character is something Paula rarely reflects upon since it has become a way of life for her. That and operating across the sexual spectrum is a game she enjoys, partly because it shocks, but more out of an almost insatiable hunger for intimacy, something which no doubt goes back to her childhood experiences.

In her adult sex life, she has experienced few long-term sexual relationships, but is starting to ache for one at present. She sees Diana as a distinct possibility and looks forward to her coming in this morning. Paula knows that Chris propositioned Diana recently, that Diana held the line, but worries that she might be tempted to cross it. Especially since Diana isn't as comfortable in a lesbian relationship as is Paula. Besides, Paula often has trouble keeping a relationship monogamous, as she discovered to the cost of her own stability and the emotions of several partners over the years. She reflects that she isn't tempted to go elsewhere with the dynamic Diana around.

Paula's thoughts and her unsuccessful attempts to read the report are interrupted by a knock at the door, and Diana comes in looking flushed. They'd spent the night together at Paula's as they often did on a Saturday, and it seems that their relationship is blooming. Paula and Diana often feature in the social columns and programmes, and the one commentator refers to them as Perth's most handsome and powerful political couple. They cop a fair bit of derision from their friends about this, but are happy to go along for the ride.

'Oh, darling, do come in and rescue me from this rubbish, literally,' Paula quips, handing the weighty tome to Diana.

Diana's face contorts as she reads the report's title page.

'Hmmm, I guess it won't be long before I have to read this for Elaine. There's just been that inquiry. I'm her rubbish er sorry, waste disposal expert, so to speak. But rather you than me at this stage.'

'Ah well, maybe I'll just wait for your policy summary then, save me reading the whole bloody thing?' Paula tries, thinking she was testing her luck.

'It's a deal, but only if you make me a strong espresso this instant and whenever we meet here?'

'Done!' laughs Paula. As she gets up, she strokes Diana on the arm and heads for the coffee machine. She soon returns with a steaming espresso for Diana and another latte for herself. She also brings in a small plate of biscotti.

'Wow, I didn't stipulate biscotti as part of the deal, but I think I will now,' jokes Diana. She puts the report down having made a mental note to get on to it this week, but hardly thrilled at the prospect.

'Easy done, as long as Nona keeps turning them out.'

'Good old Nona, I should have known.'

Diana has only met Paula's family in passing since she always seems to have her own commitments. They sip their coffees and chink cups as they both say at the same time, 'hot and strong, just as we like our lovers!' They laugh and kiss.

'But listen my sweet, I have news: I just had a call from the Premier,' crows Diana as she helps herself to another biscotti. 'I'm not supposed to know, but Elaine has got you at the top of her short list for the FRA job, the Chair, you know. I' – and here she holds up two fingers from each hand to make quote marks in the air – 'accidentally saw the names yesterday.'

'Well, I'll be damned . . . sounds fantastic, you know I'd love to do *that* job,' beams Paula, sweeping back her hair, which she's started growing long again. 'But can I really do it? I'm already overloaded here. Anyway, won't that be a politically dangerous appointment . . . you know jobs for the girls and all that?'

'Could be, but you're the obvious choice, and you are definitely *not* associated with the Party. And I know you'll find the time. Don't worry, I'm sure Elaine will conjure up the right words to justify the appointment. And if she doesn't, I will!' Diana concludes triumphantly.

The two women embrace warmly, and after Paula satisfies herself that no one is in the vicinity, they strip off and make passionate love on the mayoral couch.

Two floors below, a disconsolate Doug Dodge is making hate rather than love. He swears and mutters under his breath as he reluctantly empties his Councillor's desk. He's been forced to resign from the council, to take effect the following Monday.

His resignation follows his conviction for malicious damage and the news that the sexual harassment case, which had gone quiet, is coming to court soon, with damning new corroborative evidence. And finally, there's the release of information on Dodge's part in the brothel scam.

The local court hadn't needed much convincing that Dodge had deliberately sought out the photographic exhibition and vented his spleen on the photographs of Paula. He was found guilty and given a heavy fine. And a warning that a repeat of this type of behaviour would lead to jail. The beak was especially scathing of Dodge's behaviour given his status as an elected representative. His story is the talk of Fremantle and local residents are seen laughing and joking in the streets.

But that's just the start of Dodge's problems. The latest **Fremantle Messenger** leads with an article detailing Dodge's part in the attempted scam that would have seen the FRA's health centre used as a brothel.

The **Messenger** report quotes a police source as saying,

'We suspected there was something untoward with this application and when we checked, we found that the applicants were involved in the brothel business. We know the applicants have connections in the criminal world and are currently investigating just why Councillor Dodge sponsored the original application and made clear his support for what turns out to be a ruse. We have strong grounds to suspect that money has already illegally changed hands on this proposal.'

No one at the FRA was available for comment. Following his resignation, Fred Chewis mysteriously disappeared to an unknown overseas destination.

However, the police representative on the FRA, one Sgt Bill Murkitt has plenty to say. Murkitt had cleverly been able to extricate himself from the matter and lay the blame elsewhere. He's quoted as saying he's glad the police checks had got to the truth behind this proposal.

'I'd always suspected there was something wrong with this application, and I only voted in favour following assurances that all was above board.'

Since Chewis has disappeared, Murkitt knows that this would point the finger back to Dodge. This left Dodge with very few allies and no one to back his protestations of innocence. His story was further undermined by the young planner who had dealt with the matter when it first came to council. Having just resigned his position and gone to greener pastures, the planner felt able to say that he had been 'conned and unduly pressured by Dodge to support the application in the first place.'

Dodge denies the allegations, claiming that he was acting under orders. He wouldn't elaborate and besieged from all sides, the pressure on him to resign from council grew. It had finally become too much to withstand, when he was found guilty of the vandalism charge and then, the very next day, charged with official corruption and fraud.

This quiet Sunday morning, Dodge decides to mark his final time on council by retrieving his personal belongings from council premises and then beat a hasty retreat. He flushes as he bends to the task at his desk and filing cabinet, the building is heating up, the air conditioning not operating because of the weekend. His excessive weight makes the task physically demanding and beads of sweat fall from his brow and smudge the collection of papers and other items he shovels into a couple of large cartons.

By the time he leaves with the cartons on a trolley, he's looking dishevelled and feeling uncomfortable. His gaudy tropical shirt is marked by dark sweat stains at the underarms, his ill-fitting shorts are spotted with blue and red by ink that leaked from a set of pens he greedily stuffed into his pocket, and his shoes are covered with accumulated dust from the papers he removed.

As he emerges from the building through a rear entrance leading into a narrow laneway, he's in an even fouler mood and swears incessantly under his breath. Ignoring signs warning **Caution: Maintenance in Progress**, he struggles to push the heavily laden trolley over a large water pipe, a remnant from the unfinished plumbing job in the vicinity.

As the trolley finally mounts the pipe, his foot strikes a temporary join further along and water sprays everywhere as the join comes unstuck. The force of the resulting water jet causes the cartons to fall from the trolley and Dodge goes down while the trolley falls uselessly back to where he'd started.

'Fuck!' he shouts as he falls heavily among a pile of bursting cartons, papers and stationery all going mushy as the water continues to gush from the leak. At this point a dark figure, dressed in clothing far too heavy for the weather, emerges from behind a nearby pile of rubble and laughs ominously as he unceremoniously kicks Dodge in the ribs with a steel-capped boot.

Dodge groans as he tries to turn over and identify his attacker. But the gloved figure kicks Dodge again and again, this time around the neck and head, and warns him to stay still or there'll be more in store.

'Christ Dodge, you could get a part in a comedy routine!' the figure says, laughing all the while.

'Shit, you bastard, lay off,' Dodge manages through a growing mist of pain. 'Who the fuck are you anyway?' he asks, sensing the attack has been well rehearsed.

'Let's just say my name is M and that we have a mutual friend who's keen to catch up with you. He tells me you stuffed up the brothel deal good and proper, and now he reckons you've got it coming!' growls his assailant.

'Bloody Sizall sent you. Shit, what the fuck has he ordered you to do?' asks Dodge in desperate voice.

'You'll soon find out, but not here,' replies M. 'Just get up quietly, give me the keys to your car. We'll just be going on a short drive.'

To emphasise his intent, M takes a pistol from his pocket as he leans down over Dodge. He presses the glock against Dodge's temple and clicks off the safety catch. Dodge soon responds, groggily rising to his feet, terror in his eyes, and hands over the car keys. He grips his head in pain, blood seeping from wounds the attack has left.

They soon reach the car. His assailant unlocks it and pushes Dodge into the driver's seat at gunpoint. There's no one about. M climbs into the passenger seat and hands the keys to Dodge, ordering him to drive away.

'And don't draw attention to us or you're history,' M says, keeping the gun trained squarely at Dodge's chest.

They drive south for ten minutes or so to the defunct South Fremantle power station, which stands on the coast surrounded by mostly vacant land, a solitary monument to a former era when it was surrounded by industry. They get out, Dodge at gunpoint, and enter the derelict building, which echoes their footsteps as they make their way to a cement apron deep inside the building.

A tall figure stands waiting for them, Jack Sizall.

'Well, Doug, looks like it's your lucky day!' enthuses Sizall in a voice full of menace. 'Not only do you finish up at council, but it seems you and I are finished too. You stupid bastard, how did you let the brothel deal get away, especially after all those promises, eh?'

'Fuck, Jack, you must see that it was out of my control. Bloody Murkitt spilled the beans and blamed me, the prick, just to take the heat off himself. He's the one you should be going for, not me!' whines Dodge.

'That's not the way I see it. I don't know why you're so dark about Murkitt. I mean, just this week he was cleared of any involvement in the bungled shooting of your bloody double-crossing Mayor. You're lucky they haven't checked you out yet! And on the brothel deal, if you'd done your homework properly you would have known that stupid fucking planner, what was his name, er, Wide?'

'Narrow,' interjects Dodge.

'Yeah, him,' growls Sizall. 'Anyways it was obvious to me he would eventually spill the beans. Murkitt was merely protecting *my* interests, something you certainly haven't done. The paper made it sound as if you were going to try and pin the whole thing on me, you fucking insect!'

Sizall spits in his face.

Dodge attempts unsuccessfully to clean off the spittle.

'No, no, you've got it all wrong, I was never going to give anything about you away.'

'I've heard enough of your excuses, Doug, it's time you were taught a lesson!' Sizall said, his voice rising in threat.

"Don't shoot!' cries Dodge in alarm, seeing M raise the gun and point it in his direction.

Sizall nods, a shot is fired, Dodge feels a searing pain in his knee and slumps to the ground.

'Right, Dodge, that'll do for now,' seethes Sizall as he bends over the bleeding Dodge and shouts into his ear. 'Any attempt on your part to dob me in, and the next bullet is for your brain, understand?'

Sizall grabs Dodge's watch and throws it to M. M puts the pistol minus any bullets into Dodge's outstretched hand. They leave the building and speed away in a car that had been secreted out of sight.

Dodge is left clutching his leg in a vain attempt to ease the pain and stem the flow of blood from his shattered knee.

Shortly after they leave the scene, M uses Dodge's watch to put in a call to emergency services, reporting an apparent case of accidental shooting. Dodge is rushed to the hospital an hour later. As the ambulance speeds away from the scene, already crawling with police investigators, Dodge writhes in pain, but realises dimly that this is hardly the end he had in mind for his political career.

CHAPTER 32

UNDERGROWTH

Chris is exhausted. Two weeks into the new job, his role as Minister for planning, transport, and the environment is taking a toll on his increasingly disorganised life. He never imagined having to deal with so many issues at the one time, and even his extensive new complement of staff are unable to keep up.

Coming into his large ministerial office this morning, his tiredness is reinforced by the return of hay fever. He hasn't had enough sleep for days, a result of trying to come up to speed on the myriad problems his departments are dealing with. Even the spectacular view of the river and the sprawling metropolis beyond from his office on the thirty-fifth floor of a city tower is of little comfort.

Neither is his relationship with Diana, which despite his hopes had not become intimate again. Diana's reluctance and her growing attachment to Paula kept her from crossing the line back to Chris. Paula was also becoming a key part of the new government's face. She accepted the FRA job with fervour, looking forward to starting as Chair.

Chris hopes to finish off the large pile of briefing papers he started working through on his train journey to the city, only to be confronted by a series of meetings and delegations that had somehow found their way into his diary. After several groups come and go, he's at the end of his tether.

'OK, Mike,' he says wearily to his former electorate officer, now his chief advisor, 'what's this next bloody group, Friends of the Forest, coming in to lobby about?'

'They're the umbrella group for the forest industry, in this case lobbying for the proposed pulp mill.'

'Really . . . they should be seeing the Minister for Economic fucking Development, not me,' Chris goes on grumpily. 'They know my attitude on this one, after all I've bagged it heaps of times! But I'd forgotten about their umbrella organisation. These days the names of groups often mean the opposite of what they really are. We've just had the Friends of the Wetlands come in to lobby me to support plans to put the Rockingham Highway through the wetlands. As if I would! They claim the freeway will mean less traffic in the nearby residential areas where they live. Never mind the wetlands. The Wetlands Action Group on the other hand, who came in last week, is vehemently opposed to this road!'

'Life's confusing for the new Minister?' Mike chides.

Chris laughs. 'Right Mike, I am going overboard here. Show the fuckers in, but let's sit down later and see if we can organise a better way of doing things in here. I really don't need to see groups that don't support our environmental agenda. *And* I need to get out of the office more.'

Chris stretches and looks outside ruefully.

'I've got to take a more dynamic approach to this new job!'

'Suits me boss, the place works much better when you're not here!' Mike jokes.

Impatiently, Chris waves him out of the office.

The delegation pushing the pulp mill get short shrift. Chris is dogmatic that there's no way he can support the proposal, on environmental or any other grounds. The only chink of hope he leaves for them is a suggestion that he *might* support a mill if it used a raw material other than native hardwoods and if its industrial process isn't reliant on environmentally harmful chemicals.

This isn't at all what the so-called Friends of the Forest had in mind, and the meeting confirms that they need to work hard against this new government to try and restore a more 'sensible' one to power.

'Right might have been dodgy, but Burnside is just off the planet. He always did sound like a bloody eco-nut to me!' one of the delegation observes on the way out.

Later in the day, Chris and Mike agree over a few beers that it would be better all round if Chris saw as many groups on their home territory rather than in the ministerial offices. And he won't accept invitations or delegations from industry groups as such.

Instead, Chris's office will organise events where industry and community views can both be heard and where they might be able to work towards community-based rather than industry-driven solutions.

As to outside visits, Chris proposes to start with his old friends in Nannup, to check progress on their campaign against the mill.

'Bloody good idea' Mike agrees, 'I forgot to tell you that you've been invited down to a town meeting on that very topic next weekend. They're keen to hear what the new government has in mind.'

'Yeah, well, so am I,' Chris complains. 'Elaine has been sitting on this one for a while. I know she doesn't like the current proposal, but the influence of the timber unions on the ALP is still there. The whole topic is up for discussion in a few weeks. Meantime, Nannup, here I come!'

The job is suddenly looking more attractive.

A couple of days later, Chris is in his favourite country town again, still tired but glad to be out of the city. Francine, now his chief environmental adviser, is with him. To the delight of the locals, the new Minister and his officer arrive by bus, after taking the train to Bunbury.

There are few passenger railways outside Perth, but one of them reaches south to Bunbury, from which Nannup is only a short drive. Chris is keen to see the passenger rail network extended. In the meantime, he'll support public transport in the country just as he does in the city.

As they alight from the bus, a local jazz band strikes up, part of a colourful welcome. Nadine is first in the queue to greet Chris. Simon, Sheree and the feral forest crew are there too and smile broadly when

Chris and Francine wave in their direction. Chris hugs Nadine with relish, glad to be back among old friends. Nadine slyly puts a joint in Chris's shirt pocket, winking and whispering into his ear, 'I hear the new Minister is a real dope fiend.'

'I'm glad the green grapevine is still working well. I look forward to sharing it with you,' returns Chris, relaxing.

'Me too.'

Nadine holds on to his arm as he chats to Simon and then cuts across their conversation with, 'before you guys get lost reminiscing, you need to come to our meeting on the pulp mill. Detha Shioban will be there to put the Greens' perspective. She reckons there's a real chance Hipper'll agree to a new agenda on the mill. But we want to talk to you and them about what an ecologically friendly mill really means. Some of us are not too happy about the compromises that could be involved. I mean Right's mob claim their mill would be environmentally friendly too.'

'Yeah, but we both know that's bullshit. I was talking to Francine on the way down, telling her about the bloody Friends of the Forest who came to see me a few days ago. They weren't impressed when I mentioned that a *really* ecologically friendly mill might now be on *our* political agenda,' Chris laments.

'Well, it's a big question down here,' says Nadine, 'we've got a discussion going to see if we can resolve differences within the local community. And that could help bridge the gap between the bloody timber workers and us. Of course, many of them are desperate for a job and some are still behaving like arseholes when we run our forest actions. But others are talking to us about just what sort of mill, if any, would be acceptable.'

'Great,' says Chris, 'Francine has been researching all of that. You'll find some of her material will help.'

It certainly did at the meeting that followed. The point which raised most eyebrows and caused most reaction was centred on another approach to the pulp mill question altogether. Francine told the meeting that the only way to get a *truly* environmentally friendly pulp mill was to go for a new raw material altogether.

'Not the native hardwoods of jarrah, karri, and marri. And not plantation timber either, because that's needed as a substitute for native hardwood chips. In any case, blue-gum and pine plantations are already causing damage to the fragile soils. But good old hemp, the non-hallucinogenic, non-THC, variety.'

'I prefer the other, actually!' quips Nadine, holding up a joint.

'Give over, I know you love the other variety, so do I, but seriously, hemp offers a viable alternative to wood for the production of pulp and paper. Hemp was widely used in the past for paper-making, not to mention clothing and rope. It was only the bloody big American chemical companies with their synthetic alternatives that put hemp out of business. The rest is history. These days, you need a special licence to grow the stuff in bulk, even the non-THC varieties! But an increasing number of experimental crops have shown it has great potential for paper production.'

The crowd loves it. A jocular discussion follows, and the meeting agrees that hemp is the best choice as raw material, in fact the only acceptable one if the pulp mill is to go ahead.

Chris backs Francine to the hilt and goes on to say that he'll only back the mill if hemp is given priority.

Detha Shioban expresses enthusiasm for the idea, which has been a topic of interest in the Greens for years. At the last discussion, doubts had been raised about the commercial viability of hemp crops, given past failures.

'Yeah, that's all the bloody Greens do these days, talk! How about some action?' a wag in the audience shouts.

This prompts Shioban to undertake to raise the hemp option in discussions with the Premier. As the meeting breaks up, Chris and his crew are surprised to see Gabor Soraszem and Greg Jones of TVTV climbing out of a crowded car.

'G'day Chris, or should I say Minister?' says Greg, with a wry grin, and the two hug. It's the first time they've met face-to-face since Chris's promotion.

'Greg, what a surprise. Thought you'd be in Fremantle?' Chris inquires, grinning back.

Greg explains that as a new member of TVTV's board, he's been pressing for a TV special on hemp for a while, since it had always been one of his hobbyhorses. And so here they are to record interviews with some of the leading players.

'Pity you missed the meeting, Francine was in top form,' says Chris.

'Pity you didn't let us know about it,' shoots back Greg.

Chris makes a note to tell his press officers to put TVTV more firmly in the loop.

Francine is thrilled to have the opportunity to reach a wider audience and so gives an upbeat summary to the cameras. While waiting for their own interviews, others in Chris's party drift down to the nearby Park to enjoy the joint that Nadine had given Chris earlier. Several others light up and the usual Nannup hemp is again the order of the day.

CHAPTER 33

TRIALS OF THE HEART

Emilio Muscatelli's trial promises plenty of controversy. Paula is unable to appear as her brother's defence lawyer since when all was said and done, he had shot her. The question the jury has before it is whether the shooting was intentional as the prosecution claim, or whether it was accidental and carried out when Emilio was in a confused mental state as the defence has it. And then there's the question of duress from the gang of conspirators that Emilio claims he was acting for.

Emilio has made a good recovery from his mental agitation, and his drug addiction is now under control, thanks to support from his family and the continuing treatment programme. By the time of the trial, Emilio is working as an orderly in his sister's mayoral offices. There he has already become a popular figure, owing to a well-developed sense of humour and a clear pride in working for his sister. He also makes a mean cup of coffee, and people on return visits invariably ask for Emilio as barista. Paula's especially fond of his lattes, and having him working in her office is a particular pleasure. Their mother is chuffed and loves to fuss around them both when she delivers the weekly supply of Nona's biscotti.

But all of this is far from the minds of the Muscatelli family as they attend the momentous trial, which draws an even bigger crowd than had the committal hearing.

Lobbying of the new Attorney-General, Yoni McNamara, to have the case against Emilio dropped has failed to alter the course of events. Though sympathetic to their cause and saying so publicly, Yoni is obliged to tell them the matter is out of her hands and has to be left to the Director of Public Prosecutions.

The DPP has to be seen as independent. While this principle is frequently breached, the Hipper government is determined to restore ethical standards. In the end, the Director rules that the trial go ahead, concluding that the alleged perpetrator of a shooting has to be brought before the courts, no matter what the circumstances.

The matters raised in Paula's statutory declarations, which she attempted to tender at his bail hearing, were also submitted to the DPP and the Corruption Commission. But the authorities have so far concluded that the statements do not provide any useable evidence of a shooting conspiracy. Those supposedly involved have all denied it and produced alibis.

At the trial, Emilio is far from the bedraggled figure Paula identified as kith and kin in the lock-up. He looks fit and trim, has regained a healthy tan over the summer, and cuts a handsome figure in the dock. The court artist's impressions give him a distinguished look that helps gain public sympathy.

The **Worst Australian** and the telescreen editorials pontificate over the 'threat which the shooting poses to free speech and open government' and insist on the 'need to bring this allegedly dangerous man to trial in the public interest'. Yet it's clear as the trial proceeds that the majority are empathetic to Emilio and certainly don't want to see him jailed.

Through a leading QC, the prosecution opens the case with a long diatribe about the evil man before them. The QC ends with a claim that Emilio is a desperate and dangerous criminal, whose actions threatened the very basis of government and democracy. Emilio is a known drug dealer, an unreliable person and one who carried out the shooting as a result of a long-standing grudge against his sister. Having realised the extent of his evil doing, he now seeks, with no viable evidence, to lay the blame on an unlikely set of circumstances and a shadowy circle of criminals.

Emilio sits passively in the dock at this attack, but Darlene Pocket QC defends him ably.

'Your Honour and members of the jury. This man is accused of attempting to murder his sister. We will show that this shooting was neither deliberate nor malicious. Indeed, my client, through brave action, was able to subvert a sinister conspiracy to assassinate his sister, the Mayor of Fremantle. A conspiracy organised by professional criminals. While the crown does not acknowledge the existence of this conspiracy, we will produce concrete evidence of its existence. The jury should also know that were it not for the rules of the court, I would not be standing here today, but the accused would be represented by his sister, also a QC, and the victim of the accidental shooting.'

This is all too much for the prosecution, whose own QC rises to his feet and raises an objection, 'Your Honour, the defence talks of concrete evidence of a conspiracy. But so far, all we have in our possession is a copy of a declaration from the accused, the very document they previously tried unsuccessfully to have tendered. Do they have other documents they are planning to tender at the last minute, and if so, why haven't we been given copies? In any case, the claims in the original document have been investigated by the relevant authorities and found wanting as concrete evidence. I submit that they are, in fact, a concoction, and I ask therefore what other basis the defence will rely on to establish their unlikely conspiracy case?'

'Ahem.' The Judge clears his throat. 'The prosecution raises some interesting points, although I presume the defence has an answer, or does it, Ms. Pocket? I trust you're not overstating your case to get public attention?'

Pocket glares at the prosecution bench, but replies amicably to the Judge, 'definitely not Your Honour. As to the documents in question, they are certainly not a concoction. We will also draw on the testimony of witnesses to the events in question. These witnesses are listed in document A6 as tendered to the court, and copies are in the hands of the prosecution. We believe these people will convincingly confirm the existence of a conspiracy.'

'Very well, Ms. Pocket. Please proceed.'

Pocket quickly summarises the rest of the defence and the trial is under way.

By the end of the first week, the prosecution case is well advanced and Emilio's stocks are down. He's been painted by witnesses as an irresponsible character dealing in drugs, one who became addicted to the substances in which he traded.

He took on the shooting for personal reasons, to get back at his estranged sister. He used the alleged conspiracy as a cover. Police witnesses to the shooting, in Constable Walters and Sergeant Murkitt, testify that there was no pushing of the gunman as Emilio claims. Under cross-examination by Pocket, Murkitt was forced to admit he didn't have a clear view of Emilio during the incident, but the arresting officer Walters stuck to his story. He also claims he saw Emilio lining up a second shot when they nabbed him.

Pocket's defence demonstrates a different slant on the story. She has the court sit through TVTV's video of the incident, which had caught Emilio lining up to shoot. Most people had already seen this when broadcast. But by slowing the video down and taking it frame by frame, Pocket points out that you can also detect a falling branch brush the gunman's lower arm as he discharges the weapon. At the time, Emilio had felt but not seen this object and had mistaken it for a push. But it clearly changed the trajectory of the shot fired.

Pocket then has Emilio go through his version of events, the whole saga of his disappearance, the assumption of a false identity, and the extent of his descent into the world of heroin dealing and addiction. A world that seriously clouded his judgments.

Pocket then turns to the matter of the alleged shooting conspiracy, which Emilio claimed he had been forced to join. A new witness is called. He sports a beard and tattoos, has a close-shaven head, and exudes a hostile demeanour.

Some in the gallery, the same crew with dark glasses and suits as were at the bail hearing, groan as they see X, another standover man in Sizall's gang, recently jailed for drug importation and distribution.

This followed the raids at Nannup, from which Sizall somehow escaped. X had been forced to take the rap. The jail term was far tougher than predicted, and he was dark at Sizall as a result.

He contacted Pocket from jail, offering to testify on the conspiracy matter, having been a witness at the meeting where Emilio was set up for the shooting. He hoped information he had already provided to the DPP would help to snare Sizall on this and other charges.

Lawyers advised that this tactic would probably also help tone down the severity of charges and penalties the witness would face on other matters, including his earlier failure to alert the authorities about the shooting conspiracy.

The prosecution object to the witness, arguing that, as a convicted drug dealer who had denied the charges, he would be unreliable. Further, they argue that the matter of the alleged shooting conspiracy should not be heard at this trial. This because the ongoing investigation has so far not produced enough evidence for the DPP to press any charges.

But the Judge overrules them, stating that the matter of the conspiracy needed to be addressed since it was fundamental to the case before them.

Getting straight to the point, Pocket asks X, 'Can you tell the court what was your involvement with Muscatelli before the shooting?'

'Muscatelli didn't call himself that then, he was Gino Lamazza, bikie and drug dealer. Any rate, I was a witness to a meeting where he was set up to shoot the Mayor.'

'Paula Muscatelli, Emilio's sister?'

'Yeah, of course, but Lamazza didn't let on he was related to the fucker he was s'posed to wipe out!'

'Right, he was acting under a false identity?'

'Yeah, sure was, and he fooled all of us.'

'Evidently. Now can you tell us who was present at that meeting?'

'Fred Sizall, Bill Murkitt. Lamazza, er, Muscatelli and . . . oh and yeah, me.'

'And why were you there?'

'Usual reasons, to look after Mr. Sizall. I'm his . . . well, I *was* his bodyguard.'

The Judge intervenes and asks the witness, 'Do you realise just who you are implicating here? When you say Bill Murkitt, I presume you do *not* mean Sgt Bill Murkitt of the Fremantle police?'

'Course I do, Judge, he's as bent as they come.'

The courtroom fills with laughter and chatter until the Judge calls for order and says in and agitated manner, 'witness, please, I'm the Judge here, not you! Kindly leave out your opinions of the people you are naming . . . that is a matter for the courts!'

'OK, Judge, whatever,' X returns casually.

As this is happening, several people crane their necks around to the courtroom doors as a figure looking very much like Murkitt scurries from the court at double-quick speed. Some press follow in his wake. Pocket resumes questioning.

'Now, Mr. X, just what transpired at this meeting?'

'Er, sorry?' says the witness, looking puzzled.

'Please tell us about the setup,' says Pocket patiently.

'Oh yeah, well, like I heard Sizall and Murkitt tell Lamazza to get rid of Paula Muscatelli.'

'By get rid of, you mean kill, murder?'

'Fuckin' oath! Er I mean yeah, that's it.'

'And what did Muscatelli say?'

'He reckoned no way, but they heavied him.'

'How?'

'Told him they'd dob him in for drug deals he'd been involved in. He hated that, protested, but they reckoned *he* might just get rubbed out if he said no.'

'You mean murdered?'

'Sure. That's what's on the cards for them what gives Sizall the finger.'

'So Muscatelli or Lamazza agreed to carry out the shooting?'

'Well yeah, wouldn't you?'

Pocket looked momentarily non-plussed and laughter rippled around the courtroom.

'Less of the histrionics, if you please. Remember I'm asking the questions, not the other way around! A simple yes or no will suffice.'

'Yeah, yeah, OK, what else d'ya wanna know?'

'What happened after Muscatelli agreed?'

'Er, they said they'd give him two weeks to do the job, said he should keep quiet about the whole deal. Ya know, if he got busted he was to say it was all his idea.'

The Judge intervenes again, 'and knowing that this was going to happen, you made no effort to let the police know. Why not, there's an offence called conspiring to pervert the course of justice, you know.'

'Yeah Judge, er, Your Honour, I know that, the DPP reckon I still might be charged with it! There's no way I would've told the cops. When you work for the big boys like Sizall, the rules are different. If I'd spilt the beans, I would've been wiped out meself.'

The Judge looks quizzically at Pocket.

'No further questions, Your Honour,' says Pocket.

The prosecution do their best to discredit the testimony, drawing attention to X's long criminal record, even if it was not strictly relevant, as Pocket frequently objects. But the die may have already been cast, for as soon as the cross-examination is complete, the Judge calls an adjournment while he considers the implications.

He returns to a packed courtroom half an hour later and announces, 'given the testimony this afternoon by our new witness, Mr. X, I have no choice but to abort this trial on grounds that the accused may not have acted alone and may well have been acting under duress. I trust that now this testimony has been given, the DPP will take the matter further and bring forward conspiracy charges relating to all involved in this shooting, if appropriate. Until then, Mr. Muscatelli, you are free to go.'

Cheers and laughter fill the courtroom. Emilio is surrounded by well-wishers, and Paula comes forward and hugs him with a strength even she didn't know she had. They leave the court arm-in-arm weeping with emotion and joy. A hero's welcome awaits the Mayor and her brother outside.

CHAPTER 34

COLLUSION

Sizall is furious. He's keen to exact revenge on his former bodyguard and needs to get his contacts in the prison system on to the job. For that to work smoothly, he consults Murkitt.

Finding Murkitt is a problem however, for he had gone to ground following the damaging evidence given at Emilio's trial. He'd been suspended from the police force pending further inquiries by the DPP and the Corruption Commission, which were accelerated by the Judge's admonitions.

Eventually, Sizall tracks him down through other contacts and Murkitt reluctantly agrees to meet the following Sunday night. The meeting place is the service end of the top floor of a multi-storey car park in a side street off the strip. He knew this corner of the car park was just out of range of security cameras and the telescreen. The car park itself had been a controversial project in the centre of Fremantle, ironically partly funded by Sizall's drug money.

Sizall arrives half an hour short of closing time, in his black super-charged hybrid Commodore, to find Murkitt emerging from a little-used stairwell. The floor is empty of other cars as Sizall gets out, flanked by a new and even more powerfully built bodyguard, and proceeds arrogantly to the front of the car where the bodyguard laid out some paper and white powder on the bonnet, and retired to the shadows.

Sizall bends over the bonnet and snorts some cocaine and then invites Murkitt to join him before they get down to business.

'Top quality this shit. Just arrived from a new source, does wonders for the mind!

Murkitt sniffs deeply.

'Fuckin' oath, yeah, that feels better already.'

'Good. Now listen. We're both in deep shit unless we can get rid of that fucking former bodyguard of mine. Can you help there?'

'A bit difficult now I've been suspended,' says Murkitt quietly.

'That's your problem not mine, Bill. Just get on to it, right?'

'Hold on to your hat, mate. I'll find a way. But there's another problem in the form of Emilio Muscatelli! What the fuck are we going to do about him?'

'More like what the fuck are *you* going to do about him, Bill!' Sizall turns on Murkitt in a gloating manner.

'What the fuck are you on about?'

'Come on, Bill, you're not nearly so useful to me now you've been sprung!' replies Sizall, 'and that means you've just got to be more cooperative.'

'Shit, Jack, if you think I'm just going to become another of your bovver boys, you've got another thing coming!' Murkitt's trying to put on a brave face as the change in their relative power sinks in.

'Is that a threat?' Sizall is incredulous, his patience wearing thin despite the cocaine.

'No, but just remember that I've still got plenty on you if the investigating cops get too heavy with me. Information they could use to haul you in,' returns Murkitt smugly.

'You'll be in trouble if you keep on with that line.' Sizall summons his bodyguard with a slight incline of his head. The bodyguard wastes no time fronting Murkitt, grabbing him forcefully by the arms and frog-marching him to the concrete rail edging a porch jutting out from the top floor of the car park.

He pushes Murkitt's head down to give him a better appreciation of the fifteen metres or so between him and the pavement below. Murkitt fights down his fear but Sizall, who now draws a pistol, is enjoying the spectacle.

'Hang him over the edge, just so he knows what's at stake!'

The bodyguard uses his wrestler's strength to lift a protesting, squirming Murkitt so that he's dangling perilously over the edge. Murkitt goes still with fright.

'Just lift him back gently. We want him alive and you drop the gun Sizall,' says a voice from the shadows.

Sizall turns to see guns trained on him and the bodyguard. They're held by a couple of goons and Sizall realises that another gang honcho – probably Lilliano – is lurking behind, giving the orders. Turf warfare between the two gangs has heated up recently, and Sizall guesses that Murkitt tipped them off about tonight's meeting. Lilliano had parked a few floors below and climbed up the same stairwell that Murkitt had used.

'You two-timing bastard, Murkitt!' hisses Sizall, dropping the gun as the bodyguard lifts Murkitt back over the parapet. They now face the goons as Lilliano emerges from the shadows and spits in Sizall's direction.

'Two-timing he may be, but we need him more than you do, Sizall.' Lilliano is all contemptuous swagger. Murkitt looks relieved as he squats and takes a few deep breaths in an attempt to restore his shattered nerves.

Lilliano comes over to him and pats him on the back, lights a cigarette for him and then addresses Sizall, 'now it's your turn to be scared Jack, just go over to that wall where you were threatening to drop Murkitt. And you,' he orders the hapless bodyguard, 'stay right there.'

Sizall shuffles unwillingly over to the wall, aware that the goon's gun follows his every step.

'Now up on the wall!' orders Lilliano.

Sizall looks back with hate.

'Fuck off!'

He's looking to delay the inevitable, but complies with the order, terror written all over his ageing face as one of the goons cocks his gun.

'Your choice now Jack. Jump by the time I count to 10, or you'll be pushed.'

'1, 2, 3, 4, not jumping yet? I mean you could survive, your hide's so bloody thick, 5, 6.' Sizall is looking desperate as his bodyguard looks on helplessly. '7, 8, 9.'

One of the goons comes close to Sizall, who at the last minute tries to draw a gun hidden in his coat. He's quickly dispatched over the edge by the goon as Lilliano reaches 10. A sickening thud is heard a second later as Sizall bounces off the thick glass awnings and hits the pavement below. He doesn't move. A knot of pedestrians, until then oblivious to the drama above their heads, scream and rush forward as if transfixed when they see the body spread on the footpath.

Above, the goon satisfies himself that Sizall is dead, then ducks out of sight and signals the thumbs up to Lilliano. He moves over to Sizall's bodyguard and king-hits him with his gun. The bodyguard slumps down with a thump, and the group retreat to Sizall's car, dragging the bodyguard behind them. They shove him roughly into the boot of the car before exiting the car park.

With Murkitt hidden in the back seat, they screech down the ramps to the exit. On the ground floor the car park attendant, who has heard or seen none of the drama, is about to shut up shop for the night. Just as he emerges from his booth, he watches in horror as Sizall's car speeds past, crashes straight through the flimsy exit barrier, and heads off at high speed. At the same time, the frightened pedestrians draw his attention to the body on the pavement.

The attendant calls 000. The police arrive soon afterwards, but have little to go on until Detective Schilz arrives on the scene. 'Shit, it's Jack Sizall!' he exclaims. 'Looks like Bert Lilliano's mob must have caught up with him at last,' Schilz goes on knowingly.

'You realise it's now gang warfare?' says Murkitt as he emerges from hiding and they speed south to Lilliano's hideaway.

'Yeah, well, it'll be worth it!' Lilliano is emphatic. 'With Sizall out of the way, I reckon we can soon get the Freo patch back all to our lucky selves!'

'About time,' says Murkitt. 'But shit, you know I'm not gonna be able to help you much for a while,' he adds ruefully. 'Looks like I'm really in the shit over this Muscatelli racket!'

'Well Bill, we've still got plenty on the Corruption Commission's people. Once we remind them of that and with Sizall now out of the way, I think you'll find this conspiracy business just quietly fades away,' Lilliano says confidently. 'And if you don't get back into the cop shop, remember there's always a job here for you.'

'Jeez thanks Bert, I was beginning to think my days in crime were over,' he jokes.

'No way josé! returns Lilliano and hands Murkitt a cold beer from the car fridge. He drinks greedily, starting to recover from the earlier ordeal. *This is how I prefer to do business,* he thinks hazily.

The conversation turns to politics as they reach Lilliano''s well-bunkered headquarters, an hour's drive south. Murkitt's keen to know just how Lilliano figures he'll go under Hipper's new government. Lilliano is keen for company to share his full fridge of beer with, and so a real bender begins.

'Yeah well, Hipper's a canny bitch,' is Lilliano's assessment after a snort of cocaine. 'But if she reckons she can straighten out this State's ways of doing business, she's deluding herself. I mean, that building and development mob have been running WA for too long to give up without a fight!'

'Sure have!' agrees Murkitt enjoying another snort himself. 'But that prick Burnside is always trying to stop their fun.'

'Bloody Burnside, yeah, but basically he's pretty naïve. I mean, I hear he's got some dirt on us,' says Lilliano. 'But he's still not able to control the cops, they'll never go for us as long as we're doing business with them. And that reminds me Bill, you've gotta find a replacement contact for us while you're under suspension.'

'Already organized Bert, I'll give you the details.' Murkitt smirks as he starts on his fourth beer.

He unsteadily writes down contact details for his temporary replacement at Fremantle, someone not as wily but probably as reliable a source of inside information as Murkitt. The conversation then switches to former Premiers Right and Cloke and how their new situations will affect the crime scene.

'Hell,' says Lilliano, 'with Right and his mob going down, and with Cloke likely going down with 'em, the pickings for the likes of Roberts and his union mates are going to get thinner for a while.'

Lilliano is referring to an investigation, which has just been set up by Hipper to complete the work that the HIP group had begun. He goes on braggingly, 'but for *us*, at least for our direct income, the pollies have never been that important, in fact they cost us,'

Murkitt raises an enquiring eyebrow. Lilliano elaborates, 'they make the laws, and we have to find ways to get around them. Like the police, some pollies cooperate with us and others don't. Some are satisfied with the occasional drug supply, but others get greedy and demand hefty commissions to avoid them setting the pigs onto us. And the pigs have been getting pretty greedy too, Bill. You should know that.'

'Yeah, I was pretty pissed off about that brothel business collapsing,' says Murkitt. 'And then Sizall's mob fucking up the Muscatelli shooting. You sure have done us a favour there tonight. And by the way, I never thanked you properly for getting that idiot Dodge under control!'

'No wucking furries Bill, I reckon he's out of the picture for quite a while. And we never could have prospered so much without you at the station. Here's to our continuing partnership.'

Lilliano raises his beer, they clink bottles and empty the umpteenth for the night. They then devise a stratagem for tackling the unusual prospect of an honest government in power. By the end of the night, they reckon they have Hipper and the new power group taped.

Murkitt leaves early the next morning. He retrieves his car and heads several hundred kilometres east to Kalgoorlie, a goldfields town on the edge of the desert, one where he's spent a lot of time in the past. Here, he plans to lie low for a few weeks before taking up the next challenge Lilliano has offered.

CHAPTER 35

COLLISION

Chris wakes a happier man, although when he recalls the immediate reason, feels vaguely uneasy. As he stretches and finds the indent in the pillow beside him, still redolent, he recalls how much he and Yoni McNamara enjoyed the space together only a few hours ago.

Yoni left in the early hours after Chris fell asleep. She scrawled a note, which Chris now spies on the bedside table.

'Great night – thanks Chris' it reads. 'But beware complications.'

He guesses Yoni is referring to their drunken discussion before they decided to go to bed together. Yoni then reminded him that she was a married woman and told him that she didn't make a habit of having affairs. *Was she, like him, now feeling guilty?* he wonders.

After all, they had stepped over matrimonial boundaries and Chris still yearns strongly for Sarah Kingsmill. And then there's Diana, even though her ongoing involvement with Paula seems to preclude that yearning ever being satisfied again. Faint hope.

Starting a relationship with Yoni would probably kill off that hope permanently. But does he want to pursue an illicit affair with Yoni? He's been repeatedly warned about the dangers involved. He didn't take Diana's warning about losing his new ministry altogether seriously. And in any case, Chris thrives on danger, although he's on a virtual high-wire here. Well, he has to agree with Yoni; this is complicated!

But what the heck, he thinks, *Yoni is young, attractive, and definitely stirs the adrenalin!* Chris shrugs, gets out of bed, and quickly showers.

As he does, he recalls how the night before had developed seamlessly from a meeting between the two about the transport planning decisions that Chris and the government were facing. He and Yoni met with Mike, Francine and some of Yoni's advisers over dinner in order to explore the legal and other ramifications of attempting to enact what was originally Francine's idea. That is, getting a rail connection to Fremantle.

The concept was always going to be fraught with practical and political difficulties. A huge impediment was that Right had already let the contract for extension of the hills railway to Tough Constructions and the project was now well under way. Sure, the decision had been shown by Diana's HIP dirt file to be based on suspect grounds, and this was one of the factors causing Right's downfall.

The whole question of dodgy deals in government contracts was going to be picked over by the Corruption Commission, whose report was not due for months yet. In these circumstances, Yoni's legal team had concluded there was no way in which the rail contract could be legitimately cancelled. As to the railway's politics, voters in marginal seats were looking forward to its completion, no matter how corrupt the contract allocation process.

This prognosis had been thoroughly explored at the dinner meeting and at that stage, Chris was beginning to feel their dream of getting a line to Fremantle were doomed to failure. But then a chink of light had appeared to lift his gloom.

That was provided by the ever-alert Francine, who had discovered that the fine print of the contract only provided funds for extension of the line to Darlington, a centre in the lower area of the hills district. The intent was then to extend the line to outlying centres, but no funds had been allocated in the contract for this purpose.

'An amazing find, Francine, good on you,' Chris had said. 'But if we drop the extension, we'll face a voter backlash in the Hills suburbs.'

'True', observed Yoni, 'after all, they've been waiting over a decade for this bloody railway!'

'Sure, but in this case, the government just might be able to have its cake and eat it too,' enthused Francine. 'If we change the last section of the line from suburban electric rail line to light rail, that would be heaps cheaper. The funds saved could go on another light rail, this one from Rockingham to Fremantle. In the end, we'll have a sort of passenger rail loop from Perth to Rockingham and back to Fremantle and Perth. Could almost be two for the price of one.'

Chris was ecstatic, but Yoni chimed in, 'sounds interesting, but what's all this about light rail versus suburban rail, why would it be cheaper?'

'Well everyone asks that,' Francine said, 'thing is, light rail is a sort of modern tram, whisper quiet compared to the old rattlers. And they can run down median strips and the like. That way, they're closer to where people want to go and easier for passengers to get to.'

'Hmm, you could be on to a winner here. I reckon you and Chris should take this further, have it costed, and get some community feedback,' responded Yoni encouragingly.

This is one of Chris's tasks today, to get a study of rail alternatives going. As he dresses, he reviews his appointments for the day. First stop a meeting with Francine before heading into the electorate office, an office that was in danger of neglect now that he's preoccupied with ministerial matters. He has new staff there, and he needs to touch base with them more often.

Before heading off for his coffee, another luxury he misses out on too often, he contacts Yoni.

'Oh, hi, Chris,' she says brightly, 'did you get my note?'

'Uh-huh, sure did. But tell me, what sort of complications could there possibly be for a young couple like us?'

'Yeah right, Chris,' she replies laughing lightly, ignoring the fact that Chris is twenty years older. Then her tone becomes more serious. 'Now listen, we're no couple, and I suggest that we don't risk any complications at this stage. You're great, but I don't need an affair so early in my Ministerial career.'

'Alright, I get the message,' Chris says testily. And then trying to keep the light tone of the conversation going and not let her brush-off reach his deeper emotions, 'but just let me know if you want to get complicated at any time!'

'Sure Chris, but don't hold your breath.'

Sensing Chris's bravado and wanting to change the subject, Yoni goes on, 'hey, talking of complications, I was thinking you could probably do with a good publicly minded economist on your rail study?'

'That'd be excellent, but wouldn't such a person be a contradiction in terms?' jokes Chris, knowing Yoni has an economics background herself.

'Hah bloody hah!' she returns. She gives him the contact details for a hot-shot public economics university lecturer who's itching to work with the new government.

Reflecting as he collects his papers, Chris starts to wonder about the wisdom of having indulged in what now looks like a one-night stand. Such encounters always leave him feeling discombobulated and riding a roller-coaster of emotions, elation mixed with wishes that it could go on. But clearly, this one couldn't do that easily. And then what about Diana? Better not give anything away to her, he tells himself as he heads for coffee and breakfast with Francine.

'That's fantastic,' she enthuses, when Chris tells her about Yoni's suggestion on the rail study. 'I'll call this guy today.' She takes a bite from her rye toast with caraway, chews thoughtfully, and then asks in a teasing voice, 'but what's all this palsy-walsy with Yoni, Chris? Is there something I should know about you two?'

'Nothing at all, Francine, we just had a chat and got to know each other better, that's all, OK?' He sounds evasive and Francine can tell he's being defensive.

She says nothing but smiles to herself and makes a mental note to take the matter further with Mike later in the day. Chris tucks into his double order of bacon and eggs. Francine changes the subject by saying, 'Chris, the other thing we have to do something about soon is the Rockingham Highway. We need to get that bloody road off the map!'

'Agreed,' says Chris, frowning. 'You know some in Cabinet are still arguing for it, so Elaine is setting up a sub-committee to examine the issue more closely.'

'More delays, then,' says Francine with a sigh.

'Mmm,' from Chris through his last portion of bacon and eggs. 'They've only got a few weeks to report back. And I've recommended you for research officer to the sub-committee Francine, so you'll have the chance to convince the doubters.'

Francine grimaces and says unhappily, 'shit Chris, I appreciate your confidence, but remember that along with the hemp project and the rail study, I'm going to be bloody busy for the next few months. I'm not sure I can handle the road study too.'

'You know what they say, if you want a job done, give it to a busy person!' opines Chris as he lights up. The wind takes the smoke over Francine, who screws up her nose in disgust while trying to wave it away.

'God, I wish you'd stop smoking Chris, for both our sakes! But listen, while the highway job would be fun, I really would rather someone else did that!'

'But it's one of your pet projects.'

'Don't tell me, another chapter for the Mad Roads book?' she asks in a cynical tone.

'Of course!' Chris responds cheerfully. 'But I hear you, you need help. Maybe someone else in the office can take over the rail study and work with this economist guy. That way, you could keep an eye on it but concentrate on the highway. In a way, the stakes are higher there, as there are a couple of Ministers pushing for the highway for all they're worth.'

'Why so, surely they can see how environmentally damaging the road will be, let alone the other problems it will bring?'

'If only,' says Chris with feeling. 'No, you remember the so-called Friends of the Wetlands who came in to see us a few weeks back? The silly bastards who tried to convince us it is in the best interests of the wetlands to have a huge road built through it?'

'Those mad pricks! I thought, assumed they were all Liberals.'

'Think again. No, a lot of Liberals *are* in favour of the road, but a lot of community minded Libs, like Jill Woodall, are strongly against it. More interestingly, I hear the develop-at-any-cost clique is backing the pro-roaders, you know the bloody Clokeites.'

'So even with Cloke and his acolytes out of the Party, they're still influential?' asks Francine, miffed.

'Apparently so. Mike Chesterfield and his cronies have not yet quit the Parliament. He's got a month or so to go. Seems Chesterfield delayed his resignation date so he could qualify for a bigger super payout. Typical! And even when they quit, others will probably take up the role. There are plenty of bored backbenchers around the traps keen to test Elaine's mettle. And there's still Roberts and his boys, including Cloke, putting pressure on from the outside.'

'Will we never be rid of Cloke?' laments Francine.

'He's coming up for trial on corruption charges very soon now, or so Yoni tells me.'

'Oh, so it's Yoni now Chris, is it?

'Give over Francine,' says Chris, bristling and blushing despite himself.

Complications, he thinks again.

Meanwhile, Chris and Francine arrange a new person to work on the rail issue while Francine cranks up the highway research. The prospect fires her up, an issue close to her heart.

Before they finish their conversation, she and Chris promise themselves they'll have an office showing of a TVTV video, recently supplied by Greg Jones, of a special he and Gabor had put together on the highway.

'This TVTV thing seems to have given Gabor a new lease of life,' observes Francine as they get up from their table.

'Better for him than women,' says Chris dryly. But he immediately regrets it as Francine comes back with 'now Chris, now there's a lesson for you!'

He laughs and she waves cheekily at him as she hops on her bike to ride to the station. Chris heads for his office looking decidedly chastened.

CHAPTER 36

COOPERATION

Few political commentators in Perth believe that the new government will last. In a recent TVTV programme, set up by the mercurial Greg Jones, one of the State's well-known political pundits suggested that the very genesis of the alliance, born of a political crisis which had seen the previous administration exposed for corruption then resigning after losing the confidence of a majority of MPs, was cause enough for worry. According to this line of thought, the alliance between Labor, now without its Cloke faction, and a raft of Independents, each standing for different value mixes, looks temporary by definition.

But Chris has a different view. As a Minister, he's amazed by the innovative approach he's seen so far. What the critics fail to recognise is the inherent potency of an alliance headed by a Cabinet with a majority of women, who aim to govern through cooperation rather than domination. They're less interested in numbers than their male counterparts, they aim for consensus rather than majority rule.

In practice however, Chris has observed that in governments run by men, i.e. almost all governments, power devolves to an inner clique centring on the senior ministers of the day. This clique dominates political decisions and invariably gets its own way, helped along by a bevy of political advisers but modified to varying degrees by senior bureaucrats, a la Yes Minister!

First, decisions are pushed through Cabinet, then through the Party room, then through the Parliament. The process relies on a mixture of cajoling and insensitive use of numbers, or failing that, bribing and bullying.

Elaine Hipper has no desire to dominate. She tells the public she wants her government to last until the next election, still two years away. Cynical political watchers suggested that her *modus operandi is* based on the survival instinct rather than political philosophy.

How this philosophy will work in setting up the sub-committee on the Rockingham Highway is a test. Like Chris, Elaine sees this proposed freeway link as an irrelevant relic of times past. She carries the mantle of predecessors that had several socially and environmentally damaging road links taken out of the metropolitan planning scheme, or at least scaled down.

Elaine recognises that the road lobby is a powerful one, and that it does account for the creation and maintenance of many jobs in car dominated Perth. For these reasons, several Labor MPs support the road while others cave in to growing pressure from constituents who take up the cudgels of the road lobby with increasing enthusiasm. The question for Elaine is how can she bring these MPs round to her point of view?

When it comes to answering this question, Elaine looks to Francine as much as to Chris. She's glad he recommended her as researcher. Taking an interest in road issues, Elaine has read and approved of reports Francine has already done for government.

She decides to meet Francine before the first Cabinet sub-committee meeting. They are in Elaine's office close to the Cabinet room, an office that perversely has sweeping views of the city's main interchange leading to the Narrows Bridge.

'Welcome, Francine, forgive the view! I'm moving to another office soon, so I don't have to face this awful sight every day. Have we learnt anything at all since good old Bessie Rischbieth? They share a pot of ginger tea, a brew she likes as much as does Francine.

'Not much I'd say, judging from the arguments the proponents are currently putting forward for the Rockingham Highway!'

'True. But how do you think we can convince them otherwise?' ponders Elaine.

'I'm thinking the best way is to highlight how alternatives such as public transport will cause less damage than the road and create more jobs.'

'Sounds promising but give me some examples.'

'Fair enough. We could use the money to upgrade freight rail services, particularly to and from Fremantle and the new port to the south. We could also go for a light rail route from Murdoch via South Street to Fremantle.'

'Yes, Yoni mentioned that to me the other day. An intriguing idea, but I'm not sure how it will go down with the voting public. Chris tells me you're working on a report. You must be busy, Francine,' observes Elaine.

'You can say that again, Premier.'

'Elaine is better, Francine.'

'Thanks, er, Elaine. I've got help and that transport dude is helping with the costings. From what I've seen so far, I think you'll like his report.'

'Excellent. But to get back to the highway, I'm impressed by your ideas. Keep on about the positives and emphasise alternatives to the road. That way we can present our new policies as natural capitalism, you know, capitalism with a green emphasis. Then no one will be able to accuse us of being anti-development.'

And so it is with all the projects Francine and Chris are involved with. They always present a viable, often cheaper and certainly more environmentally friendly alternative, railways instead of freeways, light rail instead of standard suburban railways, hemp instead of wood. Francine sees with some excitement that this approach marries nicely with Elaine's preferred manner of government.

Elaine later tells Francine that her approach is also helping to soften the sceptics in the new government and was attractive to the Greens in the upper house too. This was important as the Greens had recently signed up with the alliance, giving the government a better chance of getting legislation through both houses of Parliament.

Francine's star is on the rise as a result of all of this. Elaine seeks to second her to the Cabinet office. Chris is none too happy at this idea since he needs Francine in his office. Mike is jealous, believing he has more political nous than Francine.

Maybe he does, but Mike is old school, good at numbers and political strategy, but not so good on consensus. Francine, while chuffed at the offer from Elaine, is also keen to continue with Chris. In the end, it's agreed that she split her time between the two offices. She's keeping a foot in both camps, and she relishes the chance of a direct line to Cabinet.

Diana is also enjoying her new role. She's been appointed Cabinet secretary, a big feather in her cap, since the job often goes to a politician. Elaine knows from working with Diana in recent times that she's just the person to coordinate matters coming before her potentially fractious Cabinet.

Towards the end of the first month of the Hipper government, Diana is due to meet Yoni McNamara to discuss a draft submission from the Attorney-General's office on drug law reform. The draft proposes that policies on harder drugs be modified to put the emphasis on health education rather than punitive measures.

Diana is pondering these questions and poring over the report when Yoni arrives for their meeting. Yoni's body was, as always, in good shape due to a strict diet and exercise regime. Diana takes in her looks with admiration and a little envy, particularly her shapely backside.

'Hi, Yoni, the way you look today, I reckon you're a real callipygian,' she says, smiling playfully.

'You what?' snaps Yoni, not picking up the cue and thinking the worst.

'The word means someone sporting a good arse! Elaine was telling me earlier. We don't qualify, but you're the perfect candidate.'

'Why thanks, Diana,' she says. But once the glow of the compliment fades, Diana noticed that Yoni's face looks unsettled, and as they find a quiet room, she asks Yoni if she is OK.

'I would be if your friend Chris would stop bothering me!' she responds with an imploring look.

'Chris? Why, what has he been up to?' asks Diana, puzzled. Then remembering Chris's reference to Yoni, she asks, 'is this political or personal?'

'Hmm, pretty personal I'm afraid.' Yoni looks down at the carpet. Diana tenses, suspecting something amiss. Yoni looks up and colours as she says, 'Diana, I feel a bit bad about this, knowing that you have a soft spot for Chris, and he tells me he still has designs on you.'

'What, don't tell me you two are having an affair?' Diana asks, shocked.

'No, not an affair. We did sleep together once, but I made it clear to Chris that was it, I don't need the complications, but he's been pressing me to change my mind ever since, he keeps calling or leaving unwanted messages. I'm having hell's own job trying to explain this to my husband. We're having a few problems at present, but I don't want a one-night stand added to the list,' Yoni protests.

'The bastard,' growls Diana. 'Chris is an old friend as you know, and we were intimate there for a while. But that's over and I don't want it to start again, whatever Chris may be thinking. I've warned him about the consequences of sleeping around with all and sundry . . . sorry, Yoni, I didn't mean that as a reflection on you. I take an interest in his love life, but that's more for his welfare than for any romantic reasons.'

'Oh god, Diana, I'm sorry.'

'It's not your fault, Yoni,' Diana responds softly. 'I'll just have to sort this out with Chris. I mean thanks for telling me, the prick hasn't let on about you, so it's time for me to tackle him.'

After that, the talk turns to business, and they agree it's a bit early for Yoni's report to go to Cabinet. Diana offers to talk to the independents and get back to Yoni with suggestions for compromise.

Yoni leaves soon afterwards, not before giving Diana a comforting hug. Diana appreciates Yoni's straightforward approach and they promise to meet again soon.

Diana sends a message to Chris, 'Hey, you deceptive bastard, I need to see you about your Yoni thing.'

Seeing no alternative, Chris agrees to meet at a city bar before Diana heads home.

A few hours later they have a heart-to-heart over a glass of red wine. Diana gives Chris a hard time over his chasing Yoni and points out that her warning about recommending his Cabinet position be taken away still stands.

'Well, of course, that's why I haven't told you,' Chris replies guiltily. 'But in any case, this is a one-night stand, not an affair.'

'Fine line there, Chris! Anyhow, Yoni tells me you've been hassling her for more, so it's not over as far as you're concerned.'

'Hmm, well yes, but her attitude is like a red rag to a bull.'

'Bull in a china shop, I'd say. Damage to your blossoming political career is more than likely the way you're going . . .'

Righto, I hear you, I'll stop hassling Yoni. You know, Diana, I'm not over *us*. I wish you'd come back to me.'

'Less of the violins, you old con man. I think you're just trying to sweeten me up so I won't mention any of this to Elaine.'

'As if.'

'Come on mate, I know you too well for your usual lines to stick!'

'*Well*, you're not my keeper, Diane.'

'No, Chris, but if you don't keep yourself in check, somethings going to give. I hear the telescreen monitors are chasing so-called moral crimes as much as security matters these days.'

'That's ridiculous,' Chris protests. 'We're in Australia here, not Taliban country!'

'If you think I'm exaggerating, have a word to your friend Yoni.'

'What d'you mean?'

'Well, her department is taking up a few cases of so-called moral crimes that the Feds have launched against WA citizens recently.'

'Is that right? Well I'm safe there.'

'Are you Chris, are you really?'

'You mean?'

'You know what I mean mate, just have a look at your track record over the past couple of years.'

'That's preposterous,' Chris exclaims, then more thoughtfully, 'well if they go for me, I may as well give up!'

'There's your message Chris, give up your womanising before it's too late!'

'Ha, bloody ha!'

'Well, you old cynic, it's time I got going.'

Diana gets up to go, leaving Chris to ponder her words.

He stands and tells her he'll stay for a while. He gives her a hug, mentally accepting that she's lost to him as a lover. She looks him in the eye, catches his doleful look, and says,

'Come on man, there's more to life than sex!'

'So they tell me, alcohol for example, think I'll have a whisky!'

Diana trundles off on her way home; Chris orders the drink and reflects on his options.

CHAPTER 37

FREMANTLE REVIVED?

Paula is determined to make the most of the first meeting of the FRA since her appointment as Chair. She's excited that she now has a real chance to take back Fremantle from the dodgy operators and return it to the people, a vindication for all she's been through since becoming Mayor. The FRA Chair is a job she had never contemplated, but given recent turbulent events, she's looking forward to initiating some positive action instead of being on the receiving end of more shocks.

Paula has already spent long hours in the FRA building meeting staff, preparing for her first board meeting, and discussing strategies with her colleagues on the board, old and new. McRafferty is gone, meaning Chris finally gets recognised as the local MP, rather than as a community representative.

The new community rep is Dan Whattington, a veteran campaigner and one-time Councillor. Chris knows he'll work well with Paula. And the new police Superintendent replaces the disgraced Murkitt. The Super is reported to be gradually changing the corrupt Fremantle police culture for the better. 'About time' is the cynical response as word gets around.

The only cloud on the horizon for Paula as she walks into the FRA building for her first board meeting is a more personal matter, a worrying discussion Diana initiated.

Over their usual weekly breakfast that morning, Diana told Paula about her recent conversation with Chris on matters of the heart, the aftershocks from his interactions with Yoni McNamara. She then told Paula of her reservations about continuing their relationship.

Paula had taken all this in with a bit of a shock since she's becoming increasingly fond of Diana. Although Paula didn't spell it out, she hinted that she wanted to make the relationship more permanent, something she rarely contemplates.

In the end they agreed amicably to get away for a few days to try and sort things out. They decided on a weekend at Rottnest Island, a place that neither had been to in years. Rottnest is one of Perth's traditional playgrounds just a few kilometres off the coast.

At least that could be fun, even if we have got difficult things to discuss, Paula reflects as the lift shoots her up to the top floor of the FRA building. She steps out and approvingly surveys the new layout, only just completed.

Paula had set herself up in a more modest and different office from that used by Chewis. The one he occupied was full of bad vibes, and she could almost see the imprints of Murkitt and Chewis on the office chairs. Besides, Diana as a keen student of feng shui, had told Paula that the office was badly placed if it's to be a source of Fremantle's revival.

And that's Paula's new mission. To oversee FRA involvement in a number of projects designed to breathe life back into her beloved city. And to do this in league with her own council and through consultation, not by forcing hands.

As a first step in this direction, Paula raises the possibility of a completely revamped and human scale railway land development scheme. She's already talked to Dan, Chris, and the new police Super and they were very receptive, adding ideas of their own.

The Premier expressed enthusiasm, and Diana asked Paula to send Elaine a written summary and sketch plans, something that the FRA staff were busily working on. In stark contrast to the station high-rise scheme, which Paula had literally fought at risk to her life, this one threatens no one.

Chris comments, 'great Paula, but this time let's get the five to eight storey limit off the agenda too. After I seconded your motion, I copped a lot of flak from the Freo community for supporting that. They reckoned I was being unduly influenced by you!'

'I wonder why anyone would have said that, Chris?' asks Paula, tongue in cheek.

'More malicious gossip don't you think? But on building heights, maybe we should keep it low this time, then they can say I am being unduly influenced by you!' Paula neatly turns the tables. They leave it there for discussion before the board meeting.

Paula's on time for that discussion, but Chris is running late. There's only fifteen minutes before the FRA meeting. By the time he arrives on this hot Friday morning at the tail end of summer, others have drifted in and the meeting's about to start. Chris looks uncomfortably hot in an ill-fitting suit.

Paula takes him aside and teases, 'not like you to be late, Chris. Losing my attraction, am I? Her irony is lost on Chris, but he reckons there's still a frisson as they hug. Despite her other self, Paula enjoys the physical proximity. But she also notices Chris smells distinctly of dope.

What was it he had said previously? 'A little puff before a meeting makes it much more interesting.' Then Chris's real voice cuts in. 'Sorry I'm late, got caught up with a constituent on the building height thing. I told him you seem agreeable to a lower limit,' he says pointedly.

As they unclench Chris momentarily prolongs the physical contact by holding Paula above the elbow. Leaning back and disengaging, Paula smiles and just mouths the words, 'trust me.'

Then cocking her head to one side, she becomes more serious and points her index finger in his direction, 'just remember our agreement, you old dope-head!'

Chris screws up his face and scratches his head in a show of puzzlement, but he knows Paula is referring to an agreement they reached to avoid crossing the lines back into an intimate relationship.

For Paula, whatever happens with Diana and however much Chris still occasionally stirs her blood, she still wants the brief affair with him to be a thing of the past.

For his part, Chris is reluctant. Seeing Paula today, looking so serene and confident, not to say her usual attractive self, pressed all the old buttons. Any further thoughts along these lines, not to mention their discussion on building heights, are pushed aside as the board table fills and the meeting gets under way.

Before they get to the real business, Chris, as Minister for planning, reads out a fulsome letter of congratulations from the Premier to Paula on her appointment. A round of applause greets this, although Ken Short remains impassive.

The main item on the agenda is 'new directions for the FRA station development'. Paula talks about the concept and then, looking directly at Chris and Dan says, 'low-rise development is proposed.'

Dan nods in agreement.

Chris smiles and comments, 'Err apologies, Chair Paula, but just how many levels do you mean by low-rise?'

'No more than four,' Paula says decisively as she gets up and gestures to an image projected onto a large screen.

'And as you'll see from these sketches, development will be placed away from the station in a series of elegant and sympathetic two to four level buildings for housing and community facilities. I should emphasise that unlike its predecessors, this overall development concept will go out for public comment if the board so decides.'

She glances around to see several approving looks, but a few dark faces. To hide her nerves, Paula adjusts her stylish new watch-phone, a gift from Diana that sits well on her slim wrist. After a pause, she resumes, 'the housing will incorporate sustainable elements like wide eaves, all apartments will face north for winter sun, there will be super-capacity solar panels on the roof and recycling of grey water to gardens. Socially, it'll be a mixed development that includes some high-priced units, the substantial majority in fact, they'll subsidise co-operative and rental units for people on lower incomes.'

Ken Short is chafing at the bit and uninvited comments angrily, 'well as far as I'm concerned, and I know my chamber will back me on this, rental cooperatives are not appropriate in a prestige development!'

'The time for debate hasn't arrived just yet, Ken,' Paula manages. 'Just let me finish!' She goes on, 'the community will also gain a live theatre and performance space and a museum. The idea, according to the initial proposers at Fremantle First, is to highlight the decades of protest and action around the city that had saved it from becoming the hell-hole many developers and the big boys in official positions have pushed for.'

Ken Short bristles at her reference. He glares at her and again interrupts, 'Madam Chair, I regard that apparent reference to me and the Chamber as an insult and not worthy of you as new Chair. I demand an apology!'

'Really, Mr. Short, I think you misinterpret,' returns Paula coolly while trying to mask her delight at a direct hit. 'I was really referring to the former Premier and his crew. I'm sorry if you took offence. But more to the point, tell us your real reaction to the new plans.'

'OK,' says Short, blushing slightly at having been outmanoeuvred so early in the meeting.

'I regard this plan as a squat, ugly and essentially outdated socialist version of the grand vision we previously adopted. I oppose it and regard it as an opportunity lost. False idealism has been raised above the city's interests. Why is there is no much-needed commercial development included? I'll let you know the Chamber's opinion formally at the next meeting,' he adds caustically.

'Well, for my part, I think that far from being outdated, this plan is a breath of fresh air,' chips in Dan. 'It's high time the community was listened to, after all they have spoken loudly and clearly against the previous proposal on many occasions.

'I agree,' says Chris. 'A sensitive design incorporating social and environmental elements is very welcome to me and to the new government. The previous development concept was rejected because it was completely unsuited to this city and tried to override the community's wishes. This one seems to have got the community message. It's in scale with Fremantle's heritage and the architects should be directed to ensure it harmonises. As to socialism, come on Ken, surely even you can't regard a small component of subsidised housing and an arts centre as socialism. And about the commercial development, well, that already in the vicinity, including this building, has caused vacancy problems in the CBD. Fremantle doesn't need more shops and offices near the harbour.'

'I'm impressed by the scale of the proposal and its activity mix,' says the police Super. 'If this is indicative of the new direction the FRA is to take, then more power to it. I move that the concept be approved in principle, subject to public comment.'

The debate didn't go for much longer as Ken Short and his mate from the development industry found themselves well and truly outnumbered.

As they leave the meeting the victors are all smiles. Chris catches up with Paula as she heads out. He draws her aside and says,

'great start Paula. How about a drink later to discuss strategies from here?'

'I'll take a rain-check on that one as I'm meeting Diana this evening. We're headed for Rottnest on the last plane. We have a few delicate matters to discuss,' she says boldly.

Picking up her reference, Chris smiles ruefully.

'Hmm, wish I could be a fly on the wall this weekend! I assume the situation you are going to discuss are plans for the Mayor to take the hand of the gorgeous Diana?'

'An interesting way to put it Chris, but you and I both know that Diana is a woman of her own mind. Tell me, do you really feel that strongly for her? I mean, I heard that you and Yoni McNamara were having a thing.'

Chris blushes.

'A case of displacement activity, I think. But then I am a bit of a wandering soul, I guess.'

'You said it, Chris! Monogamy has been a difficult road for me as you know, but oddly, I haven't been tempted since I got going with Diana,' she confides.

'That sounds ominous,' Chris replies, 'but as you said the ball is in Diana's court really.'

Diana is well aware of this as she meets Paula at the airport, and they board the light plane for the short trip to Rottnest. As a result, things are a little tense between them initially. But the tension soon dissipates as a fellow passenger, recognising Paula, asks her for an autograph and her opinions on the future of Fremantle.

Paula complies willingly and an animated discussion follows as the flight gets under way. As the plane banks over the city and heads into the sunset, Diana is content to listen and unwind by taking in the panoramic view of the city and its leafy suburbs.

She taps Paula on the arm as they fly almost directly over her block of units. They both smile remembering many intimate encounters they have enjoyed there in recent months.

And they enjoy many more over the weekend that follows. They have some open and satisfying discussion as they share home-cooked meals in their unit, just a short walk from the main settlement with its fabulous bakery but ordinary coffee.

In the Rottnest tradition, they hire bikes and explore the mostly car-free roads, finding a few remote beaches where they are able to swim and sunbathe in the nude, far from the madding crowds.

As they return home on Sunday afternoon, they realise that the big questions about their future have receded into the background. They agree that this is a sure sign their relationship is far from over.

CHAPTER 38

CRIMINAL TENDENCIES

As he cruises into Fremantle early on a late summer morning, Bill Murkitt is feeling nervous. He's also weary, having just driven nearly 600 km overnight from Kalgoorlie, where he's been holed up for the past month.

As he crosses the traffic bridge over the Swan River and waits at the traffic lights, he decides to head for a coffee before tackling the more difficult job that awaits him. Murkitt's on a mission, out to get revenge on Lilliano's behalf. That way, Murkitt's new boss can get on with his nefarious drug and standover business unhindered.

Having established before he left Kalgoorlie that Chris is in the city this week, Murkitt's first job is to shadow him so he could suss out the best opportunity to strike and rough Chris up, warn him off pursuing Lilliano. He knows Chris's habits well enough to reckon he'll find him on the cappuccino strip before he heads to the city.

Sure enough, Murkitt spots Chris at his usual table and sidles to a nearby café to keep watch. On this occasion, Murkitt avoids Joe's Café, wanting to keep a low profile. He hopes his changed appearance, coming from a trimmer body, close-cropped hair and a moustache, will help to prevent Freoites from identifying him.

Several cigarettes and coffees later, he follows Chris discreetly to the train station and boards a nearby carriage of the city-bound train from where he could keep an eye on his quarry. He almost loses Chris as the

MP beats the crowd out of the train and runs up the escalator, a move he's obviously used to.

As Murkitt battles up the crowded escalator in pursuit, it's to his advantage that Chris slows down a little on the pedestrian concourse leading to the city, to enable recovery of his failing breath.

Too many bloody ciggies, thinks Chris as he coughs painfully and heads to his office. He glances at his watch and realises he's cutting it fine, so speeds up again as soon as he's able. It takes all of Murkitt's police and physical skills to keep Chris in his sight until he goes through the doors of his ministerial office on St George's Terrace, the city's main business thoroughfare.

Murkitt spends several unproductive hours on the Terrace, reading magazines and news-sheets and drinking indifferent coffee at the place just over the road from the office. He eventually buys a book to help pass the time. By early afternoon, just as Murkitt's getting really bored and is thinking Chris might have exited the building by another route, he sees him emerging with a nubile but rather untidy looking woman at his side.

Francine is new to Murkitt, but he guesses from her body language and the deep conversation they're involved in that she's working for Chris. He follows them up the Terrace in a westerly direction, only to see them disappear into the bowels of Parliament House. Parliament itself isn't sitting, but Chris and Francine are there for a meeting over the proposed re-jig of the railway projects.

Murkitt decides against trying to go in since that would require production of identification and recording of names, and he was wary of over-exposing his new false ID material. He spends the waiting time walking around to prevent himself going to sleep, just settling down for short periods to read his pot-boiler.

A couple of hours later, he's mightily relieved to see Chris emerge with Francine and another woman, whom he identifies as Diana. Francine sets off back down to the Terrace while Chris and Diana head in the opposite direction, deep in conversation.

They go into a nearby café and settle into a comfortable booth in the lounge for what Murkitt feared to be a long session since he notices the waiter taking them a bottle of champagne. At his nearby table out of their line of sight, he's glad to have time for a beer or two.

Had he been able to eavesdrop, he would have heard another of the continuing heart-to-heart exchanges between Chris and Diana. Diana started out by telling Chris that she had enjoyed the time and the communication with Paula at Rottnest so much that she'd decided to continue the relationship. Chris sensed as much since he had found it hard to contact Diana in recent days.

But he still looks hurt by the announcement.

'Diana you said before that you weren't really comfortable in this relationship?'

'I think it's a matter of time. I didn't feel all that relaxed at first, that's true, but there just doesn't seem to be a barrier anymore. And Paula is just so lovely to be with, you know she's not just gorgeous, but she's also lively, intelligent, provocative.'

'Spare me the details Diana, for god's sake! It's bad enough for me, knowing you and she are going to continue together, that just shuts me out of the picture.' Chris is clearly piqued.

'Oh come on Chris, look we both know we've been attracted to each other, but I'm simply not available except as a friend. So you'll just have to find another outlet for your desires and I don't mean Yoni! Or relationships at all for that matter!'

Diana catches Chris's sceptical look.

'Well we did go through this the other night, I imagined you'd come up with a few fresh possibilities in view of the imminent dangers we canvassed.'

'I've given it a bit of thought,' Chris replies, 'and I realise drifting from one woman to another isn't what I really want. In the end, I guess it's a bit shallow. Might be fun, but thinking about it, the last three women I've been with haven't wanted to get really involved beyond the sex, even the case with you, Diana!'

'I don't think that's quite accurate Chris, you know I have a fond regard for you.'

'Alright, thanks for that. But you still don't want me around as a permanent fixture.'

'Do you want to be 'permanent'?

'Well, yes, assuming you were still available, I mean you told me you weren't, even before your Rottnest tryst. But then, I don't think we ever explored the idea of going beyond being lovers and becoming a couple.'

Diana nods thoughtfully, but smiles and touches Chris gently on the arm as he poured them each a final glass from the bottle. The conversation has helped to clear the air.

With this in mind, Chris suggests Diana join him for a meal at their favourite curry house in Fremantle a little later that night. Diana readily agrees. Chris heads for the West Perth train station while Diana says she'll finish off some paperwork back at Parliament before taking a later train and joining him in Fremantle for dinner.

Murkitt is sorry to see them head for the door as he has just started on another beer and is feeling decidedly merry. He hurriedly gulps down the rest of his pint and heads out unsteadily into the fading light.

It's one of those humid nights, a light misty rain falling, the pavement damp and slippery. Murkitt ducks behind a tree and watches Chris and Diana part company with a light kiss and a hug. He then strides confidently after Chris as he heads for the train station. At the station, Chris has a five-minute wait for the train at the otherwise empty platform. Murkitt holds back in the shadows while Chris positions himself on the platform so he could board through the last carriage from where he can get a quick exit at Fremantle.

A few minutes later, as the train approaches, something snaps in Murkitt's slightly drunken brain, and he's suddenly of a mind to sideline Chris once and for all.

'Bugger this shadowing game, it takes too fucking long,' he mumbles.

With dutch courage coursing through his veins, he rushes forward, thinking he'll push the unsuspecting Chris into the path of the oncoming train. As he advances, a yell is suddenly heard, 'Chris, watch out!'

Startled at the cry from a voice he knows well but cannot quite identify, Chris spins around to see Murkitt hurtling towards him, arms outstretched, and another figure following at a slight distance.

Chris just has time to throw himself aside. Murkitt's momentum makes it difficult for him to stop in the slippery conditions and he slides forward and off the platform into the path of the oncoming train.

The horrified driver, who catches the split second happening from his cab, is meanwhile trying to bring the slowing train to a complete stop. But it's too late and the train skids on to Murkitt's body on the rails below with a sickening thud. The wheels slice through his torso, and he's dead.

Meanwhile, the figure that had yelled the warning reaches the platform, where she bends over Chris, who had fallen over after his well-timed leap. He looks up at her uncomprehendingly and manages, 'Diana, what are you doing here? Just as well though, you saved my life!'

'Sure did Chris, how lucky can you get? I decided to share the train journey with you after all. I couldn't face those papers back at Parliament, but who the hell was that?'

'Not sure Diana, but he looked familiar.'

His voice trails off as he vomits; he's in shock. The train driver brought the train to a stop and climbed from the cabin to survey the grisly mess below and called for assistance. Startled passengers emerge from the train as the driver jumps down to assess Murkitt's fate.

'Jesus wept,' they hear him say, 'he must have been dead as soon as the train hit him.'

As he climbs back on to the platform, he approaches Chris and Diana and asks suspiciously, 'what the hell was going on between you guys?'

Chris is still suffering from shock and can't readily explain the sequence of events. Diana takes the driver aside and does so. The police and emergency services arrive shortly afterwards and one of the team, Constable Walters, recently transferred to traffic police, sees through Murkitt's disguise and informs his colleagues that a cop has just died. A disgraced cop, but a cop nonetheless.

The police are doubly suspicious of the circumstances and it takes a befuddled Chris some time to convince them he is the innocent in all of this. For the second time that night, he thanks his lucky stars that Diana is with him. She is far more coherent and believable.

As they leave the police station some time later, he takes Diana by the arm.

'Well Di, our intimacy may be over, but I tell you now you're stuck with me as your most loyal friend!'

'I could do worse, Chris, a lot worse,' Diana says as they find a taxi. They decide to defer their dinner, and head instead for their safe but separate home bases.

CHAPTER 39

OVERGROWTH

The unexpected death of Murkitt exposes his tarnished record to further public scrutiny. Since the death of Sizall, investigators had turned attention to the drug barons, the bikies and the property world. Linkages between them and the establishment are becoming clearer as pressure from the investigation mounts.

The establishment makes it clear that they're not going to yield to pressure easily. Many of the political benefactors are protected by senior figures in the major parties, both are beneficiaries of their largesse.

Besides, JD had handed over a thick dirt file on Cloke to the authorities, in order to protect himself and keep the focus on the politicians. Richard Right and Wayne Cloke are expendable. Chewis is still officially missing, although there are reports that he's moved to Majorca.

At the Corruption Commission inquiry, lawyers for JD and Thumper argue that the recordings Chris used to expose the FRA deal have been misinterpreted in order to implicate their clients. JD and Thumper cannot deny being at the meetings but they do deny being willing parties to commissions. The crucial words are gone over again and again:

Right: Well, John, Ken, have your companies got the capacity for the scale of this Fremantle high-rise project?

Dick: Sure, we think so. Ken and I agree that there should be no problems if Flexible is able to share the work with non-union builders like ABC without causing a major industrial upset. It'll need a watertight deal with the fucking building unions to implement this idea.

Thumper: That's it, Richard. We can work together, but only if those bloody unions don't cause us their usual grief.

Cloke: Well, I don't think that'll be a problem if they get the rates you've mentioned and of course if I get my slice of the deal!

Right: No problem there, Wayne. Like the rest of us, you're in for 1 percent of the contract price, which we conservatively estimate at $2 billion.

Chewis: That includes me, of course?

Right: Yes Fred, trust me!

Lawyers argue that their clients JD and Thumper had misunderstood Right's offer of a 1 percent commission, thinking it referred to a contribution *they* would be expected to make in order to secure the contracts.

This they claim was a normal expectation under both Right and Cloke when the government was awarding contracts. Right had tried to go one step further down the path of cronyism by seeking to set up a deal that would ensure everyone in on the ground floor got a percentage of the profits.

The cronies swore they would *never* indulge in such deals. Moreover, they had been horrified when the transcripts had been published since they had no idea their meetings with Right were being recorded.

This was bad enough, possibly illegal, and they were looking to sue Right as a result. In any case, their legal counsels argue, Right's the architect of the corrupt deal. And it proves almost impossible to establish otherwise. Counsel for Right and Cloke argue that the builders are the bad apples in the barrel since they had *demanded* the proposed commissions through standover tactics.

The court of public opinion doesn't readily accept this argument. As far as it's concerned, the guilty verdict applies to the politicians more than the business community. After all, everyone knows or suspects politicians are on the take.

But corrupt businessmen, aren't they the exception rather than the rule?

The Commission takes note of the public debate that rages during their hearings. And while they recommend some charges be laid against JD, Thumper, and Tough, early responses from the DPP suggest that the charges won't stick. Too big a slice of the economy is at risk for rigorous investigation against the big boys.

As to the links with organised crime, they're difficult to untangle. After Sizall's death, as Lilliano tries to take back his former Fremantle territory, he's badly wounded in a gun battle at a night club and is under intensive care in a city hospital. This leads to further reprisals. The local police are reluctant to intervene, since their own ties to the criminal world become harder to trace with the death or side-lining of gang bosses.

However, Federal investigators look more closely. After Murkitt's death, they find material at his Kalgoorlie hideout. Apparently written by Murkitt himself, a report deals with the grisly events around Sizall's death. And Murkitt's previous dealings with the bikie gangs and drug barons.

Lilliano is under close watch.

Kerry Cinnamon is also under investigation. The Commission receives evidence of his links to organised crime, evidence that Chris had earlier been informed about but had failed to pin down.

Cinnamon's casino licence is reviewed and there's speculation that it'll be confiscated. Sirolli might after all be the beneficiary, Chris wryly muses when he hears. But he knows Cinnamon still may not be charged. The guy's just too slippery and powerful for that. Dodgy characters from the top end of town are adept at staying clear of the long arm of the law.

As the inquiries grind on, Yoni McNamara makes a progress report to Cabinet. Several Ministers are becoming anxious that justice will never be done. She senses that some of her news will be excruciating to hear.

Later, as she stands in the Party room to deliver her summary to a specially convened meeting of all alliance MPs, Yoni looks to the Premier for reassurance. Elaine smiles and touches Yoni on the arm, a gesture that helps calm her attorney's nerves. Yoni clears her throat.

'Hrrrm, members you have probably heard that many of the big players in the WA crime and corruption scene seem, Houdini-like, to be capable of escaping our dragnet. The contortions of the likes of JD, Ken Thumper, and Ken Tough have been laughable.'

This prompts laughter among her audience. She catches Chris's eye. He smiles, recalling their night at the recent Cabinet dinner. The evening had given them the chance of a long chat. Yoni had told Chris she'd separated from her husband, but was in no way after another relationship. After Chris expressed his condolences and hinted this might still leave the door open for further intimacies between them, he'd finally agreed he would not press the matter.

Yoni smiles in return and continues, 'it seems our dodgy builders and their mates have found a loophole through which to escape serious charges. But remember this is their history, always operating on the margins of the law and dropping others in the proverbial shit when they look like being caught themselves!'

'Sounds like a good summary of the State's development history,' interjects Chris wryly.

'And by the way, all is not lost in our bid to clean up the development industry. Our committee will present enough hard evidence to nab both Vince Roberts and JD for a sweetheart deal they did, involving the construction of a beach cottage near Melbourne for Roberts's retirement.'

Murmurs of approval fill the room and spontaneous discussion momentarily interrupts proceedings. Yoni's into her stride now and has no difficulty allowing others to enjoin her story. The hubbub dies away as she resumes, 'well that's great Chris, even if a few other snakes may have escaped from the zoo. But *my* good news is that the DPP now says JD *is* likely to face charges relating to the FRA deal. Now that's something worth waiting for,' Yoni says with emphasis, amid a growing hubbub of approval.

She looks around the room to acknowledge the plaudits.

'But don't get too excited yet guys, there's more.' She pauses for effect. 'Charges will definitely be laid against not just one, but two former Premiers, our favourite, Richard Right, will be up on collusion, conspiracy and official corruption, for explicitly offering government contracts in return for political donations. And you will have already heard that Kerry Cinnamon's casino licence is likely to be confiscated.'

Cheers break out and get even louder when Yoni goes on, 'and while talking of the casino, the news of the day is that Cloke will finally be charged with fraud and corruption for the casino deal and with collusion over the FRA redevelopment scheme. And extradition proceedings will be instituted against Chewis.'

'About time that bastard faced the music,' puts in a backbencher.

'Agreed, but at last report, Chewis was pleading medical problems in an effort to stall proceedings.'

'Another Christopher Skase in the making!' returns the MP.

The meeting breaks up and Yoni basks in the glow of congratulations. She joins Elaine, Chris and Diana for a celebratory lunch that lasts well into the afternoon.

Much public excitement follows the charging of the two disgraced former premiers. Not since the 1980s had WA politicians paid such a high price for their misdemeanours. And even then there were questions as to whether the politicians involved had been treated too lightly by the justice system. This time around, it looks as if this lot will get their just desserts. Some of their business and criminal cronies might also end up with long jail sentences.

CHAPTER 40

IT'S A WOMAN'S WORLD

Business in the Wild West will take a long time to return to normal. The Hipper alliance takes a while to find its direction and the press has a field day with sexist comments directed at the female majority in the Cabinet.

The government sends a strong protest to Canberra about the telescreens that are increasing in number and impact. Citizens are often seen being dragged off on sedition charges. These most often turn out to be spurious and were it not for the work of Yoni McNamara and a dedicated legal taskforce, many more innocent citizens would end up behind bars.

As Diana told Chris earlier, the taskforce was also disturbed to find the telescreen denouncing others on the basis of so-called moral crimes. This under the influence of a recently appointed moral crusader to the role of Federal Attorney-General. He's pandering to moral conservatives in the Senate in order to get their support on other matters.

The HIP group still meets occasionally, knowing that the government is headed in the right direction. It's popular with the public too. It's honest and unusually receptive to community opinion on a wide range of issues.

This annoys the business establishment, so used to having their own way. In the long term, it may lead to turmoil in the corridors of power, but in the short term, it means many people feel they have an unusually receptive government, ready to adopt innovative and environmentally benign solutions to the State's increasingly urgent problems.

The government abandons Right's environmentally damaging pulp mill and adopts plans for increased production of hemp as a raw material for a very different sort of mill.

This leads Nadine to organise a weekend-long hemp festival at Nannup. Nadine is in fine form and ensures that Chris and Elaine Hipper, who make the journey south, are given their share of the glory.

However, the highest accolades go to the local ferals, who were the vanguard. And special mention is given to Francine, whose report was highly influential. A party lasts most of the weekend, and the press is discreet about rumours that the Premier was seen sharing a huge joint with her Minister to mark the occasion.

Back in Perth, proposals for light rail services from Rockingham to Fremantle are still on the cards as is cancellation of the Rockingham Highway. The whole State is abuzz with progressive initiatives.

Plans for a solar power station are well advanced, using a locally invented system that produces a prodigious increase in the output of solar panels, thus making them far more competitive. Wind turbines are also being increasingly used as an alternative.

And yet it is hardly the dawn of a completely new era. For the big boys are still there, even if their pride and reputation have been dented. Not yet for them any change of heart on the need for bigger and bigger development, or support of projects based on the old paradigm of dig and build.

For Chris this is proving a huge challenge. On a personal front Chris and Diana remain firm friends and continue to meet socially. Chris is also part of a wider group including Paula and Dan Whattington. They institute regular soirees, often focussing on Fremantle issues and the FRA's part in them.

Chris is finally spending more time swimming, bush walking and other healthy pursuits, working off some of his increased weight in the process and diverting him from more womanising.

Under Paula's skilful guidance, the FRA becomes a voice for rather than against the community. Dan and the Fremantle First group can't believe their change of fortunes.

Paula still dresses to kill, but Diana starts to steal the limelight as she experiments with the latest fashions. This sets the magazines ablaze with photos and stories, but gradually the gossip columnists lose interest.

They finally suggest that Paula and Diana are losing their status as the city's most chic couple and one goes so far as to claim that they are becoming 'just like most other couples, boring and conventional'.

For a few years at least, politics and business in Western Australia would be anything but boring and conventional.

DON'T COUNT YOUR CHICKENS

Or so it appeared. Matters of sex and the heart still too often occupy Chris's mind. He imagines he can revive his affair with Yoni, but his optimism is short-lived as Yoni decides to concentrate on her work.

Then one morning during the Christmas season, Chris is sipping his usual morning coffee on the strip when the telescreen stops its drab morning news broadcast and breaks into an unexpected sermon about the importance of men and women behaving in an upright and moral way. It condemns promiscuity and claims that immoral behaviour and deviance are increasing and sapping at the cohesion of society and the family.

The rot, the telescreen blathers on, goes right to the top. Especially in WA. It then proceeds to show some footage to demonstrate the point. It warns that the scenes to be broadcast may offend some viewers. It announces that for this reason the footage to be shown has been suitably edited so that body parts are obscured.

Chris, who up until now had been only half-attending to the diatribe is flabbergasted when on the screen before him flash scenes from each of his recent dalliances.

First, a scene from Paula's Fremantle pad. The footage is fuzzy, the faces and most of the bodies are blanked out or obscured. From the soundtrack, only *his* voice comes through the other deliberately muffled. But Chris knows instantly that it's one of their more off-the-wall encounters with apparently impossible sexual positions getting a run. Clearly enjoyed by both. Who ever thought of the telescreen?

Second, a scene from the Big Bong, Nannup. Chris knows it's a clip of him and Diana making love. The last thing they'd thought of was a telescreen.

Then, a scene from a Melbourne hotel. Similarly disturbing. No chance of Sarah being identified, but Chris knows it's the illicit night they spent at that flash hotel. Neither noticed the telescreen.

Finally a scene from Chris's flat, and he realises he failed to take account of the telescreen on the one night he and Yoni had their tryst.

Chris is mortified. And outraged at this assault on his privacy. He has recently seen a few others called out in this excruciating and embarrassing way.

'Jesus,' he exclaims, draining his coffee and wondering what to do next. An appeal to Yoni and her taskforce? Impossible in the circumstances. *You've brought this on yourself,* his conscience puts in.

'Surely, this must all be a nightmare?' Chris mutters in hope.

Nightmare it's not! Chris is surrounded by a posse of Federal police, with

Moral Safety
Bureau

badges prominently displayed on their uniforms. He's forced to the ground.

'You've got a lot to answer for there mate,' the head of the group observes casually. The others smirk at Chris's demeanour.

Chris tries to stand up, but is restrained by a particularly tough-looking member of the posse.

'Jesus Christ,' Chris says in anger. 'You can't be serious?'

'No need to add blasphemy to your record, mate. If you'll just accompany us to the station, we can get a statement from you.'

To minimise his public embarrassment and because there seems little other choice, Chris goes along with the posse to the nearby Federal Police HQ.

He demands to see a lawyer.

'Under our powers, Mr. Burnside, we can hold you for up to forty-eight hours on suspicion of crimes of moral indecency such as you are facing.'

The chief barks this at Chris, but then softens, 'however Mr. Burnside, if you'll just drop your outrage and give us a considered statement, we can then arrange for you to request bail and get some legal representation for any trial.'

'Trial? Moral indecency! What is this, Victorian England? Who the hell do you think you are, judging me? I haven't heard about these laws.'

Chris has not been mollified, so the police strip him of his belongings and shove him roughly into a holding cell for a cooling-off period.

It's an uncomfortable twenty-four hours during which time Chris is given only low quality food and the occasional toilet break.

It has given him time to think. He's decided to make a statement and seek bail, so he can at least have some hope of getting out of this hell-hole.

His statement is certainly not the conciliatory one the police suggested. He doesn't deny the acts, but insists that what he did in the privacy of bedrooms has no bearing on anything, certainly not his moral fitness.

He chose to sleep with different partners at different times and they with him. That's his and their business and should never be in the public domain. He concludes by stating that this is the most insidious star chamber he's ever encountered.

Reluctantly, the police allow the statement to be registered and put in a call to the duty magistrate for a bail application. This is set at a figure of $50 000, considered light by the chief in view of the serious nature of the offences.

Chris phones Darlene Pocket QC, not wanting to drag Paula into this, and in any case remembering she's away on a break.

Luckily, Darlene is working over the break. She promises to help. She says the moral police have stepped way over the mark as the legislation on so-called moral crimes is currently under challenge in the High Court. This is of some comfort to Chris, although maybe they're out to make an example of people in the public eye, while the legislation is still in force.

Chris later wonders just what the love life of the arresting officers, particularly the chief is like. *Two could play at this game,* he thinks.

Darlene doesn't take long to get to his cell. She quickly moves to arrange bail. Approval for the application arrives soon afterwards. Chris emerges from the lock-up in thoughtful mood, wondering how he can turn the situation to his advantage.

This mood doesn't last for long, however, as he soon hears the nearest telescreen announce that Federal authorities have requested the Hipper government to consider sacking Chris in view of the charges, now given plenty of publicity.

He's in a daze, thinks about a meeting with Premier Elaine, see if they can put things right. Her office, like all the others, is closed for the Christmas break. So he calls her private number and gets the answer machine. Gives up.

Instead, he goes out of Fremantle to Perth's CBD, where the entertainment area in Northbridge looks dull to his jaundiced eyes. He finds a bar, orders one whisky, then another, and another. And so on. Nobody seems to recognise him or care. He gets drunk before catching a late train back to Fremantle.

He doesn't feel like sleep so he visits a pub. He looks around at the crowd, some of whom are talking in merry groups, others preoccupied by their computing devices and watches. After downing a double whisky, he decides to head for home as patrons are starting to look in his direction and point.

He wends his way to his flat, hearing the telescreen droning on about declining moral standards and the arrest and charging of State Minister Chris Burnside.

Time to lie low, he reckons.

To achieve this, the next day he takes off for his favourite hidey hole, Nannup. Nadine is effusive.

'Welcome to Nannup, you dirty old man!'

'Yeah, any vacancies on the front line?'

'Not for dirty old men, but plenty for activists, mate.'

Nadine leads Chris to the resistance centre where they are running a campaign to ensure the government keeps to its word on establishing a pulp mill based on hemp.

Chris takes it in and decides on a change of direction. He fires off a letter to the Premier, resigning from his Ministries.

Save her the trouble of sacking me, he thinks.

He'll stay on as an independent, but will rekindle his activist roots. And work on changing his ways. Not in response to the moral police, against which he reckons he'll join the already active campaign.

When it comes to the crunch, that's superfluous, for the High Court throws out the legislation before Chris's threatened trial eventuates.

In the meantime, Chris comes to a realisation that there are more ways of enjoying life and the senses than he ever imagined. And of connecting with people. Once he's re-established his position in Parliament, he puts in more effort to track down his kith and kin, his only son. This will require travelling to Melbourne again.

One thing we can be sure of is that there will be no repeat of highjinks he shared with Sarah Kingsmill MP.

Or can we?

AUTHOR'S NOTE

Politics and corruption are a heady mixture: they often go hand in hand. Usually masked from the public eye in Australia, corruption is increasingly in the news.

It's common knowledge that dodgy deals are frequently on at local council level. It's well satirised in TV programmes such as *Sea Change* and *Grassroots*.

And at State level, consider Queensland in the Bjelke-Petersen years: corrupt behaviour from top to bottom of the political system, closely linked to the police force. Such cross-overs are present all over the nation. Recent TV series like *Underbelly* probe the murky organised crime scene unmercifully.

City of Sharks is set in Perth and Fremantle, Western Australia, the fast-growing metropolis where I was raised and spent many of my adult years. I was exposed to the shenanigans of politics through time as a local Councillor and then as a State politician over the period 1982–93, a time when the infamous WA Inc story unfolded.

The Curtin Foundation played a central role here: local entrepreneurs, some with a dodgy reputation, were invited to join and contribute to a Foundation established to fund future ALP elections. In return they had the ear of government, but not, the critics were assured, any sure path to government contracts. The truth, fully exposed a decade later, was somewhat different.

Similar stories and dealings with cronies and banks cost the Victorian and South Australian Governments of the day dearly too.

In the early 1980s, some of us in the ALP raised too many potentially embarrassing questions. This made us unpopular with the Party hierarchy, but a couple of us gained preselection and subsequently were elected to State Parliament.

Having been elected, a colleague or two and I joined a small number of dissident 'lefties' in the State Parliamentary Labor Party and tried to change things from within. The odds were against us, especially given the dominance of the Cabinet over the backbench and the continuing wrangles over how that dominance could be reduced. By the early 1990s, a few of us had had enough and resigned the SPLP in protest at the direction of the government and saw out our time as independents. A Royal Commission was appointed in 1991 to delve into the murky waters of 'WA-Inc', This included the Burke and Dowding government's decision to twice rescue the Merchant Bank Rothwells, which was run by one of the Labor Party donors Laurie Connell. The bank gave loans where others wouldn't, prompting Connell to be labelled 'last resort Laurie'. But the bank ran into financial trouble. Hence the rescue, which was enjoined by many corporate high flyers, including several who had donated to Labor Party 're-election funds' and had, coincidentally, been beneficiaries of State contracts.

When the Royal Commission reports came out in 1992, the findings were highly critical of many Ministers and two Labor Premiers in the period 1983-89.

- *The Commission accused the 1983-87 Premier, Brian Burke, who initiated the Labor Party's relationship with business, of 'reprehensible conduct.' He denied this, but was later goaled for apparent travel rorts.*
- *Of Mr Dowding (Premier 1987-90), the Commission concluded that he 'presided over a disastrous series of decisions designed to support Rothwells when it was or should have been clear to him and to those ministers closely involved that Rothwells was no longer*

> *a viable financial institution. This culminated in the decision to involve the Government' [again]*

The Commission also underlined the close coincidence of donations from particular businessmen and their receiving contracts from government. Three quotes from the Commission's final report are sufficient to give the flavour of their findings:

- *The Commission has found conduct and practices on the part of certain persons involved in government in the period from 1983 to 1989 which were such as to place our governmental system at risk.*
- *A common theme is apparent in the evidence of most of the donors, namely, that the Government was good for business and provided them with a strong incentive to assist in its efforts to be re-elected.*
- *Some ministers elevated personal or party advantage over their constitutional obligation to act in the public interest. The decision to lend Government support to the rescue of Rothwells in October 1987 was principally that of Mr Burke as Premier. Mr Burke's motives in supporting the rescue were not related solely to proper governmental concerns. They derived in part from his well-established relationship with Mr Connell, the chairman and major shareholder of Rothwells, and from his desire to preserve the standing of the Australian Labor Party in the eyes of those sections of the business community from which it had secured much financial support.*

But all that's a while back. *City of Sharks* is a light-hearted fictional representation of what might be not too far around the corner in the Wild West.

It's dedicated to all those who have tried to change what was or what might have been.

In writing -- and re-writing -- *City of Sharks* over the space of several years, many people made valued contributions along the way -- all improved the final version.

I am particularly indebted to: Kim Kemp for suggesting imaginative ideas on the plot; the late David Po for encouraging my early efforts at story-telling; Jo Trevelyan for providing space in which to write the first draft; Nikki Endacott for constructive feedback on that messy and confusing draft; Cherry Noel and other editorial staff at X-Libris for patience and encouragement; staff at the WA Parliamentary Library for expert and efficient guidance to records referred to above; members of the Fremantle Society, who encouraged me to become more closely involved in their tireless efforts to have the city's heritage more fully appreciated by those in positions of political and economic power ; Chris Williams for timely legal advice; Don Whittington for time-consuming, thoughtful and punctilious proof-reading that led to countless improvements in the text; as did my much-thumbed Macquarie Dictionary; Ruth Belben who, having read the final draft, offered encouragement at a time when I was losing faith in the project; and my mates Greg Smith and Michael Couani for providing quiet space at Cape Kersaint eco-lodge on scenic Kangaroo Island, that allowed extensive and much-needed revisions to the manuscript.

The usual disclaimer applies to any remaining errors or inconsistencies – I accept the blame! If I have offended any politicians – past or present – that would be a pity, for as Barry Humphries has it: 'Never be afraid to laugh at yourself, after all, you could be missing out on the joke of the century.'

Printed in the United States
By Bookmasters